CH
6—15

MOUNTAIN RAMPAGE

A National Park Mystery
by Scott Graham

D1018885

TORREY HOUSE PRESS, LLC

SALT LAKE CITY • TORREY

3 1336 09677 7561

This is a work of fiction set in a real place. All characters in this novel are fictitious. Any resemblance to actual events or persons, living or dead, is entirely coincidental.

First Torrey House Press Edition, June 2015
Copyright © 2015 by Scott Graham

All rights reserved. No part of this book may be reproduced or retransmitted in any form or by any means without the written consent of the publisher.

Published by Torrey House Press, LLC
Salt Lake City, Utah
www.torreyhouse.com

International Standard Book Number: 978-1-937226-45-9
E-book ISBN: 978-1-937226-46-6
Library of Congress Control Number: 2014957372

Cover design by Rick Whipple, Sky Island Studio
Interior design by Jeff Fuller, Shelfish • Shelfish.weebly.com
Distributed to the trade by Consortium Book Sales and Distribution

For my parents, Reg and Bev,
with thanks for sharing their love
of the Colorado mountains with me

MOUNTAIN RAMPAGE

"It may be, if we quit shooting animals on one side of a Park boundary line, that in due time we shall become sufficiently civilized to stop killing people on the other side of the boundary line."

—Enos Mills
Father of Rocky Mountain National Park, 1870-1922

PROLOGUE

The ram never heard the shot that killed it.

The heavily muscled Rocky Mountain sheep, its horns long and curled, grazed its way up the shadowed northwest ridge of Mount Landen accompanied by its herd of two dozen ewes and first-year lambs. The ridge scalloped the dawn sky high above tree level. The herd nipped at bunches of dry grass shivering in the stiff breeze between lichen-covered rocks.

The ram stopped to gaze at the forested valley far below. The ewes and lambs halted, too. Any predator attempting to approach from the forest would reveal itself long before it grew close. But predators were not a concern here on the north face of Mount Landen in the heart of Rocky Mountain National Park's Mummy Range.

The grizzlies that once constituted the ram's only real threat were gone, hunted to extinction more than a century ago. Black bears and the park's few mountain lions fed below tree line on easier prey—deer, elk, raccoons, porcupines. The bighorn had no need to fear humans; hunting was a thing of the distant past in the park. Only the long natural history of its species compelled the ram to maintain its vigilance.

Satisfied all was well, the ram lowered its head and resumed grazing. It paused again as it topped the rocky crest of the ridge. The rising sun splashed the ridge with rust and orange against a cloudless turquoise sky. The ram stood with its powerful chest thrust forward, wind whipping its thick coat. To the north and west, the surrounding peaks and folded cirques of the Mummy Range took shape in the growing light.

The bullet, moving far faster than the speed of sound, struck the ram in its side. The slug mushroomed upon impact, ripping through the animal's lungs and shredding its heart before bursting through its ribcage in a spray of red.

The ram staggered sideways. Blood frothed at its mouth, forming small, crimson bubbles. The bighorn sank to its knees.

The last pulse of oxygen to the ram's brain enabled the creature to maintain its balance, kneeling atop the ridge as the slope below exploded with motion. The ewes and lambs scattered, regrouped, and galloped as one, parting around the kneeling ram and disappearing over the serrated ridge.

The shooter lay three hundred yards down the ridge, his eye to his rifle's scope. He'd seen the ram shudder and envisioned the poof of fur as the slug plowed into the animal precisely where he'd intended. The bighorn remained upright on its knees, but the gunman knew the ram was finished. More than once, though, he'd known as much only to be proven wrong.

Bullets were odd things. A slug could plow into a creature dead-true, only to nick a rib and spin sideways through the lungs, bypassing the heart despite the outward perfection of the shot. In such a case, the mortally wounded animal might cover half a mile or more during a final, all-out run as its undamaged heart pumped and its lungs bled out.

Not this time.

The dawn breeze swallowed the clatter of the departing herd's hooves as the ram toppled off the ridge and rolled down the steep face of the mountain into a granite-walled couloir. The falling ram set off a cavalcade of loose scree, its heavy body a brown raft afloat in the gray river of rock. The bighorn slid fifty yards down the couloir to where the pitch of the face lessened. The flowing gravel streamed to a stop and the animal came to rest, half-buried, in the deep shade of the north-facing ridge.

The shooter shouldered his rifle and side-hilled off the ridge into the drainage and across the face of the mountain to the dead ram. He stood over the animal. The scent of blood and musk filled the air. The ram's tongue draped from its mouth. Its big eyes, round as marbles, stared up at him, milky and unseeing.

The curl of the ram's heavy horns rounded well past full. The shooter took a firm grip on one of the curls and tugged the ram down the drainage and into the forest, the animal's body sliding behind him on its slick coat. Grunting with effort, he wound between tree trunks and ducked beneath low branches until he reached a small opening in the woods. He pulled a hacksaw from his rucksack, cut through the ram's neck just at the back of its skull, and lowered its severed head into doubled plastic trash bags.

The shooter settled the bagged head of the ram in his pack and set off downhill through the trees toward Fall River Road in the valley below. He left the bighorn's body to rot, confident in the knowledge that, within a few weeks, nothing of the ram but an unidentifiable scattering of picked-over bones would remain in the small meadow, deep in the forest below the summit of Mount Landen.

Tuesday

One

Rosie's cry jolted Chuck Bender awake. He blinked, blurry eyed, and sat up, focusing on his six-year-old stepdaughter sprawled before him, her arms and legs jerking in violent spasms, her eyes rolled back in her head.

Rosie had been asleep in her twin bed in the cabin's tiny back bedroom, her forehead warm to the touch but her breathing calm and steady, when he, too, had drifted off, chin to chest, slumped in a ladder-back chair cadged from the kitchen table.

Chuck checked his watch. 2:30 a.m. He'd dozed for no more than fifteen minutes, but a different Rosie now lay before him.

Janelle hurried into the bedroom, a damp washcloth clutched in both hands.

Rosie cried out a second time. Only the whites of her eyes showed between her fluttering eyelids. Her arms and legs thrashed, spilling the sheets to her waist.

"Rosie. *M'hija*," Janelle whispered, her voice laced with fear. "Darling girl, my darling girl."

She crouched at the side of the bed and put the cloth to her younger daughter's forehead. Chuck leaned forward and mindlessly kneaded Janelle's shoulders, his gaze fixed on Rosie.

Janelle turned on him. "You fell asleep."

Stung, Chuck lifted his hands from her shoulders. "*She* fell asleep. Finally. I thought we were in the clear."

"You thought wrong."

He pressed his palms together between his knees. Rosie's fever had built until midnight. When, finally, it had receded, he'd figured they had simply to last out the night, that Rosie would be better by morning.

But what did he know about childhood illnesses? What did he know about children at all, for that matter?

He reached past Janelle and caught the nearest of Rosie's convulsing arms. He pressed it gently to the bed. The soft skin of her bicep was blotchy and scalding to the touch. Her fever was back, fiercer this time. As soon as he released her arm, it lashed about.

"More Tylenol?" he asked Janelle.

She put the back of her hand to Rosie's cheek. "Too soon. We already gave her two doses."

"Some ibuprofen? Isn't that allowed?"

Janelle shrugged, her back stiff.

On the opposite side of the small room, eight-year-old Carmelita rolled over in her matching bed and settled back to sleep.

Chuck stared at Rosie, his every muscle tense. He was twelve months into parenthood, still a newcomer to the world of sleepless nights and sick little girls. "The doctors' offices are all closed," he said. "The only thing open at this hour will be the emergency room."

"Then let's go."

He hesitated. "Yeah."

Janelle skewered him with a hard look over her shoulder. "Don't tell me you're worried about money."

Chuck pushed himself back in his seat. "With our deductible, we'll get slaughtered."

Janelle's voice shook. "This is not a baby-medicine type of thing, Chuck. Not anymore."

"It'll pass," he said, his voice revealing his uncertainty. "Won't it?"

"She's having some sort of a seizure. I've never seen her like this. *Nunca*. Neither of the girls."

Rosie's eyes were closed now, but her arms and legs continued to stir.

Chuck ran a hand over the top of his head, passing his fingers through his short hair. "You're right."

Relief flooded Janelle's face.

He looked into her frightened eyes. "She's my darling girl, too," he said.

Minutes later, gravel pinged off the undercarriage of the pickup as Chuck sped down the two-track from the cabin, familiar after seven weeks with the narrow, descending drive through the trees to the flat valley floor a mile south of downtown Estes Park. He slowed as he left the forest and turned onto the gravel road behind two massive log buildings—Lodge of the Rockies and, next door, Mills Conference Center. The matching, three-story, historic structures faced onto the open greensward at the center of the Y of the Rockies resort complex.

A glance in the rearview mirror showed Rosie slumped in her seat, strands of dark hair stuck to her sweaty forehead.

Rosie was her grandfather Enrique in miniature: short, stocky, and—normally—full of life, with thick, wiry hair and round, rosy cheeks. Carmelita sat opposite her little sister on the rear seat, her head against the side window of the truck, her eyes half-closed. Carmelita was thin and delicate like her mother, with Janelle's heart-shaped face and long, straight hair.

Dread coated Chuck's insides like heavy syrup. He swallowed grit from his throat as he fishtailed around the near side of the conference center. He slung the truck east onto the main road leading out of the resort, only to be greeted by a car rocketing down the open slope from the Y of the Rockies entrance two hundred yards ahead.

Chuck jammed the brakes, skidding the pickup to a stop in front of the lodge and conference center. Janelle tumbled from the rear seat of the crew cab to the floor between the seat-belted girls. A cloud of dust rose in the truck's headlights, mixing with thin tendrils of the summer's first rain.

Chuck kept his foot pinned to the brake as the oncoming vehicle—an Estes Park police cruiser, siren silenced and emergency lights extinguished—flashed past. Janelle clambered back to the bench seat between the girls. Ignoring the police car, she pointed through the windshield at the resort entrance ahead.

Chuck accelerated before sliding to a stop once more when a shiny, blue, single-cab pickup, the words "Y of the Rockies, Estes Park, Colorado" stenciled on its side, shot around the far corner of the lodge in pursuit of the police car. As the truck passed, Chuck caught sight of its driver hunched over the steering wheel.

"Parker," Chuck said. He watched over his shoulder as the truck chased the police car across the Y of the Rockies compound.

Janelle pulled Rosie close and stroked the girl's damp forehead. "Not your concern," she said. "Not now."

Chuck punched the gas. The rear tires spat loose rocks as the truck sped up the sloping drive and out of the shallow valley. The pickup bounced onto the paved road leading to Estes Park, the gateway tourist town at the east entrance to Rocky Mountain National Park, high in the mountains northwest of Denver.

Chuck gunned the truck toward the center of town and glanced out the side window to see, through breaks in trees, the police cruiser and Parker's pickup racing along the far side of the broad rectangle of well-tended grass play fields, more than a quarter mile across, that marked the center of Y of the Rockies, the former Young Men's Christian Association training center turned rustic resort and corporate retreat. The cruiser and truck sped down the row of buildings lining the west side of the fields.

The buildings, catty-corner across the expanse of grass from the lodge and conference center, included the resort's gift shop, outdoor-gear rental center, and log cabin museum. Beyond the museum were the resort's two dormitories.

Through one last break in the trees, Chuck watched as the police cruiser and Parker's pickup truck passed large, new Falcon House, home to the resort's international crew of summer workers. The car and truck slid to a stop facing the second dormitory, ramshackle Raven House, home for the past two months to Chuck's group of field school students.

In the rearview mirror, Chuck caught sight of Janelle staring out the window at the police cruiser and Parker's truck.

She uttered a single, strangled word as she stroked Rosie's forehead: "Clarence."

Two

Rosie whimpered from the back seat as Chuck sped toward Estes Park, his thoughts, like Janelle's, torn.

Why were the police and Parker headed for Raven House? What sort of mischief might Chuck's students have gotten themselves into in the middle of the night? And as for Clarence—Janelle's brother and one of Chuck's two field school team leaders—Janelle's concern was well grounded. It wasn't much of a stretch to think Clarence might have gotten himself in some sort of trouble.

Janelle tapped on the face of her phone as Chuck crossed Elkhorn Avenue and braked to a stop at the Estes Park Medical Center emergency entrance. Already, the smattering of rain was gone, replaced by a cold wind whipping beneath the covered entryway.

"Anything?" he asked Janelle as he threw the truck into park.

She shook her head. "No reply. He must still be asleep." A beat passed. "Right?"

"Right," Chuck repeated, agreeing with what they both wanted to believe.

He hurried into the hospital with Rosie in his arms, Janelle and Carmelita close behind. A gray-haired woman in blue scrubs rose from behind a computer at the front of the hospital's compact emergency room—three curtained compartments on one side, portable pieces of medical equipment sheathed in plastic along the opposite wall. The woman's nametag identified her as Irene, R.N. She pressed a button on her computer keyboard before stepping around the counter and putting a hand on Rosie's arm.

At the nurse's touch, Rosie lifted her head from Chuck's shoulder. Despite the drained look on her face, she smiled beatifically at the woman.

Chuck's heart swelled at the sight of Rosie's smile. The nurse directed him to lay Rosie in a wheeled gurney in the nearest of the three unoccupied compartments.

"You doing okay, hon?" she asked, leaning over the gurney.

"Yeppers," Rosie declared in her little-girl version of her grandfather's raspy voice. She rose on her elbows. "I'm doing *grrrreat!*"

Janelle dug her fingers into Chuck's biceps.

The nurse turned from Rosie to Chuck and Janelle and asked doubtfully, "Sick little girl?"

"Really sick," Janelle asserted. "We think she had a seizure." Her eyes went to Rosie. "Thank God," she breathed.

"It's good she's doing better now." The nurse patted one of Janelle's hands, still gripping Chuck's arm. "Why don't we get her checked in for the M.D.?"

Carmelita curled up on a hard plastic seat next to Rosie's wheeled bed, wrapped her arms around her drawn-up knees, and closed her eyes while the nurse set about taking Rosie's temperature and blood pressure. Before the nurse finished, a tall, broad-shouldered young man pushed through double doors at the back of the emergency room. A shock of bleached-blond hair tumbled to just above the man's bright, emerald-blue eyes. A deep cleft bisected his square chin, and a strand of white shells, visible in the V-neck of his scrub top, complemented a blond soul patch perched below his lower lip. A nametag on his left breast read Gregory, M.D.

Chuck straightened to his full six feet, but the ER doc still had him by two or three inches. The doctor looked far too young to be a physician, in the same way Janelle, slender and girlish at twenty-eight, looked far too young to be the mother of a pair of girls six and eight years old.

Unlike the doctor's thick, blond locks, Chuck's sandy-brown hair was thin and sparse, with more than a hint of gray. Crows' feet cut deep into the sides of Chuck's blue-gray eyes, the result

11

of more than two decades of work outdoors on archaeological digs across the Southwest. His lean build contrasted sharply with the linebacker-like physique of the doctor.

As he crossed the tile floor in his slip-on clogs, the M.D. gave Janelle, in her fitted blouse and form-hugging jeans, a full once-over. Chuck's eyes went to Janelle as well.

His young wife was Carmelita all grown up, olive-skinned and slender, dark, lustrous hair framing hazel eyes flecked with gold, a petite, upturned nose, and full lips.

The doctor stumbled and came to a stop, staring at Janelle.

Color rose in Chuck's cheeks as the doctor finally turned his attention to Rosie. "Well, hello there," he said, bending over the gurney, his voice warm and upbeat.

Rosie beamed up at him. "Are you a real doctor?"

"Why, yes. Yes, I am."

"Do you know how to ski?"

The doctor cocked his head. "As a matter of fact, I do."

Rosie's words fell over one another. "I knew it. It's because you live here, isn't it? Chuck says everybody who lives in the mountains knows how to ski. I get to learn how this winter. My name's Rosie. My sister learned how last year, but I didn't because I didn't want to. But now I want to because we live in the mountains, just like you. In Durango. We don't live in New Mexico anymore. Do you know where that is?"

The doctor nodded, providing all the encouragement Rosie needed.

"We're living at Y of the Rockies for the summer," she said. "All summer. It's a resort. It's fancy. Chuck says it isn't, but I think it is. I got to ride a horse. It's fun. We live in a cabin in the woods. But sometimes it's boring. But mostly it's fun."

The doctor grinned and put a hand on Rosie's shoulder to quiet her. He straightened. "I'm Dr. Akers," he said to Janelle. "What brings you here this evening?"

"Rosie—my daughter—" Janelle paused for no more than a millisecond, "*our* daughter—got sick. She had a fever. Then, in the middle of the night, she had a seizure of some kind."

"Can you describe it for me?"

The doctor looked down at Rosie, his hands on the gurney rails, as Janelle related the scene in the cabin. He turned back to Janelle when she finished.

"The good news," he said to her, "is that whatever was troubling Rosie clearly has passed, at least for now, and most likely for good. Your instincts were sound—your description is classic for a pediatric febrile seizure." He reached into the gurney and stroked Rosie's upper arm while keeping his eyes on Janelle. "Odds are she picked up a virus and seized when the fever peaked."

Chuck glanced away, his thoughts on how much Rosie's hospital visit—looking increasingly unnecessary—would cost.

The doctor shone a bright light in Rosie's eyes, listened to her heartbeat, palpated her abdomen, and ran his hand down the fading patches of red on her arm before turning back toward Janelle. "It's good you brought her in. Seizures can be dangerous things. At this point, I'd suggest we observe her for a bit before we do any expensive tests. We'll keep her comfortable, make sure she's headed in the right direction. That way, if it happens that we've got a zebra here, she'll be where she needs to be."

Chuck leaned in to catch the young doctor's eye. "A zebra?"

The doctor looked at Chuck for the first time. "Here in the ER," he explained, "when we hear hooves, we want to make sure it's simply a horse—something common and expected. Every now and then, though, the hooves turn out to be something uncommon—a zebra—and we want to be sure we're prepared for it."

Rosie's eyes grew large. "Like in Africa?"

The doctor gave her a reassuring smile. "Which is why I don't think you've contracted a zebra. Or a python either, for that matter. We're a long way from the Serengeti." He turned to Janelle. "I've got a couple of inpatients to check on. I'll leave you with Irene for now. Assuming all's well in a couple of hours, you and Rosie can head on home. I'll be right upstairs, just seconds away."

"Thank you, doctor," Janelle said.

The young physician rested his fingers on her forearm. "You can call me Gregory."

The muscles at the back of Chuck's neck tightened. The doctor gave Rosie's hand a quick squeeze and left the room.

The nurse motioned Chuck toward the front counter. "Time for the paperwork."

Chuck followed her across the room and took a seat in front of the counter. A multi-band police radio rested on the countertop beside the nurse's computer, its volume turned low. A male voice, barely audible, issued from the radio's small speaker. "...wrapping up...Code 12," the voice said.

Chuck recognized the law enforcement code number from his years of work on federal lands across the West. Code 12 was police-speak for a false alarm.

The tinny voice continued from the radio. "I should be 10-40 in five or ten."

Chuck let out a breath he hadn't realized he'd been holding. Logic said the voice on the radio belonged to the officer who'd responded to the Y of the Rockies resort complex thirty minutes ago—and now was readying for departure.

"Roger that, Hemphill," the dispatcher replied from the radio.

The nurse took her seat behind the counter, opposite Chuck. She rested a hand on the computer's mouse, her eyes on the monitor.

The officer's voice sounded again from the radio, this time

with a sudden, urgent edge. "Paula. You there? *Paula.*"

The dispatcher's response was immediate. "Yes, Jim. What've you got?"

Heavy breathing came over the radio; the officer was on the move.

"Paula," the officer said. "Looks like we have a potential 10-54. I repeat, a 10-54."

"A 10-54? Jim?"

When the officer's voice came back over the radio, it had lost all tones of authority. "Blood. Jesus, Paula. A whole bunch of it."

The nurse, concentrating on the computer screen in front of her, reached a casual hand to the radio and clicked it off.

THREE

Chuck struggled to make sense of the previous night's events as he trailed his field school students around the east flank of Mount Landen. Kirina led the way, fifty yards ahead. Clarence walked in front of Chuck, just behind the dozen students spread along the footpath.

The white, fifteen-passenger field school van was parked out of sight behind them, around the mountain at the side of Trail Ridge Road, five miles shy of the winding, two-lane highway's 12,183-foot high point. The road bisected Rocky Mountain National Park, connecting Estes Park on the east side of the Mummy Mountain Range with the town of Grand Lake on the west.

The morning breeze coursed over the summit of Mount Landen and swept down the rock-studded slope. The skein of clouds and spatter of rain that had descended from the Mummies and blown through Estes Park overnight were gone. In the wake of the clouds' departure, the clear morning sky heralded another in the string of cloudless days that had beset central Colorado since the last substantial snowstorm had rolled through the high country in March.

Now, a week and a half into August, the leaves and needles on the trees that made up the aspen and pine groves around Estes Park had a desiccated, pale green hue, and the park's famously rugged alpine landscape was so parched that lichen peeled from rocks like scabs. Clumps of bunch grass, brown and brittle, crumbled at the slightest touch.

The hint of rain the night before hadn't even been enough to wet the ground. The students' work boots kicked up small clouds of dust with each step along the path leading around the mountain to the mine three-quarters of a mile ahead, as they had every weekday morning for the last two months.

The breeze was cool this early in the morning. Chuck buried

his hands in his jacket pockets and burrowed his chin in his collar. He wanted only to reach the mine site, set the students to work, and put last night behind him.

Clarence fell back from the last of the students and spoke so only Chuck could hear. "You really think we should be here, *jefe*?" He glanced at Chuck over his shoulder, displaying a wan face and bloodshot eyes.

"Three days to go," Chuck said.

"That doesn't answer my question."

Chuck rubbed an eye with a knuckle.

Clarence continued. "Rosie was so sick you took her to the emergency room, the cops spent the whole night climbing all over each other outside the dorm, nobody got a bit of sleep, and you make us come up here like nothing happened?"

"Because nothing *did* happen."

"You were there. You saw what I saw, what we all saw."

"The cops thought it was a homicide. I get that. But they were wrong."

"It was a pretty big puddle."

"And that's all it was: a puddle of blood. No dead body, no nothing. As for Rosie, she's back at the cabin with Janelle, doing great."

Clarence huffed in exasperation. The wind whipped his long, raven-black hair around his neck. He gathered it in his hand and shoved it into the collar of his heavy cotton work jacket. His baggy jeans dragged at his heels, a mark of his urban upbringing with Janelle in Albuquerque's gang-ridden South Valley.

Clarence was big-boned and round-bellied. Thick silver studs pierced his ears. His nose was pressed like putty above his thick lips, which were encircled by a black goatee. Different as he was from his lithe older sister, Clarence shared Janelle's natural magnetism—she with her eye-popping looks, he with his big laugh, dancing eyes, and devilish grin.

An hour ago, in the dining hall behind the two dormitory buildings, the students' thumbs had been a blur of motion over their phones. They hadn't stopped texting until the van left cellphone range on the drive into the mountains. "You know as well as I do," Chuck told Clarence, "the kids would've spent the day tweeting and texting like mad." He shoved his hand back in his jacket pocket. "No telling what Sartore's going to make of it all."

"As if he doesn't already know."

"I texted him." Chuck hadn't received a response from the professor before they'd left phone range. "I'll call him as soon as we're back this afternoon."

Clarence clambered over a waist-high boulder protruding from the middle of the unimproved trail. "Sartore's not the only one you're avoiding today. What about Janelle?"

"Rosie was fine this morning, like last night never happened."

"Except it *did* happen." Clarence spun from the boulder and headed on down the trail. "You know Jan's not at all okay with your coming up here today."

Chuck threw his leg over the boulder. "She's got the truck. The doctor said she could bring Rosie back for another look, no charge, if she needed to. But he was pretty clear that everything was okay. Said it was just a virus." Chuck continued despite himself: "Young guy. Tall, blond hair, blue eyes. *Very* accommodating."

"Ready to swoop in, was he?"

"I'm still not used to it."

"*Digame, hombre.* Every dude lays eyes on her, it's like they want to swallow her whole. Even now, with the ring on her finger. Objectification, isn't that what they call it?"

"Ooo. Big word." Chuck pushed himself off the boulder and followed Clarence along the trail. "You'd know all about that, wouldn't you? What with all your pretty little *objects*."

"Hey," Clarence retorted. "We're talking about my sister here."

He toed a loose piece of granite off the trail. "That's how you won her over, you know. She was a person to you from day one."

Chuck spun the gold band on his finger. "Still is. A fire-breathing one. And yes, I know full well I'm risking my life coming up here this morning."

"Then why are we here?"

Chuck sighed. How could he admit to Clarence his real reason for adhering to schedule today? How could he confess to being that self-centered?

For the past two decades, as founder, CEO, and sole full-time employee of Bender Archaeological, Inc., Chuck had bid for and worked archaeological assessment contracts on his own or, on occasion, with the temporary help of recent anthropology school graduates such as Clarence. Chuck's contracts involved surveying and excavating sites of potential archaeological significance destined for development on federal, state, and Indian reservation lands. He left Durango for weeks at a time to complete the field portion of his work before returning home to prepare his final reports, cataloging the thousands of ancient artifacts he dug up and preserved on behalf of his clients before the bulldozers moved in.

Chuck's work had provided him a decent living—and no small amount of notoriety within archaeological circles for his many significant discoveries over the years—straight through to the day a year and a half ago when his then-temp worker, Clarence, had introduced him to Janelle. Four months later, after a whirlwind courtship and Albuquerque City Hall marriage, Chuck discovered upon heading back out on the road that the satisfaction he'd once found in working alone in the field had disappeared. Instead, he ached for the companionship Janelle and the girls gave him, missed the cacophony they brought to his former solitary existence.

Clarence turned his head when Chuck didn't respond. "I

asked you a question, boss."

Chuck looked past Clarence at the students—the six male members of Team Nugget and six women on Team Paydirt—as they made their way along the trail.

Silver-haired Ernesto Sartore, Chuck's anthropology professor two decades ago at Fort Lewis College in Durango, had called in April from out of the blue to offer Chuck a job running a group of students through Fort Lewis' eight-week field school in historical archaeology at the site of long-abandoned Cordero Mine, high in Rocky Mountain National Park.

"You're the top graduate our School of Anthropology has ever produced," Sartore told Chuck. "All your published papers, your finds displayed in museums across the country—you're our rock star."

"I'm not so sure about that," Chuck demurred, pleased by the unexpected praise from Sartore, with whom he hadn't been in contact for years.

He accepted Sartore's offer when Janelle agreed to bring the girls and spend the summer with him in Estes Park, thanks to her scheduled summer leave from the school receptionist position she'd found upon moving to Durango after their marriage last fall. Chuck called Parker, an old high-school buddy from Durango, and secured the secluded cabin at the back of the Y of the Rockies complex for himself, Janelle, and the girls, and use of Raven House for the students, with Clarence and Kirina providing live-in supervision.

Upon the start of the field school in June, Chuck, for the first time in his life, experienced the satisfaction of coming home to family at the end of each work day, and his insistence on sticking to schedule this morning was born of that contentment. He'd brought the students up into the mountains as planned today despite—or, more accurately, because of—last night's events; he wanted to assure no glitches during the final three days of the program put his plan to run another field school for Sartore next year at risk—he wanted to spend another contented summer with Janelle and the girls.

"You agree with Parker?" Chuck asked Clarence, changing the subject. "You think the thing with the blood isn't that big a deal?"

Clarence stopped and faced Chuck in the middle of the trail. "Tell you the truth, more than the blood itself, what really confuses me is the anonymous phone call."

Parker had told Chuck, and Chuck had told Clarence, that a 911 emergency phone bolted to a post in the grass fields at the center of the compound had been used in the middle of the night to alert the police to "something suspicious" next to Raven House. According to Parker, the unknown caller had spoken with a muffled voice, likely through a cloth wrapped around the receiver to avoid leaving fingerprints.

Clarence continued, "Somebody comes across some blood on the ground? That I can buy: a cook or dishwasher from Falcon House gets his hands on some chicken blood from the kitchen and dumps it on the ground—gross out your buddies, trick them into walking through it in the dark, snap a pic and put it online, whatever."

"Sounds like something you'd do."

"Sure. But if I did, I wouldn't call the cops about it. And if someone else saw it on the ground and felt the need to report it, why'd they work so hard to hide who they were?"

"Maybe if they were tricked into stepping in the blood," Chuck theorized, "and they wanted to get the person who did it in trouble without getting in any hot water themselves."

"The whole thing's strange, you ask me. Those cops, though?" Clarence blew a derisive jet of air through his lips.

"What about them?"

"So serious. They stayed till dawn—for a puddle of blood."

"It's Estes Park, population what, five thousand? Their whole careers are spent dealing with jaywalkers, shoplifters, people going thirty in a school zone. This is big stuff for them."

"Still. Crime scene tape? Spotlights? All the pictures they took? I'm telling you, if this had happened in the South Valley, the cops wouldn't even have shown up."

"You saw me talking to the guy in charge, Hemphill, the one I heard on the radio thinking he'd found a homicide. He seemed okay to me. Just trying to do his job."

"That's because you're from a small town, too, bro."

"He's watched a few too many cop shows on TV, that's all."

"Maybe," Clarence said. He shot Chuck a look. "Or maybe he knows something you and I don't."

Four

The sun was well up and the day quickly warming by the time Chuck gathered the students before him at the mine site.

Cordero Mine sat on a flat triangle of open, rock-strewn ground well above tree line on the east flank of Mount Landen, a mile around the peak from Trail Ridge Road. Ore cart tracks, bent and rusted with age, ran a hundred feet from the mouth of the long-abandoned mine's single underground tunnel to where the mountainside fell away to the east. A dark tongue of dumped tailings extended down the steep slope from the end of the tracks. The site was devoid of structures, save for a collapsed log cabin at the lip of the embankment that had housed miners a century ago.

The field school students stood in a half-circle in front of Chuck, their hardhats tucked beneath their arms. Several of the students cast tired looks at Chuck. Sheila, usually the liveliest of the group, appeared particularly wiped out.

Chuck lifted a consoling hand to the students. "I know you didn't get a lot of sleep last night. But we only have three days to go, and Professor Sartore wants to make sure you get your money's worth."

Sheila opened her mouth in an exaggerated yawn. "All I want to do is take a nap. I couldn't even make it for my spirit time today."

Sheila took a few minutes to herself each morning after breakfast, wandering up the slope into the forest behind the dormitories. She was a short, stocky Navajo steeped in spirituality and mysticism. Her cheeks were round and merry, her chestnut eyes generally filled with mirth. All summer, she'd rebelled—good-naturedly—against the field school, claiming her participation was due only to the fact that completing the course was required for her to graduate.

"I'm an anthropology major," she explained. "I just want to study my *Diné* people. But they say I have to do some field work if I want my degree, so here I am."

She had predicted the students' presence at the abandoned mine site would stir up ghosts—known on the Navajo reservation as skinwalkers. The male members of Team Nugget had declared their readiness to take on any and all angry spirits that dared haunt them.

Chuck lowered his hand. "The sooner we meet today's work goal, the sooner we can leave. We're almost there—today and tomorrow here at the mine, Thursday at Raven House finishing up the last of the logbooks, and Friday we are—" he held his hardhat in one hand and drummed it with the other "—outta here." He looked around the group. "Okay. Team Nugget in the tunnel, Team Paydirt's got the cabin."

The six young men of Team Nugget groaned in unison.

Acting on a suggestion from Professor Sartore, Chuck had selected the mine tunnel along with the collapsed miners' cabin for excavation during the final four weeks of the eight-week field school, following the students' survey and assessment of the entire mine site. The intrigue of working underground made the mine tunnel the students' preferred work assignment—at first. However, the reality of spending long hours in the cold, dark tunnel soon set in.

"We got the shaft three days last week," whined Jeremy, Team Nugget's chief complainer. "The girls were only in there for two."

Jeremy was thin and pale, with bony arms, angular cheekbones, dark brown hair slicked back from a high forehead, and eyes so large they shoved his eyelids out of place in their sockets. His pronounced Adam's apple rode up and down the front of his long neck whenever he spoke.

"You know the schedule," Chuck said. "Every other day. Paydirt was in there yesterday. You're on for today."

The mine tunnel, six feet wide by seven feet high, extended two hundred feet into the side of Mount Landen. A floor of heavy planks topped by the ore cart tracks ran the length of the tunnel. At the start of the summer, Chuck had placed pin flags to divide the tunnel floor into four equal sections. The students had dismantled, examined, and reassembled the floorboards and tracks of one flagged section each week for the past three weeks. The last week of the field school called for studying the final, deepest fifty feet of the tunnel.

Yesterday, under Kirina's direction, the members of Team Paydirt had dismantled the iron tracks and floorboard planks to within fifteen feet of the gray granite wall at the end of the tunnel. Team Nugget was to disassemble the last of the tracks and floorboards today, leaving tomorrow to root through the stony debris beneath the floorboards by hand—traditional trowel excavation of the tunnel's rocky base having proved impossible—and Thursday to reassemble the final stretch of floorboards and reattach the tracks.

Kirina addressed the members of her team. "Let's hit it, ladies."

Along with Chuck's suggestion to hire Clarence for one of the field school's two team-leader positions, Professor Sartore had suggested hiring Kirina, a graduate student from Northern Arizona University in Flagstaff, a few hours southwest of Durango. From day one, Kirina had impressed Chuck with her no-nonsense style. He'd learned over the course of the summer that her flat face, receding chin, and small, inset eyes hid a backbone of steel.

At one point, Chuck had overheard Jeremy refer to Kirina as "Hatchet Face," at another, he'd caught Jeremy referring to her derisively as "one of those square-faced dykes who swing both ways." If Kirina had heard those or any other derogatory remarks about her over the summer, she hadn't let on. She worked the students hard at the mine site, but always worked harder herself. Best of all, she did a far better job than Clarence of keeping an eye on the students during their off hours at Raven House, enabling Chuck to relax and enjoy his evenings and weekends with Janelle and the girls.

Kirina was a semester away from completing her Ph.D. in archaeological anthropology at NAU. In her mid-twenties like Clarence, she'd worked a number of digs during her grad-school years, making it easy for Chuck to put her in charge.

Chuck settled his hardhat on his head while Kirina led the members of Team Paydirt across the plateau to the site of the collapsed cabin. The students had numbered and stacked to the side the timbers from the collapsed cabin, and had staked and strung the cabin's cleared floor area using long iron spikes and white nylon cord to form a rectangular grid five units long by four units wide. So far, the students had excavated seventeen of the meter-square units a foot or two deep, to where the rocky soil beneath the cabin gave way to bedrock. The final three units of the twenty-unit grid awaited excavation over the next two days. Thursday, the students would refill the excavated grid and replace the cabin logs where they'd lain after their collapse a century or more ago, returning the cabin site to its original condition as required by Professor Sartore's contract with the National Park Service.

Kirina popped the lid off a plastic equipment bin next to the excavation grid and distributed trowels to Team Paydirt. Chuck walked with Clarence and Team Nugget to the mouth of the tunnel, which extended underground where the triangle-shaped plateau narrowed to a point in a fold in the face of Mount Landen. A rusted iron door in a thick metal frame was bolted into the mountainside, covering the mouth of the tunnel. The bottom half of the heavy door was solid iron, the top half a lattice of inch-wide iron bands welded to form six-inch squares. Hanging from the frame were a heavy chain and keyed padlock that served to secure the door when the site was unoccupied.

Chuck pulled the door open with a noisy creak and stepped aside, allowing Clarence to lead his team into the tunnel.

The six teammates, close friends from their past three years at Fort Lewis, were among the annual wave of high-school graduates who found their way over the mountains to "the Fort," as the college was known, from the cities and suburbs lining Colorado's Front Range.

Jeremy's irascibility aside, Chuck liked the members of Team Nugget. Though they wore the air of easy privilege about them like cloaks, all six were willing enough to put in the long hours and physical labor required of the field school despite the fact that only two were anthropology majors. The other four had signed up for the course simply as a way to spend the final summer of their college years together before going their separate ways after their upcoming senior year.

The team members put on their hardhats and clicked on their headlamps as they followed Clarence through the door. Chuck turned on his headlamp and followed. A stream of outside air coursed past him, drawn into the tunnel.

A mining engineer Chuck had hired at the beginning of the summer to assess the security of the mine tunnel had declared it safe from the risk of roof collapse, pointing out that no explosives, which might have damaged the tunnel's structural integrity, had been used in its construction.

"They did it the old-fashioned way," the fire-hydrant-shaped engineer told Chuck, putting his finger to one of the countless indentations in the wall where miners had chipped away at the granite interior of the mountain, lengthening the tunnel pickaxe blow by pickaxe blow.

The mining expert led Chuck deep into the tunnel, walking on the floorboards between the ore cart tracks three-quarters of the way to the bare back wall of the mine before turning and declaring it safe.

The engineer tapped the thick floorboard planks with the sole of his boot. "I like that they installed rails to cart out the tailings. And the quality of the floor, too. Shows they thought they were in it for the long haul." He directed the beam of his headlamp at the wall of the tunnel. "It's too bad, all this effort—pick-work, flooring, rails—and they just quit." He turned to Chuck. "I've seen it before, though. Probably ran out of money. Happened all the time."

"At least they didn't go too deep before they moved on," Chuck said.

The engineer faced the tiny rectangle of daylight that marked the doorway at the mouth of the mine one hundred fifty feet away. "They must've dug thousands of these things back then. Hell, tens of thousands." He grunted. "Just another empty hole."

FIVE

Chuck trailed Clarence and Team Nugget down the mine tunnel. The six students fell silent, subdued by the darkness and the tunnel's chill. They positioned the solar-powered LED floodlights to illuminate the day's work area and set about dismantling the final, fifteen-foot stretch of ore cart tracks and underlying floorboards. Each time they removed one of the planks, the young men crouched shoulder-to-shoulder around the newly uncovered rectangle of debris, looking for anything of interest.

At the start of their work in the tunnel three weeks ago, the students of both teams had groused about the extent to which Chuck required them to sift through the layer of gravel that comprised the base of the tunnel.

"We're searching for a needle in a haystack," Jeremy complained.

"Which is exactly what you signed up for," Chuck responded. "Olduvai Gorge, Tanzania. August, 1951. Hundred and ten in the shade. Louis and Mary Leakey scraping away at the side of a hill blazing day after blazing day. And what is it they found?"

"Frosty the Snowman," joked lumpy, disheveled Carson.

"Broken bits of stone tools," Chuck corrected. "Tiny pieces of bone. Tooth fragments. It was years before they came across the skull that made them famous."

"Oh, my God!" Carson exclaimed with an exaggerated shiver of fear. "A skeleton!"

"Everybody loves the mystique of archaeology's biggest discoveries," Chuck continued as Carson traded a fist bump with Jeremy. "Olduvai in Tanzania. The Valley of the Kings, Egypt. Machu Picchu, Peru. But the truths archaeologists work to uncover aren't tied up all neat and tidy in ribbons and bows. They're covered by jungle growth, buried in dirt and rubble, or—" he pointed at the base of the tunnel "—hidden beneath floorboards in an abandoned mine. Gravity is an archaeologist's best friend. Stuff falls down, other stuff covers it up, and it all lies there, waiting to be dug up and studied."

Jeremy gave a dismissive sniff. "Nothing's ever fallen in here."

"The laws of gravity aren't suspended underground," Chuck said. "Which is why each time we remove another board from the floor is so important." He added a note of wonder to his voice. "Who knows what might lie below?"

By now, Chuck knew the same thing the students knew: they wouldn't find much, if anything, amid the broken rock and rubble, just as they and Team Paydirt had found little of note upon disassembling the rest of the tunnel's floor over the last three weeks.

That, in fact, was the point, as Professor Sartore had explained to Chuck when he'd suggested the students excavate the tunnel. While the excavation of the cabin site was sure to provide a trove of finds, the tunnel would provide the opportunity for the students to realistically judge whether they wanted to go into the field of archaeology after experiencing the tedious, day-in-and-day-out work and dearth of discoveries that, in truth, comprised the bulk of archaeological inquiry.

Aside from a few rusted, Civil War-era peg nails dropped beneath the boards during the tunnel's construction, the students had uncovered only three items of interest: a broken pick-axe tip, a soggy box of matches, and a brass lipstick container. Of the three items, only the pickaxe tip dated from the tunnel's initial construction in the 1860s. The matches and lipstick container were from the 1950s, about the time park officials affixed the iron door to the mouth of the mine, putting an end to the increased exploration of the tunnel that had come with the completion and opening of Trail Ridge Road.

Fortunately, the teams' finds beneath the collapsed cabin numbered in the dozens—intact bottles, rusted tin cans, broken china and crockery and glass, and a few leather boot soles, dried and curled with age—precisely the type of items the National Park Service sought, by encouraging archaeological digs in its parks, for eventual display in park visitor centers and museums.

Chuck shuttled back and forth between Team Nugget and Team Paydirt throughout the morning, assuring himself Rosie was on the mend and banishing any thoughts of how Janelle would receive him when he returned to the cabin at the end of the day. Not long before lunch, he stood with Clarence between the tripod-mounted floodlights illuminating the final stretch of the mine tunnel. They looked on as the team pried loose their sixth floorboard of the morning, this one little more than a body's length from the end of the tunnel.

For the past few days, in a welcome attempt at overcoming the monotony of dismantling the floor of the tunnel unrevelatory plank by unrevelatory plank, Team Nugget member Samuel had taken to injecting some showmanship into the lifting of each loosened floorboard.

As his teammates prepared to remove the next plank, Samuel, green-eyed and sporting a prodigious, leprechaun-like red beard, stood beyond the other team members on the last of the intact flooring, his back to the chipped stone wall at the end of the tunnel. He spoke into his fist, assuming the role of a play-by-play announcer, his voice artificially deep.

"All is hushed," he intoned into his imaginary microphone.

Samuel's teammates crouched, unmoving, over the loosened plank.

"The members of Team Nugget, acting as one, work their fingers under the floorboard," Samuel continued.

Chuck couldn't help but smile as the five team members did as Samuel described, eliciting a quiet squeak from the loosened board as it moved in its place.

Samuel pounded the intact floor at the end of the tunnel

with his boots. "What might be hidden beneath one of the last boards to be lifted from the floor of the famed Cordero Mine?" he asked. His breath, lit by the floodlights, clouded in the moist air of the tunnel. "Could it be an ancient scroll? A map to hidden treasure? A key to a long-forgotten tomb?"

He paused. The team remained still, allowing the tension to build. Chuck bit his lower lip, caught up in Samuel's patter. It didn't matter that five times already this morning the team members had found nothing beneath the planks they'd lifted; Samuel's invented suspense was exhilarating nonetheless.

Samuel dropped his voice to a whisper. "And now, the Nuggeteers remove the ancient hunk of wood and peer beneath it."

The students lifted the heavy, moisture-laden plank, holding the board level so the shadow cast by the floodlights and their headlamps hid the narrow rectangle of gravel beneath it until the last possible second.

Samuel's voice grew louder as the students edged the plank away. "We begin to see what's underneath the floorboard," he exclaimed. He drummed his boots, and, while still speaking into his fist, he waved his free hand like a gospel preacher. "Yes, yes, it's...it's...we can almost see it now. It's a...I can't believe my eyes. Something shimmering. Hold up. What's that?"

The students set the plank aside.

"Diamonds," Samuel crowed jubilantly. "Rubies. Sapphires." He jumped into the air and landed with a resounding *thump* on the floorboards at the end of the tunnel. "A treasure like none other."

Samuel leapt again in feigned ecstasy. He landed on the floorboards with another loud *thump* while the five kneeling members of Team Nugget aimed their headlamps at the bare patch of ground formerly hidden beneath the plank.

Chuck leaned forward until he caught sight over the students' shoulders of what the team members were seeing—no rubies, no sapphires, just the rocky rubble spread by miners a century and a half ago beneath the paired timbers that ran the length of the tunnel, serving as a foundation for the floorboards.

On the far side of the kneeling students, Samuel turned his face to the tunnel ceiling and cried out, "The Seven Cities of Gold, the Treasure of the Sierra Madre, the Holy Grail—all pale in comparison to what has been discovered here today!"

He jumped into the air, pressing his hands to the roof of the mine. "Incredible!" he shouted as he landed, his weight depressing the floorboards with a dull crunch before they gave way with a splintering crash and Samuel plunged, screaming, from view.

Six

Chuck stumbled backward, slapping an arm across Clarence's chest.

The three students grouped on the near side of the newly removed floorboard tumbled backward along with Chuck and Clarence. Carson and Jeremy, on the far side of the plank, threw themselves forward, scrabbling for anything to hold onto as the floor fell away behind them. Before they, like Samuel, disappeared, each managed to grab the snapped end of one of the two rotted timbers that had served as the floorboards' foundation.

The three remaining students crawled on their hands and knees past Chuck and Clarence. Chuck scrambled forward, reaching a hand to Carson, hanging chest-deep in the black hole that had opened beneath the collapsed floor. Chuck pulled Carson out of the hole and into Clarence's waiting arms.

Jeremy fought for purchase, his fingers slipping on the wet, broken timber at the edge of the hole, which extended the width of the tunnel and all the way to the tunnel's back wall.

Chuck jammed a boot against the timber, anchoring himself at the edge of the six-foot-by-six-foot opening. Jeremy latched onto Chuck's ankle with both hands. Only Jeremy's head and neck showed above the edge of the hole. The rest of his body dangled into darkness. He gulped in terror, his Adam's apple jerking up and down.

With the addition of Jeremy's weight, Chuck's foot slid along the moist timber, inches from the gaping hole. He threw himself away from the opening, his arms outstretched, reaching for something, anything, before his foot broke free and Jeremy dragged him into the pit.

A pair of hands grasped him from behind. "Got you," Clarence said in his ear, toppling with Chuck to the ground between the timbers, his arm wrapped tight around Chuck's chest. Clarence extended his free hand past Chuck to Jeremy, who grabbed it and scrambled up and out of the hole.

As soon as Jeremy crawled past him, Chuck shook himself free of Clarence, rolled to his stomach, and extended his head over the edge of the pit, shining his headlamp into the darkness. To his immense relief, Samuel was not impaled on shattered floorboards at the bottom of the opened hole. The bearded young man clung to the side of the hole, eight feet below the floor of the mine tunnel, his feet kicking in space, his hands grasping the remnant of a handmade wooden ladder affixed to the wall of what appeared to be a downward extension of the mine.

A pair of rusted, iron stanchions secured the splintered, three-rung length of the ladder to the rock face of the vertical shaft. One of the stanchions broke free and the length of ladder dropped several inches on one side, nearly sending Samuel plummeting to the bottom of the pit.

"I can't hold on much longer," Samuel said, his voice strained, staring up at Chuck with fear-filled eyes. He toed the damp rock wall before him, searching for a foothold but finding none.

Chuck scanned the squared-off walls of the vertical shaft. He needed rope, webbing, carabiners, but he had no climbing gear at hand nor the time necessary to effect such an involved rescue.

He spoke over his shoulder in a staccato burst. "Grab my ankles. Now. *Everybody.*"

He shoved himself forward, counting on Clarence and the members of Team Nugget to respond to his terse command. His body canted downward as his torso extended past the edge of the hole. Hands wrapped themselves around his lower legs from behind.

"All the way," he said, worming his body past the lip of the opening. "Far as you can lower me."

Harsh exhalations of exertion sounded from behind Chuck as Clarence and the students lowered him headfirst into the vertical shaft. His hardhat slipped from his head and tumbled past Samuel, the beam of its headlamp wheeling off the walls as it fell. It struck one side of the shaft and ricocheted to the other before coming to rest, its lamp still shining, amid the wreckage of the collapsed floorboards and ladder some sixty feet below.

Chuck hung upside down, his face to the rock wall. The tops of his feet rested like angle irons on the lip of the vertical shaft, locking him in place.

He reached downward, past his head, but his outstretched fingers found only blank rock wall and moist air.

"Chuck," Samuel gasped, his voice flagging.

"Lower," Chuck called to Clarence and the students, his voice muffled against the rock wall. "You've got to get me lower."

He relaxed his feet. No longer using his own strength to help hold his body in place, he plunged downward several inches. Alarmed cries sounded from above as Clarence and the students halted Chuck's descent, their hands tight around his ankles.

Again Chuck reached past his head. This time, his groping fingers found the ladder rung to which Samuel clung. Chuck swept his hands along the rung until he came to Samuel's fingers, wrapped like steel bands around the wooden dowel. Stretching, Chuck reached lower and took hold of Samuel's wrists with both his hands.

"Let go," Chuck panted. "Grab my wrists."

"No," Samuel said.

"You've got to. We're running out of time. First one hand, then the other."

"I can't," Samuel said, his voice trembling.

The splintered length of ladder ripped free of the last stanchion holding it in place. Samuel swung away from the wall with an anguished cry, held aloft only by Chuck's grip on his wrists. He released the ladder rung and grabbed Chuck so that the two were attached wrist-to-wrist like a pair of trapeze artists.

"Up," Chuck said through gritted teeth, addressing Clarence and the students above. "*Up*."

Clarence and the members of Team Nugget pulled on Chuck's ankles, their groans filling the chamber, but Chuck and Samuel didn't budge.

"Can't...do...it," Clarence wheezed.

Blood pounded in Chuck's head, his grip on Samuel's wrists weakening.

"Climb past me," he told Samuel.

"I can't," Samuel whimpered.

"Do it," Chuck commanded, and pulled upward with his right arm, lifting Samuel's hand a few inches. "I'm letting go."

"No!" Samuel cried.

Chuck continued as if he hadn't heard. "Reach up my back, grab hold of my belt. Give it everything you've got."

"*No!*" Samuel gasped.

"On the count of one." Chuck didn't pause. "*One*."

Chuck slid his right hand free of Samuel's grasp, keeping his left hand wrapped around Samuel's other wrist. Samuel swung free, locked to Chuck by only one hand. Calling upon what must have been his last reservoir of strength, Samuel clambered monkey-like up Chuck's body from his belt to the hammer loop on the leg of his canvas work jeans to the lip of the hole and out.

Freed of Samuel's weight, Clarence and the team pulled hard on Chuck's ankles, bringing Chuck up a few inches, their heaving breaths echoing in the chamber as they struggled with the awkward angle.

"No...leverage," Clarence panted.

Chuck ran his hands across the face of the wall. It was wet and slick. He found a protruding nubbin of rock, but as soon as he leaned into it, his hand slipped.

He twisted sideways and stretched out a hand toward the lip of the hole.

"Have to switch," he gasped.

Hands reached into the pit, seizing Chuck's wrist.

Chuck twisted farther, reaching upward with his other hand till at last someone grasped it.

He hung sideways in the hole, bent like a pretzel, before hands, now clutching his wrists as well as his ankles, hauled him up and out.

Chuck collapsed on his back in the tunnel, his heart thumping. Clarence sat beside Chuck with his head between his knees. The students gathered on the far side of the floodlights, well away from the hole.

Chuck sat up when he caught his breath. "Everybody okay?" he asked the students.

Samuel bent to give Chuck an awkward hug. "You saved my life," he said, choking back tears.

"I did my job." Chuck rose and looked around at the other students. "Everybody did."

"This is *so* not what I signed up for," Jeremy declared. "I'm gonna call a lawyer soon as we get back to town."

Chuck stepped in front of him. "And claim what?"

"Pain and suffering."

"Show me your cuts and bruises."

"My what?"

"Show me your *pain*, your *suffering*."

Silence filled the tunnel.

Chuck shifted his gaze to Samuel.

"Don't look at me," Samuel said. "I'm alive. I'm fine."

Jeremy stared at his feet.

Chuck clamped his hand on Samuel's elbow. "What say we get out of here?"

He followed the team members and Clarence down the tunnel, exhausted by Samuel's rescue on the heels of his sleepless night, eager only to get back to the cabin and curl up in Janelle's arms.

He squinted past the students at the rectangle of light marking the mouth of the mine a hundred feet ahead. He would give the students the rest of the day off. Let them spend the afternoon texting and tweeting all they wanted.

Why not, in fact, have the students spend the remainder of the week at Raven House? There really was no need for them to return to the mine site. Instead, they could spend the last days of the field school sorting and cataloging the many items they'd discovered beneath the collapsed cabin.

If they headed for Trail Ridge Road as soon as they emerged from the tunnel, he'd be back at the cabin in less than two hours to make sure Rosie was still on the mend.

He warmed at the thought of the long, contented summer evenings he'd spent at the cabin with Janelle and the girls these last seven weeks—right up until Rosie's seizure and trip to the emergency room last night. To assure another field school directorship with Sartore next year—and another summer with Janelle and the girls—Chuck had simply to explain away the mine-floor collapse to the professor as the fluke it was, play down the discovery of the blood by the police, and make sure nothing else got in the way of bringing the field school to a problem-free close on Friday.

He followed Clarence and the members of Team Nugget out of the tunnel to find Officer Jim Hemphill of the Estes Park Police Department standing in the glaring sunlight, holding out a five-by-seven-inch color photograph.

"Anyone recognize this?" Hemphill asked.

Chuck shaded his eyes with his hand and squinted at the picture. His brain registered three colors: brown, red, and gray.

The brown was the background color of the photograph, consisting of dirt and dry grass. The red was a smear of liquid—blood, presumably—on the pictured object lying on the ground between tufts of grass. And the gray was the object itself, an open pocketknife with a four-inch tungsten handle.

Chuck recognized the knife immediately.

It belonged to Clarence.

SEVEN

Hemphill waited, the photograph outstretched. Chuck held his breath and waited, too.

Hemphill cleared his throat. "I told you we might need to check in with you again."

Chuck inclined his head. The members of Team Nugget edged away from the officer to stand with Kirina and Team Paydirt near the collapsed cabin. Clarence remained at Chuck's side, the mountain rising behind them.

Officer Hemphill, in his early thirties, stood a tad under six feet in his black leather sneakers. His large front teeth, pillowy cheeks, and flared nostrils gave him the inquisitive appearance of a squirrel.

Hemphill's pant legs were dusty from his hike to the mine. A pair of sunglasses hung from the front pocket of his creased shirt below his brass badge, and a department-issue windbreaker was draped over his arm. A baseball cap rode low on his forehead, the cap's crown embroidered with the gold letters *EPPD*. Hemphill jiggled the photograph, causing sunlight to glint off its glossy coating. "I'm hoping you'll recognize this. We asked the workers in Falcon House, but none of them claimed it."

"Where was it?" Chuck asked.

"Outside the back door to Raven House."

Chuck's chest constricted. Should he cover for Clarence? No. Lying to Hemphill would lead to no good. Besides, everybody—the residents of Falcon House included—knew who the knife belonged to.

Over the summer, Clarence had spent many of his evenings whittling with his knife while he hung out on the front steps of Raven House, visiting with the field school students and the international workers from Falcon House next door. He made no secret of storing the knife in his backpack, which he left

41

stacked with the rest of the students' packs in the unlocked Raven House common room each evening, ready to be stowed in the van first thing in the morning for the drive to the mine site.

Clarence spoke at Chuck's side. "That's my knife."

Hemphill showed no surprise. He lowered the picture. "Can you tell me why we found it on the ground behind your dormitory with blood all over it?"

Clarence looked straight at Hemphill. "I don't know how it ended up where you found it, and I have no idea how it got blood on it, either."

The officer tapped the photograph against the side of his leg. "But you say it's yours."

"I'm *saying* it's mine because it *is* mine, or one that's identical to it, anyway."

"Where'd you last see it?"

Clarence pointed at the group's packs, lined at the edge of the site. "I keep it in my pack."

"Do you mind?"

Clarence led Hemphill and Chuck across the site to the daypacks. Kirina and the students looked on in silence.

Clarence picked out his backpack, a black North Face with a large compartment for food, water, and clothing, and a small, outer pocket for sundries. He checked the outside pocket and came up with nothing. He rummaged inside the main compartment, extracting his rain jacket, a sack lunch, and a liter bottle of water, but no knife.

He turned to Hemphill. "It's gone."

"You live in Raven House, right?"

Clarence nodded.

"Any reason it might be back in town, in your room?"

"I keep it in my pack. I use it to make the crew's excavation sticks."

In response to Hemphill's furrowed brow, Clarence explained, "They're for digging out and cleaning found objects. Everyone thinks trowels and dental picks are best, but for close-in work, you want wood because it doesn't scratch. I make different sizes, with blunt and sharp points."

"You know your way around a knife," Hemphill observed.

Clarence's eyes filled with fury. Before he could cut loose on the officer, Chuck jumped in. "What's that supposed to mean?" he demanded.

"Just an observation," the officer said, his voice flat.

Chuck made no attempt to hide his anger. "Sounds like you're making use of the same keen observation skills you used last night. Take a million pictures, keep my students up all night, and for what? A little bit of blood soaking into the ground." He exhaled, attempting to calm himself. "Look, you and I both know what happened. Somebody took a chicken from the cafeteria, cut it up, dropped it, made a mess, whatever. Probably one of the cooks. He doesn't want to admit to it because he's afraid he'll get in trouble." Chuck pointed at Clarence's pack. "A guy who would steal from the cafeteria would have no problem stealing somebody's knife, too."

"I considered that," Hemphill said. "Then I got back to HQ, put a drop of the blood we collected on a slide, and stuck it under our microscope."

"*HQ*," Chuck mimicked, his voice dripping with sarcasm. "CSI: Estes Park."

Hemphill's face flushed, but his voice remained steady. "I was a paramedic before I joined the department. It's pretty simple, really. Red blood cells are distinctive from animal to animal. Pig to cow, cow to chicken." He paused. "Chicken to human."

Chuck straightened. "I take it your microscope told you something."

"We won't know for sure until we get the official test results back in a few days. But the red blood cells on the slide had the distinct donut shape that is unique to one creature and one creature only—Homo sapiens."

"You're saying last night's blood was...is...human."

"That's the early indication."

At Chuck's side, Clarence drew a breath.

Chuck's heart thumped hard in his chest. No wonder Hemphill was still on the clock after working the scene through the night—and why he'd deemed it worthwhile to hike all the way to the mine this morning. "But you don't have a body, right?" Chuck asked. "And no one has turned up injured at the hospital?"

Hemphill's silence provided the answer.

Clarence faced the police officer. "That's my knife in your picture. You and I both know it." His voice rose. "But I sure as hell didn't stab anybody with it."

Hemphill stiffened, his arms tight at his sides.

Chuck clenched and unclenched his jaw. "If you have no more questions," he told the officer, "then I think we're done here."

Hemphill pivoted and held the photograph out to where Kirina and the students stood in a knot beside the excavated cabin site. "Can any of you tell me how this knife might've ended up behind your dorm building last night? Or how it could have gotten blood on it?"

Chuck opened his mouth, ready to break in before the students said anything incriminating. But what if one of them offered information that would free Clarence from suspicion? Chuck settled back on his heels.

Hemphill allowed several seconds to pass. When none of the students responded, he said, "Thank you for your attention."

He turned and spoke only to Clarence. "We'll be in touch."

EIGHT

Not until the police officer was well away from the mine site did Chuck turn to the students.

"Lunch break," he said.

Kirina clapped her hands. "You heard the man."

The students removed their sack lunches and water bottles from their packs and spread out around the site in twos and threes, sitting on boulders or the stacked cabin logs or cross-legged on the ground. They leaned close to one another, whispering and directing furtive glances at Clarence, who stood in place, shifting his weight from one foot to the other.

Chuck picked up his pack and motioned for Clarence to do the same. "Let's get out of here," he said, leading Clarence across the mine site to where Samuel sat looking at his sandwich.

Chuck gave the young man a reassuring tap on the shoulder. "You did great in there."

Samuel offered a pallid smile. "So did you."

"Let's you and me never do that again, okay?"

Samuel aimed his chin at the mine tunnel. "I'm never going back in there."

"You won't have to. No one will."

With Clarence following, Chuck crossed to the far side of the mine site and angled up Mount Landen's northeast ridge. Though he was breathing hard by the time he reached the ridge crest, he hadn't escaped the questions presented by Officer Hemphill's appearance at the mine.

Clarence reached the top of the ridge a minute later. He bent forward, his hands on his knees, his stomach heaving. When his breathing calmed, he straightened and joined Chuck in looking north off the ridge into Fall River Valley far below. The valley was bisected by Fall River Road, a tan ribbon snaking through the trees. The park's original route to the high country predated the construction of Trail Ridge Road by several decades. These days, the road was a little-used gravel byway.

High above the valley to the north and west, the three tallest peaks of the Mummy Range, Ypsilon, Chiquita, and Bighorn, jig-sawed the skyline. The midday breeze coursing over the ridge was warm, the sky clear and blue.

By this hour on any normal summer day in the Mummies, massive thunderheads should have been building above the mountain peaks, leading to afternoon storms that would lash the high country with rain, sleet, hail, even snow. But this was no ordinary summer. In contrast to the heavy summer rains and raging floods that had washed out roads and devastated downtown Estes Park a few years ago, this summer the park was gripped by drought attributable, scientists said, to the extremes of global climate change, just as the floods had been.

Though the months-long drought was hard on the park's flora and fauna, the string of cloudless days had made the students' work at the mine easy these past weeks. Collapsible nylon shelters, toted by the students to the site at the beginning of the summer to protect their excavation work from downpours, remained stowed in stuff sacks at the edge of the site. Not once over the last seven weeks had the students been forced to don their raincoats.

Chuck and Clarence sat facing west on a pair of rocks, the summit of Mount Landen high above them, Fall River Valley more than a thousand feet below.

"Time to figure this thing out," Chuck said.

"What's to figure?" Clarence asked. "My knife, human blood, white-man cop ready to lock me away."

"We're not in the South Valley, Clarence."

"I'd be better off if we were. At least a few Albuquerque cops have the same skin color as me." He flicked an angry hand. "You saw how he treated me. He's got my arrest warrant all ready to go."

"He's just getting started on his investigation."

"Easy for you to say. It's not your knife they found."

"No one knows if a crime's even been committed yet."

"Doesn't matter. Whatever happened, he figures I did it." Clarence gave his Latino accent free rein. "*El Chicano. El spic.*" His voice grew bitter. "I never should've come here this summer."

"What are you talking about?"

Clarence gave Chuck a level look. "Jan knows. Even the girls have felt it."

Chuck studied the north slope of Mount Landen. Narrow, stone-walled couloirs cut into the bare, alpine slope every couple hundred yards. Where the pitch of the slope lessened, the couloirs came together to form a funnel-like drainage that twisted and turned before disappearing into the forest on its way to the river below.

He pressed his fingers into his thighs. For a year now, Janelle and the girls had shared their lives with him—a middle-aged white guy making his way through the world with his brown-toned stepdaughters and mocha-hued wife. He'd seen the heads turn; he'd read the appraising looks in people's eyes.

"They don't mean anything by it," he told Clarence.

"So what. We're still plenty different from the upstanding, white-bread folks of Estes Park, and different is all that matters."

"You're overreacting. We'll head back to town, find a lawyer, get this thing sorted out."

"*No.* No lawyers. I'm not guilty of anything. Somebody took my knife. I had nothing to do with it. I don't need a lawyer."

"We've got to make sure—"

"I said *no*," Clarence repeated. "What we have to do is figure out what happened. And we have to do it on our own, before the cops stick it to me."

"They've got nothing to charge you with."

"They'll come up with something. Just you watch."

"I *was* watching. I saw a cop doing his job."

"We need to think beyond him—to the students, the workers next door. Somebody saw something. They had to. You can get Kirina to talk to the students. I'll talk to the Falcon House people. They won't say anything to the cops, but they'll talk to me."

Chuck lifted an eyebrow. At the beginning of the summer, he'd made it clear that the field school's female students were off limits to Clarence, full stop, no exceptions. Chuck had seen the looks every one of the Fort Lewis girls, even Kirina, had aimed at Clarence when he was at his most alive and magnetically electric. To his credit, however, Clarence had taken Chuck at his word and had focused his charms on the flock of female, college-age resort workers from Eastern Europe boarding for the summer in Falcon House.

"You really think," Chuck asked, "that whoever sliced somebody with your knife is going to turn around and confess what they did to you?"

"Somebody's sure to know something. And there's plenty who will let me know what they know."

Chuck eyed Clarence. "How many are we talking about?"

Clarence avoided Chuck's look. "It's been a whole summer."

"It's been a month and a half."

"I don't put notches in my belt."

"*How many?*"

Clarence addressed the line of peaks marching away into the distance. "Three or four. Five, maybe."

Chuck shook his head. "Unbelievable. And how many guys over in Falcon House do you suppose you've managed to piss off in the process?"

Clarence twisted to face Chuck. "All the guys living in Falcon House are a bunch of *campesinos* from *México*—cooks, janitors, dishwashers—sending their money home and counting the days till they can get back to their families."

"And the young women?"

"They're on their big summer adventure from Romania, Bulgaria, places like that. Ready to par-*tay*. They're way out of those *Méxicanos'* league."

"But not yours."

"Nobody's out of my league."

"I bet you made one of the Mexicans jealous."

"So he did what, took my knife and stabbed somebody with it? What sense would there be in that?"

"I'm still thinking it through," Chuck admitted.

"While you're doing your thinking, let me tell you what I already know. Nobody's going to come forward and tell the cops, 'Hey, guess what. I stole Clarence's knife and slashed somebody with it and they stood there and bled for a while and then they ran off into the woods and now they're gone.' Which means the focus is going to stay right on *me*."

"All the more reason to get a lawyer."

"Wrong. The cop said they're going to call me in for more questioning, right? Later today, probably, or maybe tomorrow. When they do, I want them to see I got nothin' to hide. If I come in all lawyered up, they'll figure it's me for sure. They'll focus everything they've got on nailing me to the wall." Clarence took a deep breath. "I have to show them I'm a victim of circumstance, that whatever crime was committed—*if* a crime was committed—was somebody else's doing."

"Who do you suppose *did* get their hands on your knife?"

"Could've been anybody. It's not like I was hiding it."

"Somebody must've grabbed it to do some whittling, like you," Chuck reasoned. "They cut themselves by accident. They can't bring themselves to say anything. Not yet, anyway."

"You saw how much blood there was. They'd've had to cut themselves pretty deep."

"Maybe they were drunk."

Clarence rolled his eyes.

"Really drunk," Chuck insisted.

Clarence grunted. "Wasted," he said flatly.

"Blotto," Chuck offered.

Clarence's mouth lifted in the start of a smile. "Blasted."

Chuck nodded. "Blitzed."

Clarence grinned. "Pulverized, dude. Totally, absolutely obliterated."

Chuck chuckled and bent over his pack, digging out his lunch. The faint rattle of tumbling rocks reached him from where Mount Landen's rugged northwest ridge etched the skyline half a mile away.

He looked up in time to see a Rocky Mountain sheep clamber into sight over the top the ridge. The sheep, a ewe, was followed by another ewe, then another. Gradually, three dozen more sheep ambled over the ridge, their hooves sending small stones clattering into a steep couloir below them. The animals fanned out, nipping at the dry, brown bunch grass on the slope as they made their way across the north side of the mountain toward Chuck and Clarence.

Chuck scanned the grazing sheep, looking for trophy rams. His eyes fell on animal after animal. Each was a ewe, a first-year lamb, or a juvenile male with nascent, half-curl horns—yet a herd this big should not be without two or more adult rams with broad chests and fully curled horns.

Chuck slid his sandwich from its baggie and bit into it, waiting to spot the heavy-horned rams sure to trot over the ridge to unite with the herd at any moment.

The sheep continued to graze their way across the north

slope of the mountain. By the time Chuck finished his sand-wich, the sheep were well clear of the ridge—and not a single adult ram had topped the rocky crest to join them.

NINE

Chuck's phone pinged several times to announce incoming texts when the van reentered service range on the way back to the resort. Throughout the van, phones dinged and chimed, prompting the students to stop talking to one another and set their thumbs to work.

Chuck pulled the van to a stop at Raven House fifteen minutes later. The students grouped at the rear door to retrieve their packs, then stood with their packs in hand, waiting for Chuck to address them.

Chuck slipped between the students to the rear of the van, grabbed his pack, and backed away a few steps. What was there to say?

His eyes roamed from old, rundown Raven House with its warped, clapboard exterior to new, stucco Falcon House capped by its shiny, green metal roof. Between the two buildings, amid tufts of buffalo grass, he spotted the shallow divot dug by the police the night before to gather the blood that had soaked into the ground.

Someone knew something about Clarence's knife and the human blood, and that someone was either one of the students standing before him, or one of the Falcon House employees.

Who might it be? He hadn't a clue.

He glanced across the fields toward the cabin. Janelle's glare as he'd left this morning had made clear the risk he'd taken in heading to the mine with the students so soon after Rosie's seizure. He assumed Rosie hadn't suffered a relapse today because he'd gotten no voicemails or texts from Janelle—though the absence of any of her usual, chatty messages was a bad enough sign by itself.

When they realized Chuck had nothing to say, the students turned and headed up the walk to Raven House. Chuck slung his pack over his shoulder and motioned Clarence and Kirina to his side.

"Stick close to the dorm," he told them. "I want to know who's talking to who, whether anybody's acting shady."

A corner of Kirina's mouth drew up. "*Acting shady?*" She crossed her arms over her chest. "I can tell you one thing. Whatever this is, no one from Team Nugget is involved. My girls aren't thieves, and they're not knife-wielding maniacs either."

Clarence declared, "My guys aren't involved either. I'm sure of it."

Breaking the students into two work teams had been Clarence's idea. Chuck had expected problems when the students had self-selected their teams along gender lines. To his surprise, however, the members of the two teams had gotten along well with each other at the mine and during their off hours throughout the summer.

"Nobody's accusing anybody of anything at this point," Chuck said. "Just keep your eyes open, okay? Both of you."

He hurried across the fields, past the lodge and conference center, and up the curving drive through the woods to the cabin. He owed Professor Sartore a call, but Rosie took priority—as did squaring things with Janelle.

He released his bottled-up breath when he saw the pickup still parked where he'd left it upon returning from the hospital the night before. But a vehicle he didn't recognize—a rugged SUV with a Rocky Mountain Elk Foundation sticker on its bumper and a mountain bike attached to a rack on its roof—was parked next to the truck. Janelle opened the cabin's front screen door as Chuck approached, allowing Gregory, the young doctor from the emergency room, to step onto the wooden deck ahead of her.

Gregory hailed Chuck from the uncovered porch with a

wave and a wide smile. "Yo, dude."

Chuck stopped at the bottom of the short flight of stairs leading to the deck. "Hey."

Janelle, trailing Gregory out the door, came to an abrupt halt at the sight of Chuck. "Gregory called and asked if he could make a house call," she explained.

Gregory flipped his blond hair out of his eyes with a toss of his head. "I finished my shift. Figured I'd swing by, make sure Rosie was cool."

Chuck's eyes went from the young doctor to Janelle and back. He addressed Gregory, keeping his voice even. "I take it everything's...*cool*?"

Janelle spoke first. "I told him she was doing fine when he called."

Gregory shrugged. "I got a few hours of shut-eye last night, after you guys left. Usually I go straight home and hit the sack at the end of my shifts."

Chuck knew he should say something appreciative. Unlike the doctor, however, he hadn't gotten any sleep last night. Besides, his appreciation would be expressed through his payment of the medical bill.

"Guess I'll get going then," Gregory said when Chuck didn't speak. The young physician turned and pointed a friendly finger at Rosie and Carmelita, who stood together behind the screen door. "Glad to see you doing so well, Rosie. And you, Carmelita, take good care of your little sister for me, okay?"

"Okay," Carmelita said with a shy smile before looking at her feet.

Chuck stood aside to allow Gregory to descend the stairs. When the doctor was well down the drive in his SUV, Chuck climbed the steps to Janelle and summoned a smile. "She's really doing okay, huh?"

Janelle rigidly accepted a peck on the cheek. He turned at the sound of pounding feet to see Rosie hurtling herself across the porch at him.

"Chuck!" she cried, diving into his arms. "I'm all better now. I'm the bestest ever."

Chuck lifted her and settled her on his hip, her legs dangling past his knees. "You are, are you?" He looked to Janelle for confirmation.

"She slept late this morning," Janelle said. "She's been her usual, rip-roaring self since lunchtime. It's all I've been able to do to get her to stay inside and take it easy."

Chuck lowered Rosie to the porch and crouched to speak to her and Carmelita, who had trailed Rosie onto the deck. "Why don't you two rip-roar back inside. Your *mamá* and I will be along in a minute."

Rosie followed Carmelita into the cabin. Chuck tossed his pack on one of the plastic deck chairs arrayed on the porch and motioned Janelle to follow him down the steps. He dropped the truck tailgate and took a seat on it. She hoisted herself up beside him.

He allowed the quiet of the surrounding forest to sink in, the only sound the call and response of a pair of magpies flitting from branch to branch through the ponderosa trees above their heads.

Janelle turned to him. "Where do we start?"

"She's really okay?"

"She's sniffling a little, but it's pretty much gone, like the doctor said."

"Gregory," Chuck said, an unintended edge to his voice.

"We're talking about Rosie," Janelle replied, her chin held high.

The afternoon sun reflected off the tiny jewel affixed to the side of her nose. The gold flecks in her hazel eyes shimmered. Chuck swallowed. God, she was beautiful. The young doctor's ogling of Janelle last night had lacked any semblance of professionalism—but who could blame him for taking advantage of the opportunity for another look today?

Chuck took Janelle's hand in his. "I'm sure Clarence has texted you by now."

She shook her head no.

Chuck stifled a groan. He kept it brief—the tunnel-floor collapse, the appearance of the officer at the mine with the photo of Clarence's bloody knife, and the suspicion that the blood was human.

Janelle slid her hand free of Chuck's as he finished: "The cop said they'll follow up. Later today, maybe tomorrow." He read the look in her eyes. "And no, I'm sure Clarence doesn't want you to say anything to your parents."

Too late, she looked away.

Chuck continued, "He's refusing to let me get him a lawyer. Says it'll make him look guilty."

She turned back. "But you disagree."

"I do. He's got a point, though. There's no actual crime involved. Not yet, anyway."

"What do we do next?"

Chuck closed his eyes. All he wanted to do next was sleep.

He opened his eyes and looked down the drive toward the Y of the Rockies lodge and conference center. "Parker," he said.

TEN

As he drove down the two-track, Chuck called Professor Sartore. In addition to the text he'd sent the professor in the morning, he had emailed Sartore a brief rundown of the previous night's events before setting off for the mine after breakfast.

"What the hell is going on up there?" Sartore barked over the phone. "I've already heard from three different sets of parents."

"You know college kids," Chuck said. "They love drama."

"How much drama are we talking about?"

"More than I'd prefer. But things are settling down."

"That's not the sense I'm getting. What's this I hear about your brother-in-law's knife?"

Chuck braked to a stop where the driveway reached the gravel road. He filled Sartore in on the appearance of the cop at the mine, picturing the professor's bushy white eyebrows working up and down in consternation as he listened.

"You understand," Sartore said when Chuck finished, "this is a multi-year contract we've signed with the park service. The plan is to start with Rocky Mountain and expand from there. Yosemite, Grand Canyon, Yellowstone. The opportunities for Fort Lewis and the School of Anthropology—and for you, too, I might add—are significant."

"I know, professor."

"And this is the first year," Sartore said, gaining steam. "The very first summer."

"Yes, sir."

"This whole thing with your guy's knife?" Sartore thundered. "And blood? And now you're saying it's human? It's absolutely the last thing we need." The professor's heavy breaths came over the phone. "Don't you have something else you want to tell me about?"

"I was getting to that."

"Go right ahead."

"A small section of the tunnel floor gave way. No one was hurt."

"The parents who called made it sound like it was the end of the world."

"College kids," Chuck reiterated.

"I hired you for a reason, Chuck. I tracked you down after all these years. You're my adult up there, my boots on the ground. There's as much opportunity for you in the summers ahead as there is for the college. But not if things keep going the way they are right now. You've got to keep a lid on things there, understand?"

"Perfectly, sir." Chuck hoped the professor was thinking the same thing he was: three more days, just three more days.

"Keep me up to speed on this situation with the knife," Sartore said. "And make damn sure nothing else happens up there, because right now, your ass is on the line."

"Got it, professor."

Chuck pulled around the conference center and threw the truck into park, steaming. Who was Professor Sartore to put him on the spot for events beyond his control?

He cut the engine and sat behind the wheel while he calmed himself down. The truth was, he couldn't blame the professor for being so concerned. A lot had happened in the last twenty-four hours, none of it good. If he wanted to work for Sartore again next summer, he had to do as the professor said—keep things quiet from here on out.

Besides, it wasn't as if the professor's outburst came as a surprise. His volcanic temper was legendary on the Fort Lewis campus. Chuck remembered Sartore ripping into students for unsatisfactory work two decades ago. The professor hadn't changed in the years since.

Chuck took a steadying breath and got out of the truck,

heading toward the conference center. The massive log building and the matching lodge next door had been constructed by the Civilian Conservation Corps during the Depression in the 1930s. A banquet room took up most of the first floor of the conference center. Smaller meeting rooms honeycombed the second. Chuck had texted ahead to set up the meeting in Parker's office, which occupied a front corner of the building's third floor.

Chuck climbed the steps to the top story, knocked on Parker's office door, and entered when the resort manager called out for him to come in.

Parker's large office was done up in L.L. Bean chic. A plaid Pendleton blanket lay over the back of a leather sofa against one wall. Lacquered rainbow trout on plaques hung above the couch. A life-size, chain-saw sculpture of a bear hewn from a thick stump of wood filled a corner of the room. The bear stood on its hind legs, paws upraised, mouth open in full roar.

The resort manager stood behind his desk at a wide picture window overlooking the fields and, across the expanse of grass to the south, additional resort buildings, including scattered rental cabins, rows of condominiums, a snack stand, and, off to one side, horse stables.

A few hundred yards farther south, two-story brick buildings lined three blocks of Elkhorn Avenue, comprising Estes Park's compact business district. Beyond, on a hillside facing town, perched the famous, eggshell-white Stanley Hotel with its distinctive red roof.

In his Durango High School days, Parker had been a slight, fidgety student, prone to biting his nails and obsessing over girls, grades, and his bad acne. Chuck's former close school friend hadn't changed much in the intervening years. Parker was still given to quick, nervous gestures and to voicing seemingly every concern that crossed his mind. He was still thin, too, with a long, aquiline nose, darting eyes, and a close-cropped beard that almost hid his acne scars.

Parker waved Chuck toward one of the horseshoe-shaped club chairs in front of his expansive oak desk. The resort manager wore jeans and a bright blue polo shirt, the Y of the Rockies logo on its breast.

He turned to look out his office window, his fingers drumming the top of a binocular case on the windowsill, before pivoting back to Chuck. "Jim called me."

"The police officer?"

"He told me about the knife. Said it belongs to your foreman."

"My crew leader, Clarence."

"He's your wife's brother, right?"

"That's him. He's worked for me for a couple years."

"He's not that old, as I recall."

"Twenty-five. Out of the University of New Mexico School of Anthropology. Says he had nothing to do with it. I believe him."

"Like you have any choice—your brother-in-law." Parker dropped into his suede-leather office chair, its arms outlined by brass rivets. "You know I did you a favor, having you stay here this summer, setting you up with your own cabin, letting your students room in Raven House."

"We're paying you good money, and you know it. Besides, you didn't seem to think this whole thing with the blood was that big a deal last night."

"That was before I heard about the knife."

Chuck sat forward. "No crime has even been alleged at this point."

"You have to understand my position. The owners..." Parker's voice trailed off.

"The owners what?"

"They're new. A couple of oil-and-gas guys, brothers, out of

Texas. They kept me on as manager, even gave me a raise. Just in time, too, with Joanie off to Colorado State next week. But they're control freaks. They don't like it when things get messy. They're all about 'standards.'"

"Name one thing my students have done this summer that has not lived up to your 'standards.'"

"That's not what I'm saying."

Chuck pressed on. "You and I both know the source of your problems."

"What do you mean by that?"

"Clarence and Kirina, my other crew leader, have had to call me more than once this summer on account of your people in Falcon House."

Parker straightened in his chair. "You never told me anything about that."

"It was always late, past midnight. A little too much drinking, a little too loud with the partying. They settled down when I talked to them. I didn't want to bother you."

"But you're telling me now."

"You're the one accusing my people of whatever's going on over there. You need to remember that this pool of blood on the ground wasn't necessarily found next to Raven House. It was found *between* Raven House and Falcon House—between your people and mine."

"But it's still your brother-in-law's knife we're talking about, isn't it?"

"All I'm asking, Parker, is that you give Clarence the benefit of the doubt until we learn more from the police."

The resort manager steepled his fingers in front of him, his elbows on the arms of his chair. "Your wife's brother."

"My wife's brother."

"You want me to sit around and wait for whatever the police decide to do."

"Not much else we can do, the way I see it. I got the sense from the officer that it'll be a while before they get any official lab response on the blood they found. The field school ends Friday. Three days and we'll be gone."

"Three days." Parker folded his hands in his lap. "I'll be counting."

Chuck descended the main stairway, his footsteps echoing in the building's cavernous central hall with its enormous support beams and huge, elk-antler chandeliers hanging from thick chains. He pushed through the heavy, wooden entry doors and stood aside as a troop of chattering Girl Scouts, green sashes over their shoulders, filed into the lobby.

He pulled his phone from his pocket and walked toward a pair of Adirondack chairs arranged on the covered porch at the front of the building. He lowered himself stiffly into one of the chairs, its high back creaking as he leaned against it. A couple leaned on the railing and looked out at the fields, where a group of youngsters played kickball, another bunch of kids shot arrows toward a tall, wooden backstop on the far side of the expanse of grass, and, just across the conference center parking lot, a dozen adults stood in line at the edge of the yellowing grass, fly poles in hand, honing their casting skills under the tutelage of a gray-bearded man wearing a multi-pocketed fishing vest and a hat ringed with feathered flies.

Chuck texted Clarence. *Any word from the police?*

Clarence's reply was immediate. *Nothing yet. I'm thinking tomorrow.*

Stay close. Don't go anywhere.

Wouldn't think of it.

Chuck checked the time on his phone. Coming up on four o'clock. Clarence was probably right—the cops, having been up all the previous night, were finished for the day.

The chair squeaked as Chuck shifted to pocket his phone

and rested his head back, closing his eyes. The yellow pine slats were dry but sturdy, unlike those mine floorboards. He'd walked back and forth along those floorboards dozens of times over the last three weeks, their knots and nails aglow in the light of his headlamp. Starting at the tunnel's mouth and continuing nearly its full length, the boards were cut to uniform size, roughly five feet across, long enough to cover most of the bottom of the tunnel from one side to the other, but short enough to account for variations in distance between the side walls—all except the floorboards at the back of the mine.

The planks covering the last few feet of the tunnel bottom were different, he now remembered. Each of those boards had been cut to fit precisely from one side of the tunnel to the other, leaving no open space showing on either side.

He caught his breath. The section of floor at the back of the mine had been constructed with a specific goal in mind: to hide all signs of the vertical shaft.

ELEVEN

The drive into town took less than five minutes. Chuck turned down Elkhorn Avenue, past the bookshop and knickknack stores, and parked in front of Estes Park's public library, a sleek, stone-and-glass structure built on the banks of the Big Thompson River at the east edge of town. He pushed through the heavy glass front doors and headed for the research librarian's desk at the back of the main floor.

Chuck had posted daily progress updates on the field school's blog site throughout the summer, along with reports of the students' upcoming work schedule. Anyone who knew of the vertical shaft's existence and was following the updates would have known Team Nugget was set to uncover the shaft upon dismantling the last of the floor in the tunnel today.

What if someone hadn't wanted the shaft uncovered, and had gotten hold of some blood to make the puddle, expecting that the anonymous report of it to the police would force Chuck to keep the students in town and away from the mine, at least for today, and perhaps for the remainder of the week? What might there be about the vertical shaft that, all these years later, was still worth keeping secret?

Chuck slowed to take in the view through the two-story wall of windows rising beyond the research desk. The Big Thompson River meandered past the back of the library through the heart of the flat, park-like valley from which the town of Estes Park derived its name. A mile farther east, the river entered V-walled Big Thompson Canyon and plunged, roiling, to the plains. Through the upper windows at the back of the library, Longs Peak, the 14,255-foot monarch of Rocky Mountain National Park, rose ten miles south of the Y of the Rockies complex, the mountain's sheer east face, known as the Diamond, purple with afternoon shadow.

In the early 1900s, mountaineering guide Enos Mills summited the peak almost three hundred times as he led groups of flatlanders up the arduous route to the top of the mountain. Mills claimed the term "naturalist" for himself and devoted his life to a single cause: alerting an entire generation of Americans to the beauty and preservation value of the magnificent mountain wilderness seventy miles northwest of Colorado's capital. His tireless work led directly to Congress' 1915 pronouncement of the four-hundred-square-mile expanse of rivers, streams, high alpine meadows and jagged peaks directly west of Estes Park as the nation's thirteenth national park, forever protected from human development.

The librarian seated at the research desk observed Chuck with twinkling eyes. She was well into her seventies, her mouth a bright red slash of lipstick beneath a powdered nose and rouged cheeks. A mauve blazer covered a silky white blouse fastened at the throat with an opal brooch. Her curled hair, dyed brunette, was shellacked into place. A cane fashioned from a gnarled tree branch leaned against her desk.

"Never grows tiresome," the librarian said. Her voice was earthy and well-worn, almost masculine.

"You've got the best seat in town," Chuck responded.

"That's what they tell me every time I ask for a raise."

Chuck glanced around. A middle-aged man read a magazine in an upholstered chair at the foot of the rear wall of windows. Several other easy chairs, aligned to take in the view of the river and Longs Peak beyond, were empty, and the aisles between the stacks of books leading away from the windows were deserted. The hordes of summer tourists in Estes Park obviously had more important things to do than visit the local library, and the locals were busy serving the visitors.

"I'd like to learn what I can about Cordero Mine," Chuck told the librarian. "On Mount Landen, near Trail Ridge Road."

The librarian crinkled her nose. "Cordero? Never heard of it."

"You're not alone. I've been assigned to do some archaeological work on it with a crew of college students. I spent some time in here a few weeks ago trying to do some preliminary research, but I couldn't find a single mention of it."

The librarian's face lifted in a bewitched smile. "A mystery," she said. "I like it."

She took hold of her cane and pushed herself to her feet. She was under five feet tall, her shoulders bowed and misshapen. She limped heavily as she rounded her desk. A three-inch lift was glued to the sole of one of her brown, square-toed shoes to make up for a distinct difference in the length of her legs.

The librarian led Chuck down one of the aisles away from the wall of windows.

"Walk this way," she told him. She wiggled her buttocks and gave a quiet snort of laughter as she shuffled down the aisle between the stacks of books, leaning on her cane.

They came to a row of computers lining an inner wall. The librarian took a seat in front of one of the machines and pulled a rolling chair from the next computer over for Chuck. Her knobby fingers danced across the keyboard in front of her.

Chuck watched the monitor over her shoulder as she worked her way from the Larimer County Records Department to the department's mapping center to a bird's-eye view of the Mummy Mountain Range. Controlling the computer's mouse with nimble rolls and clicks, the librarian zeroed in on Mount Landen.

"Where is it?" she asked.

Chuck pointed at the east flank of the mountain, above tree line.

The librarian used the mouse to zoom in from above until the collapsed logs of the miners' cabin became discernible in the grainy satellite photo.

"Ah-ha," she said.

With deft movements, she created a blinking, dotted-line box around the mine site, freed the boxed section from the satellite photo, and somehow transferred the freed section to another website, this one administered, as near as Chuck could tell, by an obscure branch of the U.S. Department of Mineralogy. There, the librarian pasted the box into a waiting screen, entered a series of coordinates in a search bar—numbers she'd memorized, apparently, from the Larimer County website— and clicked *enter*.

The Department of Mineralogy website popped up with a lengthy number of its own.

"Gotcha," she proclaimed.

Before Chuck could say anything, the librarian sped on with her search, copying the number and moving to yet another website, this one operated by the State of Colorado. There she pasted the number into another search box and clicked the mouse.

This time there was a slight pause before the site displayed a few cryptic lines of text against a light-blue background:

Joshua Weed, Hiram Longstrom
Application No. 681, Claim No. 394
September 8, 1861

The librarian sat back from the computer and crossed her arms in front of her in satisfaction. She lifted a gnarled finger from the fold of her elbow and pointed at the screen. "No wonder you didn't find anything. See the date?"

"A few months after the start of the Civil War, right?" Chuck asked.

"Yep. No wonder there's no more information about it than this. The federal government had a few more important things to do than record and follow up on the last few mines being punched in the ground at the tail end of the Pikes Peak gold rush way out here in the middle of nowhere."

"What about the name, Cordero?"

"Let's take a look." The librarian took command of the computer once more. Screenshot after screenshot flashed across the monitor as she worked. She pointed at the screen. "There. See?"

A hand-rendered map of Rocky Mountain National Park glowed on the monitor. Fall River Road appeared as a curving line on the map, but Trail Ridge Road, opened in 1932, did not. And there, high on the east side of Mount Landen, as if by magic, was a black dot with the words "Cordero Mine."

"Where'd that come from?" Chuck asked in surprise.

"Look at the lower right-hand corner," the librarian said.

Chuck squinted, leaning forward. In the bottom corner of the map was an unintelligible signature. Below the signature, in careful, handwritten print, was the annotation:

Alfred Cordero, Lead Cartographer
Rocky Mountain National Park Cartographic Expedition
July-October, 1918

Chuck rubbed his chin with his finger. "You mean to tell me, some mapmaker decided to name an abandoned mine after himself?"

"It wasn't uncommon. Expeditions across America in the 1700s and 1800s named geographic features after current politicians in hopes of securing funding for their next adventures. Expedition leaders and their cartographers almost always took advantage of the opportunity to name things after themselves along the way, too."

"But a mine?"

"By the time the 1900s rolled around, pretty much everything was already named. I imagine Alfred Cordero couldn't resist naming a piece of what was left for himself."

"So he decided to stick his name on something somebody else had built."

"Look where it's located," the librarian noted. "Dead center in the park. He put his name right in the middle of his map, where anybody and everybody would see it."

"A mapmaker," Chuck said, shaking his head.

She spun away from the computer to face him. "You sound disappointed."

"I am." He hesitated. The librarian's blue-gray eyes gleamed with interest, prompting him to ask, "What's your name?"

"Elaine. Elaine Bartholomew."

"I appreciate your help, Elaine. I really do. But what you found was less than what I was looking for."

"That much is obvious."

He took a breath, let it out. "Something happened today," he said. "Actually, a lot of things happened today. But the thing I'm trying to find out about..." He clicked his tongue off the roof of his mouth in frustration, started over. "What if I told you somebody worked really hard to hide something in that mine?" He pointed at the screen. "An entire vertical shaft, running straight down from a horizontal tunnel, perfectly overlaid with floorboards to make sure no one would know it was there."

Elaine's penciled eyebrows rose, deepening the wrinkles on her forehead.

"The Cassandra Treasure," she said.

TWELVE

"The *what*?" Chuck asked.

Elaine turned to the computer, speaking as she tapped the keyboard and clicked the mouse. "I moved to Estes Park after I finished teaching in Denver. Retirement didn't agree with me, so I applied to work here at the library. That was ten years ago. The Cassandra Treasure was one of the first things I heard about." She pushed her glasses up on her nose and peered at the screen. "Here we go."

Elaine rolled back from the computer so Chuck could take a look. The monitor displayed a newspaper article from the *Estes Park Trail-Gazette* dated May 6, 1972.

Former Mayor Declares Cassandra Treasure a Hoax

Stanton Gillispie, former mayor of Estes Park, declared the local tale of the Cassandra Treasure a "hoax" at the annual Estes Park Founders Day celebration dinner last week.

For years, Estes Park has been rife with the rumor of the treasure, a fortune in gold said to be lost or hidden in the Mummy Mountains west of town. But the former mayor used the opportunity as keynote speaker to proclaim his contention that the Cassandra Treasure is nothing more than a childish story.

"I think we need to stand down on this whole thing," Gillispie told the *Trail-Gazette* the day after his speech. "It's embarrassing for us as a community to be seen as a bunch of people who would believe in this sort of nonsense."

In his address, Gillispie pointed to the lack of evidence of the Cassandra Treasure as indication the whole idea was made up.

"It probably originated with some locals having fun among themselves and took off from there," Gillispie said. "I would just as soon we quiet down about it from now on. The people of Estes Park are better than that."

Chuck turned to Elaine.

"There's nothing else," the librarian told him. "Not in the newspaper, and not, more recently, online. No chat-room mentions, nothing. The locals appear to have taken this Gillispie guy at his word."

"But you heard about it."

"Just the one time. A high-school student came in. She was working on a paper. She said her grandfather had told her about a treasure hidden up in the mountains above town. I did a search with her, came up with the *Trail-Gazette* story. That's why I remembered it just now."

"The treasure supposedly was gold."

"The *gold* rush is what everybody came out here for."

"You don't believe it?"

"Of course not. I mean, how many hidden treasures have you ever found?"

Chuck leaned back in his chair. "Quite a few," he said. "My entire career has been dedicated to finding them. I've been an archaeologist for a lot of years."

Elaine pooched her red lips. "Then maybe you're the one to disprove the idea of the Cassandra Treasure once and for all. Or find the thing."

"By doing what?"

"For starters," she said, "this shaft you uncovered—what made it worth hiding?"

As he left the library, Chuck looked up at the high peaks of the Mummy Range looming to the west. He rolled his shoulders, working the stiffness out of them. The librarian's question was dead on. Why had someone gone to so much trouble to camouflage the shaft's existence?

He drove west on Elkhorn Avenue, passing the turnoff to the resort. He showed his pass to the East Entrance Station ranger and drove up Trail Ridge Road, climbing into the Mummies. He pulled to the side of the road just before he left cell-phone range and texted Janelle.

Good visit with Parker. Checking on the mine. Out of service for a bit.

He drove on up the road before Janelle could reply, parked at the mine trailhead, and rummaged in the cross-bed toolbox bolted behind the truck's cab, filling his rucksack with gear. The late-afternoon sun silhouetted the tops of the peaks to the north as he hurried along the trail, almost jogging, making use of the waning light.

He reached the mine well before full darkness descended, not that it mattered—where he was headed, absence of light was a given. He pulled his seat harness from his pack, stepped into its leg loops, and cinched it tight around his waist. His hardhat with its affixed headlamp rested at the bottom of the shaft. In its place, he slipped the elastic band of a camping headlamp over his head, centered it on his forehead, and switched it on.

The tunnel gobbled up the light of his headlamp when he entered. A too-still silence filled the mountain. He shivered, stricken by the sudden, unaccustomed desire to retreat.

He couldn't remember ever feeling this uncomfortable on his own in the field; in little more than a year with Janelle and the girls, he'd forgotten how to be alone.

"Come on, Chuck," he scolded himself, fog from his breath gathering in the beam of his headlamp. He walked the length of the tunnel, turned on the floodlights, and set to work, double-anchoring his climbing rope to the floor's base timbers with loops of nylon webbing ten feet back from where the floor had collapsed. He threaded the rope through his rappel device, attached the device to the oversized, D-ring carabiner clipped to his seat harness, and backed to the edge of the vertical shaft, paying the rope through his brake hand as he went.

He peered over his shoulder at the opening behind him. Everything was as he remembered it—the splintered floor timbers at the edge of the six-foot-square hole, the rusted stanchions that had affixed the broken length of ladder to the shaft wall, where Samuel had clung until he'd clambered up Chuck's body to safety.

Chuck leaned farther back on the rope and aimed his headlamp at the bottom of the shaft. The beam illuminated his and Samuel's hardhats, two spots of white sixty feet below, with broken pieces of the floorboards and ladder scattered around them. Longer pieces of the shattered ladder's rails rose from the bottom of the pit, leaning against the shaft walls.

He let the rope slide through his hand at a steady rate and walked backward down the shaft with small, catlike steps, leaving the glow of the floodlights behind after the first few feet.

The upper thirty feet of the vertical wall down which he walked was solid granite, its rock face dull gray in the beam of his headlamp. Halfway down the shaft, however, the granite gave way to a series of vertical black striations etched in the stone.

The black streaks grew thicker as Chuck descended past the shaft's midpoint. He tightened his grip on the rope, arresting his descent two-thirds of the way down. He swung the beam of his headlamp around the walls of the shaft. Some of the bands of black, bounded by granite, were as narrow as six inches, others as wide as a foot.

Chuck touched one of the black bands in front of him. It gave slightly beneath his fingertips. When he removed his fingers, indentations remained.

Curious, he dug his fingers into the black streak. The black matter crumbled at his touch; it had the consistency of moist coffee grounds. He brought a handful of the stuff to his nose and sniffed, finding that the substance exuded an alloy-like tang.

He turned his hand over and dropped the black material, which landed at the base of the shaft with a wet *plop*.

He looked more closely at the black bands striping the wall in front of him. Many of the striations were concave, as if some of the crumbly black matter had fallen away. Several of the cavities in the black bands extended as much as an arm's length into the wall of the shaft.

He resumed his descent. The striations continued to broaden. After another ten feet, the black bands made up most of the walls around of him, broken in only a handful of places by thinning strips of granite.

"Huh," he wondered aloud, the sound of his voice reassuring in the cold heart of the mountain.

He reasoned that the miners who'd dug this vertical shaft must have come upon the tops of the black striations while chipping the horizontal tunnel into the otherwise solid granite interior of Mount Landen. They'd turned the mine ninety degrees, tracking the expanding striations downward.

But why would have done that?

Hard-rock mining in the 1800s was about the search for crystalline seams of quartz running through granite. If prospectors were lucky, those seams led to veins of gold ore. In rare instances, seams grew thicker, and thicker yet, as miners followed them, leading, ultimately, to rich deposits of gold ore called "lodes" or, in extreme cases, "mother lodes" that resulted in unimaginable riches for the very few who discovered them.

Yet the black material lit by Chuck's headlamp bore none of the crystalline characteristics of quartz veins.

Puzzled, he descended to a couple of feet above the bottom

of the pit. Below him, resting in a few inches of water gathered at the base of the shaft, the broken remains of the fallen ladder reflected in the light of his headlamp.

He slid another foot down the rope, noting that the vertical shaft ended where the solid gray granite petered away to nothing and the expanding striations came together to form a full pocket of the crumbly, black material. He reached the sole of his boot to steady himself, his foot coming to rest on the face of the shaft where a narrowing sliver of granite ended in a knife-like point and two striations of the black substance joined to become a single dark mass, moist and glistening in the light of his headlamp.

Where his boot came in contact with the wall, the black material fell away from both sides of the granite point. The water-saturated gunk cascaded downward, leaving the jagged shard of granite in place. More of the material gave way beneath his foot, then still more, until a black avalanche of the stuff fell away from both sides of the sliver of granite, creating a flowing, black waterfall that oozed across the bottom of the pit.

In front of him, the granite shard bulged outward. A muffled *crack* sounded inside the wall of the shaft, and the sliver of granite, two feet long and several inches across, shot outward, slamming him in the stomach.

The impact caused Chuck to lose his grip on the rope. He fell to the bottom of the pit with the heavy stone in his lap.

He cried out as he sprawled sideways in the shallow pool of freezing water, the side of his head striking one of the broken planks, the chunk of granite tumbling away. He put his arms over his head to protect himself as smaller pieces of granite rained down on him from the collapsing wall.

The avalanche of black material oozing from the side of the shaft rose around him until, in seconds, he was covered. He opened his mouth for air, but only the black material flowed in.

Thirteen

Chuck sat up, choking and sputtering, as the last of the gunk falling from the wall settled around him. He spat grit from his mouth, filled his lungs with air, and clambered to his feet. The viscous black material rose to his thighs, the floorboards and ladder pieces afloat on its surface. His boots slipped on the mucky bottom of the quicksand-like pool.

His headlamp projected only a feeble beam. He swiped its lens with his finger. Light sprang forth. He knuckled his eyes clean and flashed the beam around him. The wall of the shaft in front of him had stabilized, at least for the moment. The climbing rope still hung beside him, attached to his harness.

The black muck at the bottom of the pit was bitterly cold and he was soaked to the skin. A shiver wracked his frame. He bent forward, elbows pressed to his sides, and blew into his hands. The cold would soon rob him of the ability to climb out of the shaft.

He shrugged his pack off his shoulder and around to his chest and dug into it, coming up with his pair of aluminum ascending devices. With a wary look at the wall in front of him, he attached the oblong devices to the rope one above the other, their attached nylon webbing loops hanging down into the muck. He clipped the higher of the two devices by its loop to the oversized carabiner on his seat harness. As he struggled to shove his foot into the loop of webbing hanging from the lower of the two ascending devices, he lost his balance, his shoulder striking the wall of the shaft.

"Oof," he grunted.

The blow caused more of the black matter to ooze from the wall and settle around his legs. A softball-sized chunk of granite fell from the wall as well, bruising his forearm before falling into the black pool.

He gritted his teeth against the pain and settled his boot in the nylon loop. The instant the loop took his weight, his foot slalomed through the muck, knocking a piece of ladder out of the way. He hoisted himself up the rope and stood with his full weight in the loop, ankle-deep in the pool, his face to the mineshaft wall. He shoved the higher of the two ascending devices up the rope and leaned back to put his weight on the device and lock its ratchet into place. Working fast, he slid the unweighted lower device up the rope until it rested against the upper device.

He returned his weight to his foot and hoisted himself to a standing position in the lower loop, now twelve inches above the muck. Again he pushed the device attached to his waist higher on the rope, and again he leaned back until it took his weight. This time, however, as he transferred his weight to the upper device, he toppled sideways, performing an awkward pirouette until he came to rest with his back to the near wall of the shaft. He fought to regain his balance, pumping his legs like pistons, his headlamp illuminating the shaft's far wall.

He stopped, hanging sideways, and steadied his light on the opposite shaft wall. There, six feet away, a slit-like crevice opened. The beam of his headlamp reflected off a light-colored object deep in the crevice, wholly out of place in the bottom of the shaft.

The cleft, barely two feet wide where it met the shaft wall, tapered to nothing eight feet back. The object stood out against the black walls of the narrow fissure near the cleft's terminus.

Chuck recognized the shape of the object from his years of archaeological digging.

He calmed his breathing and steadied the beam of his headlamp.

The object was smooth, round, and bone-white—the size, shape, and color of a human skull.

FOURTEEN

Chuck reached back to steady himself. The semi-solid wall oozed again at his touch. A stream of black gunk fell away from his fingers, followed by pieces of granite loosened by the collapsing black material. The freed granite chunks—none, fortunately, larger than his fist—bounced off him and plopped into the muck below.

He spun to face the disintegrating wall and fought his way to a standing position on the rope. Covered in grit and shivering with cold, he weighted and unweighted the ascending devices in quick succession, climbing away from the bottom of the pit as the last of the loosened black material fell from the wall below him and silence returned to the mine shaft.

He passed the halfway point of the shaft, where the black striations gave way to solid granite, and kept climbing, the glow of the floodlights above growing brighter.

Was the object he'd seen in the crevice indeed a skull? He couldn't say with certainty; he hadn't had time to find out for sure as he'd struggled to escape the collapsing wall of the mine.

He heaved himself up and over the lip at the top of the shaft and sat, gasping, with his back to the wall of the mine tunnel. Still soaked from his immersion at the bottom of the pit, he was shivering hard by the time he caught his breath. He gathered his gear, turned off the floodlights, and headed down the tunnel, glad to be on the move.

He shifted his pack, centering it on his shoulders, as he made his way out of the mine. He hadn't accomplished much in descending to the bottom of the shaft. He'd nearly died for a brief glimpse of an object that perhaps had something to do with the shaft's concealment, and he'd been forced to leave it behind. Whatever secrets Cordero Mine might hide, it still hid them—which was perfectly fine as far as he was concerned. Staging an attempt to retrieve the object in the crevice held no interest to him at the moment. Better to get back to Estes Park as quickly as possible, and head for Durango with Janelle and the girls as soon as the field school ended on Friday.

The steady stream of cool air pouring into the tunnel chilled him as he headed toward the mouth of the mine. Night had fallen. He increased his pace, anxious to return to the warmth and light of the cabin.

He pulled his phone from his pocket and wiped the face of its waterproof case with the butt of his hand. Just past eight o'clock. If he hurried, he might make it back before the girls fell asleep. He smiled as he imagined the girls' response to his grit-covered appearance at their bedsides, and a tingle of anticipation ran up his spine at the thought of the hot shower he would enjoy right after he kissed them goodnight.

He looked at the end of the tunnel fifty feet ahead, and froze.

The heavy metal door was closed.

FIFTEEN

Chuck charged down the mine tunnel, the bouncing beam of his headlamp illuminating the iron door.

"Hey!" he cried out as he neared the end of the tunnel.

No response.

He lowered his shoulder and rammed the door. An arrow of pain shot down his back, but the door did not budge.

He reached through the welded lattices that made up the top half of the door. His searching fingers found the chain wrapped around the door and frame. The padlock, which had been hanging open in a link of the chain these last weeks, was secured through the chain.

He peered through the lattices. The mine site was deserted.

"Hey!" he called again through the lattices. "*Hey!*"

Nothing.

He took off his pack and slumped to a sitting position, his back to the locked door.

Who could possibly have known about his visit to the mine this evening? Answer: no one. *He* hadn't even known he was coming here until he'd climbed into the truck outside the library and turned the key in the ignition.

Had someone spotted him leaving town and followed him? Or, had someone trailed him all the way from the resort?

He squeezed his eyes shut, thinking.

The library was next door to the Estes Park Police Department at the east edge of town.

Had Hemphill seen Chuck exit the library? Had the officer followed Chuck up Trail Ridge Road? Why would Hemphill have done so? And, more to the point, why would he have locked Chuck in the mine and run off?

Locking Chuck in the tunnel wouldn't result in his death; surely he could hold out against the cold for the few hours it would take for him to be found. Which led to the question: what could anyone possibly gain by temporarily trapping him in the mine?

The cold of the metal door seeped through his soaked jacket and shirt, burrowing into the muscles of his upper back. The temperature inside the mine was its normal, fixed fifty degrees, not uncomfortable in a dry jacket and long pants, but brutally cold in soaking wet clothing.

Chuck stood and looked out at the stars gleaming through the top half of the door. He stuck his hand through the lattices. The air temperature outside was roughly the same as inside the tunnel.

He weighed his options. He kept a butane lighter stowed in a sealed plastic bag in his pack for emergencies, but he didn't dare start an oxygen-eating fire in the enclosed tunnel—not that, in any case, he'd have any success setting the moisture-laden floorboards alight.

He turned away from the door. Thanks to his text, Janelle knew he was at the mine. How long would she wait before she sent Clarence to check on him?

He set off down the tunnel, swinging his arms and taking long strides to generate body heat. Back and forth he marched, pounding the reattached floorboards in the first 150 feet of the tunnel with his boots to work blood into his feet.

He considered stripping off his pants, jacket, and shirt, but the residual insulation provided by his soaked clothing was better than no insulation at all. He focused on steady movement aimed at maintaining his body's warmth at a level that would dry his clothes from the inside out while not robbing his stores of energy too quickly.

With no sunlight to replenish their batteries, the floodlights at the end of the tunnel burned out within an hour. He walked steadily, the way ahead lit by his headlamp, each fifty minutes of movement followed by ten minutes of rest.

By eleven, his clothes were no longer soaked. He slowed as midnight approached, punished by his second straight night without sleep.

He took to stopping for five minutes after every twenty-five minutes of movement. Finally, unable to keep his eyes open any longer, he sat down and fell asleep slumped against the cold rock wall of the tunnel just inside the locked door. He awoke shaking uncontrollably and unable to bend his numb fingers.

He rolled to his knees, climbed stiffly to his feet, and looked through the lattices at the newly risen, nearly full moon hanging in the sky above the eastern plains. He lifted one foot, let it fall to the floor, and repeated the process with his other foot, his feet as cold and unfeeling as his hands.

Where was Clarence?

He vaguely recognized the first stages of hypothermia—his brain growing numb along with his body. He wandered sluggishly down the tunnel, barely capable of remaining upright. He stepped off the last of the reaffixed floorboards and continued along the gravel bottom of the mine, where the floorboards and ore cart tracks from the last section of the tunnel were stacked to one side. The gaping hole at the end of the tunnel appeared without warning in front of him. Before his listless brain could react, he took another step. His foot landed at the edge of the pit, the sole of his boot skidded forward on the gravel, and his feet flew out from under him. He gyrated his arms and toppled backward, striking his head.

Dazed, he stared at the gray roof of the tunnel in the light of his headlamp, his feet hanging over the lip of the shaft, the back of his head throbbing. He pushed himself away from the hole and cradled his head in his hands. He struggled upright only to collapse sideways, his shoulder to the wall of the tunnel, his eyes closed.

He clung to one thought: he had to keep moving.

Sixteen

He stumbled back to the mouth of the tunnel. Moonlight lanced through the latticed top half of the door. He pressed his hands to the door's cold surface and leaned his forehead against its iron strips.

He turned and weaved his way halfway down the tunnel before pivoting well shy of the vertical shaft and returning to the door. Up and down he shuffled until, finally, a shout sounded through the door from the far side of the mine site. "Chuck! Chuck, are you there?"

Adrenaline surged through Chuck. He ran to the door. "In here!" he called through the lattices. "I'm locked in!"

Clarence rummaged for the padlock key in the storage boxes, hurried to the mouth of the tunnel, and unlocked the door. He wrenched the door open, the hinges screeching. Chuck stumbled past him.

Clarence aimed the flashlight from the field school van's glove box at Chuck's blackened clothes. "What the...?"

"I wanted to see what was at the bottom of the shaft," Chuck explained. "Bad idea."

Rather than leave the mine-mouth door unlocked as he had throughout the weeks of the field school, Chuck chained and locked the door, pocketed the key, and joined Clarence in heading back around the mountain. He warmed as he followed Clarence along the trail, his clothes drying in the cool night air.

Clarence had headed straight for the mine when Janelle had called. "I knew you couldn't resist coming back," he said. "Did you find anything?"

Chuck kept his eyes on the short length of trail lit by his headlamp behind Clarence's heels. What use was there in mentioning the unknown object in the crevice? "Nothing I could be sure of."

"And you have no idea who might've locked you in there?"

"I've come up with exactly nobody."

"Jan's going to be absolutely freaked."

"If she hears about it."

"You're not going to tell her?"

"She's got enough to deal with as it is."

"*Por cierto.*" Clarence ticked his fingers in succession. "Blood on the ground, my knife, asshole cops, collapsing floors, and now you, locked in the mine. This whole thing's getting more screwed up by the minute."

"No more word from Hemphill?"

"No. Which is good news, far as I'm concerned. The longer he stays away, the better. I say we pack our things as soon as we get back to town. Call it quits and get the hell out of here."

"They'll just put out a warrant for your arrest—and you'll look all the guiltier in their eyes."

"We still can't leave?"

"Sorry. We have to stand our ground."

Chuck made his apologies to Janelle as soon as he reentered cell-phone range in the truck, explaining that his return to the mine site to assure the tunnel door was secured in the wake of the floor collapse had taken longer than he'd anticipated.

The anger in Janelle's voice was unmistakable. "You're a married man now. A father," she said. "This waiting until you're about to go out of service range before texting me? Totally unacceptable."

"I know," he admitted. He steered the truck with one hand, trailing the taillights of the field school van as Clarence led the way. "It's just, things are moving so fast. I'm thinking of stuff and making decisions on the fly."

"You know how much I like your independent streak," she said, softening. "I appreciate the breathing room we give each other—just not too much, you got it? We're a family now—you, me, the girls. I know it's a balancing act, but you have to understand what that means."

Back at the cabin, he hosed off his pack and set it in the bed of the truck to dry, stripped off his filthy clothes and shoved them out of sight beneath the deck, and went inside for a shower. He was so tired by the time he crawled into bed that it was all he could do to kiss Janelle's exposed ear, her head buried in her pillow, before collapsing. He fell asleep within seconds.

His eyes sprang open at the buzz of an incoming text. He grabbed his phone from the nightstand and squeezed it in his hand beneath his pillow, stifling its vibration. He lifted his head to check on Janelle, who shifted position beneath the covers, but didn't wake up.

He slid the phone into view. Less than an hour had passed since he'd fallen asleep. The text message was from Clarence: *Noises outside between the dorms.*

Chuck slipped out of bed, eased the dresser drawers open to grab a fresh flannel shirt and pair of jeans, and crept downstairs and out the front door. He dressed on the deck and set off for Raven House on foot, lighting the way ahead with his phone.

He stuck his phone in his pocket when he left the shadowed woods at the bottom of the drive. The moon, now high in the sky, provided plenty of light out in the open. He rounded the conference center and crossed the fields in the middle of the resort, aiming for the swath of buffalo grass between Falcon House and Raven House.

He slowed as he angled between the buildings, choosing his steps with care. The windows were dark, most curtains drawn. Clarence's face was visible behind the screen in the open window of his unlit, second-story room.

Any more sounds? Chuck texted him.

Clarence's face turned downward as he texted his reply. *No.*

Chuck pointed toward the rear of the dorms and texted, *This way?*

Again Clarence's head dipped. *Yes.*

Chuck set off for the woods behind the dorms. He breathed through his mouth to accentuate his hearing as he stepped onto the paved path connecting Raven House and Falcon House with the single-story dining hall that served the residents of both dormitories. A thick stand of trees stretched around the cafeteria on three sides. Beyond the dining hall, the forest continued up and out of the valley and on into the national park to the west.

He peered up the slope into the darkness. Somewhere in the trees above, a twig snapped. He turned his head, listening. A pair of whispering voices reached him, then went silent.

He stood, unmoving, for long, agonizing seconds. Had what he thought were whispers merely been the night breeze sifting through the trees? Perhaps. But the snap of the twig had been real.

He reached for his phone, thinking to shine its light into the trees in hopes of seeing—what? As he pulled his phone from his pocket, a blood-curdling shriek came from uphill in the forest, directly in front of him.

Seventeen

The shriek cut off abruptly. Chuck charged off the sidewalk and up the slope into the woods. Before he could click on his phone light, an outstretched tree branch, invisible in the darkness, gouged his arm.

He spun away from the branch and fell to his knees. Scrambling to his feet, he turned on his light, illuminating the few feet ahead of him.

"Who's there?" he cried out.

He turned off the light and stood, panting, just inside the line of trees at the edge of the forest. The night air smelled of dust and pine. Moonlight broke through the trees, speckling the forest floor with gray.

He stilled his breathing. A faint moan reached him from up the slope, then the sound of crunching pine needles as someone, invisible in the darkness, ran away.

Chuck turned his phone light back on. Its beam penetrated the gloom, lighting only the immediate forest around him. He sprinted uphill, swerving around bushes and dodging tree trunks. He paused after fifty feet and swung his light in a circle.

The crackling footfalls of the retreating person came from far up the slope. Another moan sounded in the darkness nearby, to Chuck's left. He hurried toward the sound. Within ten yards, a pair of feet shod in white canvas tennis shoes, toes pointing upward, appeared at the edge of his phone's small circle of light. He swept the beam up a pair of bare legs.

He ran to the prostrate body. In the light of his phone, he recognized Nicoleta, one of the international workers from Falcon House, a cashier in the Lodge of the Rockies snack bar from whom he'd bought treats with Carmelita and Rosie on several occasions.

Nicoleta lay on her back, her arms flung wide as if attempting to grip the sloping earth. She wore tight denim shorts and a red-and-white blouse. No—her blouse was white, but drenched with blood.

Chuck dropped to his knees and scanned Nicoleta's body with his light. A leering red slash ran from ear to ear beneath her chin. She'd been knifed or, perhaps, garroted. Whichever the case, her neck was cut so deeply that her head was nearly severed from her torso. Blood coursed from her wound, spreading into the pine needles that carpeted the forest floor and seeping downhill.

Chuck gagged, nearly vomiting. He reached for Nicoleta but paused, his hand outstretched, unsure where or how to help her.

Her entire body shuddered. She moaned again, producing little more than a wet, gurgling sound that came from her slashed throat rather than her mouth.

Still holding his light, Chuck lifted the back of Nicoleta's head with his free hand, attempting to close the grievous wound at her neck. The young woman looked blankly up at him before her eyes closed. He dropped his phone and took one of her hands in his, her palm slippery with blood. She exhaled a long, raspy breath from her severed windpipe and lay still.

He rested her head on the ground and retrieved his light. He put his fingers to her neck above and below the slash but found no pulse. She did not take another breath.

Chuck stared at the gaping wound on the young woman's neck. No amount of chest compressions would be of any use. There was nothing he could do. Nicoleta was dead.

He smoothed her dark hair, tucked her arms beside her body. He sat back, teetering on his haunches. The blue-white beam of another phone light bobbed up the slope toward him through the trees.

"This way," he called out, his voice shaking.

Clarence spoke from behind the bouncing light. "Chuck.

What the hell?"

"Clarence," Chuck replied dully. "Clarence," he repeated.

Chuck turned Nicoleta's head gently to one side. No bruises discolored the china-white skin of her face. Save for the wound at her neck, she appeared asleep.

Clarence stopped at Chuck's side. His phone light joined Chuck's in illuminating Nicoleta's still form.

"*Dios mio*," Clarence breathed, standing over Chuck.

"911," Chuck said. "Call 911." His brain kicked in before Clarence could dial. "No," he corrected himself. "Don't. You're not here. You can't be here."

Chuck punched the emergency number into his own blood-smeared phone and spoke to the dispatcher as if by rote, giving basic details, setting things in motion. He ended the call.

Clarence stumbled off into the darkness. He leaned against a tree, his head hanging. After a moment, he returned to stand over Nicoleta. "She's dead? You're sure?"

"Yes. I watched her as she...as she...there was nothing I could do." Acid burned in Chuck's throat. He fought for control. "Tell me what you heard down by the dorms. Be exact. I'll tell the police when they get here."

His phone buzzed in his hand—the dispatcher calling him back. He didn't answer.

Clarence kept his eyes on Nicoleta while he spoke. "Somebody was arguing. They were behind the dorms. I was sleeping light, believe me."

"What did you see?"

"The two of them on the walkway."

"What did they look like?"

"I couldn't see much in the darkness."

"Was there a struggle?"

"They were pretty fired up, I could tell that much. So I texted you. But then the argument ended. It got real quiet and they

89

headed up into the trees."

"Did you hear anything else?"

"No. I almost texted you again to tell you not to come. I mean, they made up. But the argument was different somehow."

"Different?"

"It didn't feel right, like it was something more than just a lovers' quarrel. I'm not sure how to explain it."

"And after they argued, they headed into the forest?"

"Which is where she screamed...and he killed her."

"That would explain what didn't sound right about the argument: you heard the murderer make up his mind—you heard him decide what he was going to do."

"Yeah," Clarence said, sounding far from certain. "Something like that. Assuming it was even a 'he' that I heard."

The wail of sirens rose in the distance. Voices murmured at the edge of the forest as others—alerted, no doubt, by Nicoleta's scream—gathered behind the dorms.

Chuck looked down the slope through the trees, where beams of light were headed toward them. "You have to go," he told Clarence. "Loop around and get back to Raven House."

"Why can't we tell the truth?" Clarence begged, a deep-seated ache in his voice. "I can let them know what I heard, what I saw."

Chuck weighed the pain in Clarence's voice. He aimed his phone light at Clarence's face. "You knew her, didn't you?"

Clarence stared into the light, bug-eyed. "Wh-what?" he stammered.

Chuck clamped his jaw around each word: "Did...you... know...her?"

Clarence licked his lips. He raised a hand to shield his eyes from the light. "Yeah," he admitted, speaking softly, almost to himself. "I knew her."

WEDNESDAY

EIGHTEEN

Chuck groaned.

"It was early on," Clarence said. "The start of summer." His eyes strayed to Nicoleta and his voice broke. "Just a couple of times."

Chuck turned his light back to the young woman. His head pounded. The lights climbing through the forest from the dorms were drawing closer. "Go," he told Clarence without looking up from Nicoleta.

Clarence didn't move.

"*Now*," Chuck said.

Clarence didn't speak. He turned off his light and scurried across the slope, disappearing into the darkness.

Chuck rested his hand on Nicoleta's forearm. It was still warm to the touch. He aimed his light down the slope to find that the first of those making their way up the slope were two young women from Falcon House. Before they reached Nicoleta, Chuck rose and walked down the hill to meet them.

"We have to leave this to the police," he told them, his arms out to keep them back.

The young women held up their phones, lighting the body sprawled on the ground twenty feet away from them. They clung to one another and sank, sobbing, to the ground.

Kirina arrived seconds later, accompanied by more Falcon House residents.

"I told the students to stay inside," she said.

She tried to push past Chuck, but he stopped her. "The best

thing we can do for her now is let the police do their work."

A pair of paramedics arrived, flashlights and equipment boxes in hand. The emergency lights on the roof of their ambulance flashed through the trees from the parking lot in front of the dormitories. They rushed past Chuck and knelt on either side of Nicoleta's body, ignoring his pleas that they, too, wait for the police. The paramedics were still crouched over her a few minutes later when two uniformed police officers hurried past Chuck and joined them.

The younger of the two officers took one look at Nicoleta and backed away, a hand pressed to his mouth. The older one, gray hair showing beneath his cap, bent over the kneeling paramedics and conferred quietly with them. He turned and addressed the gathered group, his voice deep and authoritative. "I want to talk to whoever found this young woman. Everybody else, show's over. I need you to head back to your rooms."

Kirina and the residents from Falcon House took a last look at Nicoleta lying motionless on the ground between the paramedics before peeling away and returning down the slope in ones and twos.

Chuck stepped forward. "I found her."

"Don't go anywhere," the older officer said. "We'll want a statement from you."

"Of course."

Parker arrived with Officer Hemphill and more police officers a few minutes later. Parker wore jeans and his blue Y of the Rockies shirt. Hemphill was in uniform, his pants sagging where he'd missed a belt loop on one side.

The paramedics packed their gear and departed while the additional officers erected portable spotlights carried up the hill from their cars. One officer encircled the scene with yellow crime-scene tape, moving from tree trunk to tree trunk. Another set a black case on the ground, extracted a bulky camera, and took pictures of Nicoleta's body from numerous angles, the flashes of the camera lighting the trees around her like skeletons.

Hemphill conferred with the other officers and studied Nicoleta's brightly illuminated body before ducking beneath the crime-scene tape and circling through the trees. When he returned, he motioned Chuck and Parker to him at the edge of the spotlights.

He turned to Chuck first. "It was you who found her?"

Chuck described everything he'd seen and heard, beginning with when he'd stood on the sidewalk at the back of the dorms. He explained that he recognized Nicoleta from her snack-stand job.

"What were you doing outside at two in the morning?" Hemphill asked when he finished.

Chuck was ready with his answer. "After the thing with the blood, I figured I needed to do some checking around, keep an eye on things."

"At two in the morning?"

"*Especially* at two in the morning."

"And you just happened to be wandering around precisely when this young woman screamed, back in the trees?"

Chuck nodded.

Hemphill gave him time to elaborate. When he didn't, the officer blew air noisily between his lips. He dropped his eyes to his black sneakers, then raised them to Chuck and Parker. "You know the last time anyone was murdered in Estes Park?"

Neither answered.

"Decades," Hemphill said. "Seriously. *Decades*. And now this." He eyed Chuck. "And you, chasing shadows in the middle of the night."

Chuck said, "If I'd been here *chasing shadows* five minutes earlier, Nicoleta would be alive."

The officer looked away.

"What's next?" Chuck asked him.

Hemphill pointed at the older of the first two officers on the scene. "Harley over there came from St. Louis six months ago. He'll lead us through it. He's processed more homicide scenes than he can count. Thought he was coming here to get away from all that."

"How long will it take?"

"Hours. All morning, into the afternoon. We'll take daylight photos before we move the body. We'll search the woods in daylight, too."

"There won't be any tracks. The ground's too dry."

"We'll search anyway. I'll take your statement when we finish."

"I just gave it to you."

"I'll need an official transcript. Everything you saw, anything else you can think of. Our Mobile Command Center is on its way. It'll be stationed below, at the dorms. I'll meet you there when we're done up here, or, at least, getting close. Say, three o'clock?"

Chuck inclined his head. "Three o'clock."

Parker addressed Chuck. "I'm thinking the best thing to do may be for you to shut down your field school and get your kids out of here."

Hemphill spoke before Chuck could answer. "That's a no go. I'd like to talk with the students this afternoon, too. All of them, one at a time." He narrowed his eyes at Chuck. "Including your brother-in-law, of course."

"The young woman works...worked...for Parker," Chuck said. "She lived in Falcon House. My students have nothing to do with this, nor does my brother-in-law."

"The knife, remember?"

"Which has to do with Clarence, not the students."

"I'd still like to talk to them."

"What if I give you their phone numbers?"

"All interviews will be conducted in person."

"Professor Sartore, at the college, might pull rank and let them go," Chuck said. "He's in charge of the field school. I'm just running it for him."

"I'd prefer that the students stay, but I can't require it," Hemphill said. "All interviews, even of suspects, are voluntary—without getting involved in subpoenas, that is."

"But any decision, one way or another, as to whether to participate in the interview process can't help but play into how you view your investigation," Chuck ventured. "Am I right?"

Hemphill looked Chuck in the eye. "A young woman has been murdered, you get that? *Murdered.* My job is to find out who killed her. How much you and your students assist me with my investigation—or don't—absolutely will be taken into consideration, along with everything else we find out about what happened."

Chuck glanced at Nicoleta, surrounded by officers swabbing and snipping at her body, gathering samples of blood, saliva, and hair in small plastic bags. His shoulders sagged. "Okay," he said. No doubt the hillside behind Raven House would be crawling with police officers throughout the morning, the police cars and the department's command vehicle parked out front. "I'd like to get my students away from here while you do your work. I'll have them back for your interviews."

"No later than three," Hemphill said.

"The field school is scheduled to end day after tomorrow—Friday, mid-morning. I don't see how I can possibly get them to stay any longer than that."

"We'll see where we're at when the time comes."

Back at the cabin, Chuck showered for a second time that night. Nicoleta's blood sluiced from his hands and arms. The water disappeared down the drain in red swirls, taking a portion of his soul with it.

When he slipped beneath the covers, Janelle turned to him, her face tight with anger. "Again you just up and take off without saying anything?"

He lay on his back and locked his hands behind his head. It was after five, the patch of sky visible through the skylight above the bed growing light with the coming dawn.

Janelle rose on an elbow beside him. He wanted to take her in his arms and lose himself in the feel of her body pressed to his. Instead, he rolled up on an elbow to face her and filled her in, his voice slow and measured, as if reciting a fictional tale rather than the grim reality of Nicoleta's murder in the woods behind the dorms and the aftermath with the police.

"There's a murderer here in the resort?" Janelle asked as soon as he finished, her voice shaking. "The girls, Chuck. Did you check on them before you came upstairs?" She moved to leave the bed.

He laid his hand on her arm. "They're in bed, asleep. I checked. They're fine."

She sat up, pulling her knees to her chest and drawing the sheets around her. "We have to get out of here. *Now*."

He sat up beside her. "Whoever did it is long gone."

"The night's almost over. We'll leave as soon as the sun comes up."

"The officer in charge, the one I told you about, Hemphill, is pushing pretty hard to make us stay. Besides, the safest place we can be for now is right here at the resort. There are a million cops working the scene."

"What about Clarence? They're going to come after him, aren't they?"

"His knife is the only piece of evidence, to anything, they have at this point. Who knows what they'll have found by later in the day, though."

"They've got to find another link, a real one. This Hemphill guy—do you have any idea if there's anything to what he's thinking, that one of the students might be involved?"

"He's grasping at straws. He doesn't know anything yet."

"He ought to be focusing on Falcon House. That's where the victim was from."

"I'm sure he will. But he's not going to forget Clarence."

She cursed in Spanish beneath her breath. "What about you? Does he suspect you at all?"

"Why me?"

"You're the one who found her. You know how it goes: what better way to cover your tracks? And who else could get their hands on Clarence's knife more easily?"

"You sound like Hemphill, assuming the two things are related."

"The blood was human. And now somebody's dead. It's only logical."

"I'm telling you, I don't think the blood is related to tonight."

"Now look who's grasping at straws."

Chuck flopped backward on the bed. Janelle was right.

She continued, hovering over him. "What was it Clarence said, that he heard somebody arguing?"

"He said there was something more to it, but he couldn't put his finger on it."

"Whatever he heard, it was enough to make him text you." Her voice took on a portentous tremor as she huddled beside him in the half-light of dawn. "And now there's a record, for the police to find when they check your phones, of the two of you communicating with each other minutes before the murder."

NINETEEN

Chuck raised his downcast eyes, taking in the mine site at the end of the trail. Nothing appeared amiss. The door to the mine tunnel remained as he and Clarence had left it a few hours ago, chained and locked, the plastic storage bins stacked in place beside the collapsed cabin at the edge of the plateau, picks and shovels leaning against the bins.

The students had been more than accepting of Chuck's proposal that they return to the mine this morning in order to stay out of the way of the police working the crime scene behind the dorms. Clearly, they were as anxious as he was to stay away from Raven House until their interviews.

The weather was the same as that which had greeted them at the mine site all summer, clear sky overhead, cool breeze growing warmer as the sun climbed in the east.

Chuck wandered away from the group, overwhelmed by the memory of Nicoleta's scream, her vicious neck wound, her last breath, the feel of her hand in his. He lay on a patch of brown grass at the far side of the plateau, his head on his pack, face to the morning sun, eyes closed, fingers interlaced on his chest.

He half-listened as Kirina took charge, Clarence uncharacteristically silent at her side. She told the students they would spend the morning refilling the excavated squares beneath the collapsed cabin, after which they would return the cabin logs to their former resting places atop the dig area. Upon accomplishing those tasks, she explained, they would head back to the road one last time, carrying the storage bins and tools with them.

Chuck propped his head higher on his pack and looked out over the plains to the east as the students set to work. After lying awake until sunrise with Janelle stiff and unmoving beside him, he'd helped her get the girls up and dressed before driving with the three of them down through the trees to the lodge.

Janelle led the girls inside to have breakfast surrounded by hotel guests after she assured Chuck that she and the girls would remain out and about in town, and would not return to the cabin until he came back from the mine.

Chuck hadn't called Sartore. Better to let the initial police investigation play out before checking in with the professor at the end of the day. Maybe, by then, Chuck would be reporting the arrest of one of the Falcon House workers to him.

Sheila, the Navajo student, broke away from the group and took a seat on the ground beside Chuck. "Threes," she said. She squinted at the morning sun.

"What's that supposed to mean?" Chuck asked, his eyes focused on the hazy expanse of flat land spread before them at the foot of the mountains. There were cities out there, houses and stores and restaurants, all of them filled with people going about their daily lives, none of them having washed someone's blood from their hands in the middle of the night, none of them even aware of Nicoleta's murder.

"Bad things come in threes," Sheila said.

"That's just superstition."

"It's not superstition, it's fact. And last night was number three. First, the blood. Second, the floor falling in. And now, that poor cashier, Nicoleta. One, two, three."

Chuck turned to her, closing one eye against the sun. "You're telling me all the bad stuff's finished?"

She rolled her head around her shoulders in a mini-trance, her eyes closed. "It is," she said, opening her eyes. "I know it."

Chuck wished he had Sheila's certainty. Even more, he wished she knew what she was talking about.

He stood and picked up his pack. No need to inflict his dark thoughts on her.

He climbed the ridge away from the mine, the sun warm on

his back but the clouds in his head black and threatening. He topped the ridge and looked north across the Mummy Range. What he would give to just keep walking, to climb from peak to peak and never return to Estes Park and the police interrogation awaiting him there.

He turned and looked down at the students shoveling dirt and rocks into the excavated squares beneath the site of the collapsed cabin, Clarence and Kirina at work with them. A gust of wind curled beneath the brim of his Fort Lewis Skyhawks baseball cap, lifting it off his head. He made a grab for the cap as it became airborne but managed only to swat it, sending it spinning like a Frisbee into the face of the breeze.

The cap sailed over the far side of the ridge into a steep, granite-walled couloir worn into the mountainside, coming to rest on a chunk of rock fifty feet below the ridge crest.

Chuck descended the couloir, testing each foot placement before trusting it with his weight, his hands to the granite face behind him. As he bent to pick up the sky-blue hat from the rock, he noticed, between his feet, something entirely out of place in the couloir: a reddish-brown drop of dried blood.

TWENTY

Chuck turned his face to the clear, blue sky. He'd seen enough blood the last two days. He had no desire to expend any more mental energy on the stuff.

But what was a dried drop of blood doing way up here? He sighed and crouched over his discovery.

The blood was splattered around the edges and dried to a sheen. He scraped at it with his fingernail. Aside from the fact that the drop of blood had to have fallen here sometime since the last of the winter snow had melted out of the couloir in May, it was impossible to tell its age.

He scanned the couloir below. A larger splotch of dried blood coated a rock ten feet farther down the narrow ravine. More dried droplets were sprayed across a scattering of rocks a few feet below that.

Had a bighorn sheep nicked its leg on a shard of rock while passing through the couloir? No. The amount of blood on the lower rocks was too voluminous to fit that notion. In fact, only one explanation accounted for the amount of blood splattered on the rocks below: something had been shot here in the couloir, sometime since May—despite the fact that all hunting in the park was illegal.

Chuck climbed down to the dried spray of blood and checked out the ravine farther down. A single thunderstorm anytime since the shooting would have washed away all evidence of the kill. Instead, starting thirty feet below where he now stood, scrapes marked the edges of rocks where an animal had been dragged to the base of the couloir after the creature's death.

He centered his cap low over his eyes. What had been dragged off the mountain?

He climbed down the couloir, following the slide marks of

the animal. Whoever had killed the creature had made no attempt to hide the trail—not that the killer had any reason to do so; there was no logical reason for anyone to be here on the steep, remote north side of the mountain.

From the base of the couloir, the drag trail followed the broad drainage downhill as the steepness of the mountain's north face lessened. The trail of dark rubbings on rock wended its way around boulders and bypassed low cliffs until, nearing tree level, it headed straight for a narrow opening where the drainage entered the forest.

As he neared the trees, Chuck spotted a second drag trail descending from the mountain's northwest ridge. He studied the ridge and saw yet another drag trail leading off the mountainside.

The two additional trails joined the first just above tree line. In the forest, he followed the conjoined trail over logs and across moss-covered rocks. He eyed the ground as he walked, but the forest duff was too thick to show any telltale boot prints.

The weather-beaten firs grew close together along both sides of the drainage, their intertwined branches cutting out much of the morning light. The gloom of the shadowed forest and the drag trail of the slaughtered animals—not to mention Nicoleta's murder hours earlier—filled Chuck with foreboding. He stilled his breathing and crept through the forest in silence, following the trail until the odor of rotting flesh, carried by an upslope breeze, swept through the trees.

The stench slammed him full in the face. He came to a stop, unexpectedly overcome by a wavering vision of Nicoleta's body, arms out-flung, neck slashed.

The breeze picked up, carrying more of the awful smell with it. He bent forward. His knees nearly buckled. He never should have left the students and Clarence and Kirina on their own at the mine. In fact, he never should have come to the mountains with the students this morning in the first place.

What was to be gained by following the drag trail to its source? He had bigger problems to deal with. He should turn around, return to the mine, and head back to town with the students this very instant.

But what had happened here on the mountain?

The breeze let up and the odor subsided.

Chuck held his breath and descended another thirty feet through the trees to a fen no more than fifty feet across. The small, open area wasn't wet enough this summer to constitute a true bog, though it was damp enough in non-drought years to preclude the growth of trees. This rainless summer, the fen was a compact meadow of tall grass already turned, weeks early, from early-spring green to late-autumn brown.

Still holding his breath at the edge of the fen, Chuck spotted several clouds of black flies buzzing above the grass. Beneath each swarm of insects lay a pile of rotting flesh.

TWENTY-ONE

Spaced at irregular intervals around the fen were the headless carcasses of half a dozen Rocky Mountain sheep in various stages of decay. All the creatures had been in their prime before they'd been killed. Their broad chests, humped above the grass, gave way to brawny hindquarters of large, muscular rams, not smaller ewes. So powerfully built were the rams' collapsed forms that they appeared capable, even in death, of leaping without effort from one rocky crag to another.

The slaughtered animals' fur was intact, legs and torsos lying as they'd been left, uncut by any butchering to make use of their meat.

Chuck stepped forward and turned a slow circle in the center of the clearing, taking shallow breaths of the fetid air. Rage boiled inside him. The sheep had been slaughtered in some sort of a perverted rampage. Who had killed these magnificent creatures, and why?

He clamped his nose between his finger and thumb and studied the carcasses. All the rams had suffered the same fate: their heads cut and carried off, their bodies left to rot.

Chuck considered what he knew about Rocky Mountain bighorn rams. While some remained with their herds of ewes and lambs throughout the year, others, in spring and summer, ran in all-male groups, grazing high above tree level where their keen eyesight and unrivaled sense of smell protected them from predators—save a high-powered bullet fired by a poacher from afar.

It was easy to surmise what had transpired on Mount Landen over the course of the summer. After the first among them was killed and dragged down the mountainside, the remaining rams had continued to frequent the high alpine tundra of the mountain's north face. And why wouldn't they? The slope had proven safe for generations; nothing in their evolutionary makeup warned them away after the death of the first among them, or the second, or third.

Based on the size of the carcasses, whoever had killed the rams had harvested the most trophy-worthy of the bighorns that roamed Mount Landen. But with just the rams' heads removed, Chuck knew it wasn't trophies for fireplace mantels the poacher was after. It was their horns, the bigger the better.

For many years, Chinese men had believed that ingesting ground-up rhinoceros horn acted as an aphrodisiac, which had led to the decimation of the world's wild-rhino population by poachers. As powdered rhino horn became increasingly unattainable on the black market, a rumor started up on the internet that the horns of Rocky Mountain bighorn sheep held the same magical sexual powers as rhino horns. The demand wasn't going anywhere, so somebody came up with a new way to supply it—and here in front of Chuck was the clear result of the latest aphrodisiac craze.

Also clear, because the carcasses were still here, rotting in the forest, was the fact that no one yet knew what had taken place.

That, at least, was about to change.

Chuck retraced his route out of the trees and back up and over the ridge.

"About time," said Kirina when he returned to the mine site. "We've refilled the excavation units. We're ready to put the logs back in place."

Chuck cast an approving eye at the site of the collapsed cabin—now a flat patch of dirt and rock where the excavation had taken place.

"Leave no trace," he said, quoting the ethic of wilderness travel that was equally applicable to archaeological work.

He helped Kirina, Clarence, and the students return the logs to their original, collapsed positions, studying "before" pictures on Kirina's tablet computer for accuracy as they worked. When they finished, the site of the collapsed cabin looked as it had at the beginning of the summer—a jumble of protruding logs at the edge of the plateau—as required by Professor Sartore's contract with the park service.

The contract required that the floor in the mine tunnel be returned to its original, intact condition as well. In the wake of the floor collapse, however, Chuck decided that part of the contract was null and void.

He pointed at the picks, shovels, boxes of gear, and unused rain shelters stacked beside the collapsed cabin. "Shouldn't be a problem carrying everything back to the van in one go," he told the students. "Take a good look around. We won't be coming back."

"Good riddance," muttered Jeremy.

"We're giving it back to the ghosts," Sheila said to him.

"To your skinwalkers, you mean," Jeremy replied.

"Not skinwalkers. *Ghosts*," Sheila asserted. "They haunt the Stanley, down in town, and they're up here, too."

"Your skinwalkers are afraid to leave the rez?"

Sheila stuck out her tongue at him. "They're not afraid of anything. They just like to stay close to home."

"Let's get out of here," Chuck said before Jeremy could direct another dig at Sheila.

Back at Trail Ridge Road, Chuck joined Clarence and Kirina in stacking and strapping the tools and gear bins in the van's rooftop luggage basket as the students climbed inside and dug into their sack lunches. He checked the time as he turned the van around and headed toward town. Just past noon. Three hours before they were due back at Raven House for their police interviews. Plenty of time for what he had in mind.

Twenty-Two

Three miles before the East Entrance Station, Chuck turned left onto Fall River Road. Trees pressed close on either side of the dirt road, which followed the Fall River west and upstream away from Estes Park along the north side of Mount Landen, roughly paralleling Trail Ridge Road on the mountain's south side.

The students leaned back in their seats in silence, lunches completed and legs outstretched, their eyes following the van's progress up the valley. Neither Clarence nor Kirina asked where Chuck was taking them; they appeared to be as content as the students to avoid returning to town for as long as possible.

After a two-mile climb through the forest, the road leveled, broke from the trees, and entered a long, flat meadow where beavers had dammed the river, creating ponds linked like jewels along the valley floor. Trout broke the calm, sun-dappled surface of the pools. A pair of mallards, flushed by the van's approach, took flight from a small pond beside the road. To the south, the summit of Mount Landen rose half a vertical mile above the valley floor.

They reentered the trees at the far end of the meadow and neared the three-walled head of the valley. Chuck slowed, peering around each bend until, just before the road began its steep ascent out of the river basin, he spotted a turnout gouged into the side of the mountain. He eased the van to a stop in the middle of the road, hopped out, and crouched, studying the pullout.

Pressed into the dusty earth at the edge of the roadway between patches of gravel were tire tracks in the shape of lightning bolts. The absence of rain revealed that the vehicle responsible for making the tracks had parked at the turnout numerous times throughout the summer.

Chuck used his phone to snap pictures of the overlapping

tracks. They were thick and deep—made by a vehicle far bigger than an ordinary passenger car.

He crossed to the dirt embankment cut into the side of the mountain to accommodate the parking spot. Lug-soled boot prints in the soft earth showed that someone had made repeated forays up and down the mountain from the road. He snapped more pictures of the treads.

He turned the van around, parked at the edge of the pullout to preserve the lightning-bolt-shaped tracks, and rolled open the van's big side door. "Grab your water bottles," he told the students. "There's something I want you to see."

He led the students past the boot prints in the soft, roadside soil and up the slope into the forest, Clarence and Kirina in the rear, following the route of whoever had passed this way several times this summer. The person—almost assuredly a male, based on the size of the prints—had made no attempt to hide his passage. Chuck followed the route without difficulty, linking places where grass and weeds had been crushed beneath the hiker's feet with spots where moss, dry and flaky this rainless summer, had been kicked from fallen logs, and where small rocks had been dislodged from their former resting places.

The unknown hiker's path led straight up the mountain, cutting across elk and deer trails as it climbed. Looking up, Chuck caught a glimpse of Mount Landen's open north slope through a break in the forest.

He knew what lay ahead, yet even as he followed the route toward the rotting carcasses, he couldn't help but marvel at his surroundings. He was outdoors, hiking in the woods, on a summer day, far from all the trouble back in town.

Squirrels scurried up tree trunks ahead of the group. They scrabbled sideways around the trees to keep the trunks between themselves and the students, poking their heads out for brief looks and chattering noisily as the group passed. Gray jays tracked the students, flapping from branch to branch and announcing the group's progress up the mountain with deep-throated caws. The forest smelled of pine and vanilla. Twigs broke under Chuck's boots with crisp snaps, releasing small puffs of dust from the forest floor.

After thirty minutes of uphill progress, the path split in two. A right fork continued up the mountain to the open slope above, while a left fork angled through the stunted trees just below tree line.

Chuck led the group along the left fork. He stepped aside when they reached the fen a few minutes later, allowing the students to line up at the edge of the small meadow next to him.

The morning breeze had carried the scent of the rotting carcasses away from the students during their hike, but here, within the tight ring of trees, the reek of the rotting carcasses was overpowering.

The students recoiled, hands over their mouths and noses. Samuel fled the way they'd come, his arms clasped across his stomach.

Jeremy spoke through his fingers. "Why'd you bring us here?" he demanded of Chuck. "Is this your idea of some sort of sick joke?"

Chuck looked at his boots, suddenly ashamed of himself. Why *had* he brought the students here?

He should have let them relax in the sun beside the beaver ponds in the valley below before heading back to town for their interviews. But he'd brought them to the scene of the sheep slaughter instead.

Jeremy was right. What had he been thinking?

He waved for the students to retreat from the fen. "Let's back off and regroup."

He called ahead for a halt a couple hundred feet from the meadow. The students turned, lined along the path, Samuel having rejoined them along the way.

Chuck attempted to explain himself. "I spotted the tire tracks in the pullout and the boot prints headed up the mountain. I wanted to make sure where they led."

Jeremy's eyes grew round. "You knew where you were taking us all along?"

"I had a pretty good idea. And I had my reasons." Chuck paused, seeking the right words to justify his actions. "What have we just spent the summer doing?" he asked the students.

They looked at one another. Sheila raised a tentative hand.

"Historical archaeology," she said. "Digging up the recent past to learn more about it."

"Correct. And with everything we've done, if you think about it, perhaps the single most important thing we've learned this summer is how far humans will go in the pursuit of one particularly powerful human desire: greed."

The students cast uncertain glances at one another.

Chuck pointed up through the trees at the summit of Mount Landen. "Think about where we've been digging, way above tree line. The miners who worked up there in the winter more than a hundred years ago faced blizzards, sub-zero cold, and avalanches, not to mention lightning storms in the summer, along with all the dangers of the mining operation itself—for what?"

"For gold," Samuel said. He reprised a bit of his act from the mine tunnel: "The mother lode! All the riches in the world!"

"Samuel's exactly right," Chuck told the group. "A hundred years ago, gold was used for one thing and one thing only: ornamentation. These days, at least, there are a few industrial uses for the stuff. But back in the 1800s, gold was all about showing your friends and neighbors how wealthy you were. To do that, people would pay a fortune for the stuff, and miners would risk their lives, day in and day out for years on end, digging it out of the ground."

Jeremy pointed past Chuck at the fen. "I don't see what any of that has to do with what you just showed us."

"They're one and the same," Chuck explained. "What you saw back there is an example of what people still are willing to do—what they're willing to risk—a century and a half after the Pikes Peak gold rush, to come up with something others will pay big bucks for."

He told the students about the Chinese appetite for aphrodisiacs, the headline-making news of the black market's shift from rhino to Rocky Mountain sheep horn, and how, as a result, the park's rams had found themselves in the poacher's crosshairs.

"You mean," Kirina asked when he finished, "somebody killed all those rams back there just for their horns?"

"Only the rams' heads are gone," Chuck affirmed. He looked at the ground in front of him, then up at the students. "Maybe you guys are right. Maybe—especially after what happened last night—I shouldn't have brought you up here."

Samuel said, "No. I totally get it. My dad's a hunter—a real hunter, not some sleaze-bag poacher. I just want to make sure somebody takes out the rat bastard who did this."

Chuck exhaled. "So do I," he said. "I'll be reporting this, of course. But in the meantime, one thing we can do is make sure the poacher knows we know what he's up to. He's killed six rams on Mount Landen—on *our* mountain. Let's make sure he doesn't kill any more."

"What do you have in mind?" Kirina asked.

Chuck addressed the group. "I want you to walk all the way around the meadow through the trees, kicking over stones, rolling logs, tossing downed branches around—anything we can do to show him we've been here."

"Good," Kirina said. She took over, directing the students to spread themselves along the slope and leading them up the mountain through the forest, looping around the meadow.

Clarence approached Chuck after Kirina and the students set off. "The poacher—how many times you figure he's been here this summer?"

Chuck frowned, unclear where Clarence was headed.

"He couldn't possibly have made a successful kill every time he came," Clarence said. "What do you figure, he shot one every fourth time? Every fifth?"

"Something like that."

"Which means that, all told, this guy has to have driven through the East Entrance Station at least a couple dozen times this summer. Double that when you figure entering *and* leaving."

Chuck's eyes grew wide with understanding. "The guy's a regular," he said.

Twenty-Three

"We should talk to the East Entrance Station rangers," Chuck said.

Clarence shook his head. "What was it you told us at the beginning of the field school? Zillions of people visit the park every year, something like ninety percent of them in the summer. And of those ninety percent, most drive through the East Entrance Station on their way up Trail Ridge Road."

"So you're back to saying it could be anybody."

"Just the opposite. We can assume the guy's a local, right? He lives here, which is how he's been able to keep doing this for the whole summer. And that means, even with all the cars coming and going through the entrance station, he'd likely be recognized, eventually, by the park rangers at the station, no matter how nondescript his car.

"Whoever he is, he's a known entity. He raises no suspicion, no matter how often he comes and goes."

Chuck clicked his tongue in approval. The deep tracks in the pullout were made by big, heavy tires. Who could enter and leave the park on a regular basis, in a large vehicle, without leading to questions?

"An ambulance?" Chuck wondered aloud. Then he answered himself. "No." An ambulance carried a crew of two, but the path up the mountainside, trodden by only a single pair of boots, indicated the poacher worked alone.

"A passenger van like ours?" Clarence asked. "For hauling tour groups in and out of the park?"

"I don't think so," Chuck said. "It would have to be filled with passengers to avoid suspicion." He took a few seconds, thinking. "How about a park staffer driving a park vehicle?"

"Afraid not," Clarence replied. "The idea that a ranger could blow off his duties for hours at a time, day after day, over the course of the summer to poach Rocky Mountain sheep? Impossible."

Kirina appeared from higher on the mountainside. "There's something up here I think you should see," she called down to them.

She led Chuck and Clarence to the well-defined drag path winding its way through the trees from the upper mountain. The students stood along the path, overturned rocks and logs demarcating the stretch of forest they'd already crossed, pristine forest floor beyond.

Chuck and Clarence crouched beside Kirina at the edge of the path. She pointed at a small puddle of blood, no more than an inch across, pooled in a cupped portion of a broken tree branch lying on the forest floor. "There."

Chuck studied Kirina's discovery. The bullet wound in one of the rams must have spurted a pulse of blood as the poacher dragged the animal to the meadow, and the brief cascade of blood had pooled in the cupped portion of the rotting branch. Three hours ago, Chuck had walked right past the puddle, focused on the fen ahead.

The sun, breaking through the trees, lit the small pool's viscous, red surface.

Chuck peered at it. The blood should not be viscous, nor should it be red. It ought to be dried to a hard, dark sheen.

He touched the surface of the puddle with a fingertip. His finger came away shiny red. He looked down the slope into the small, sunlit meadow a hundred feet away as he worked the blood between his finger and thumb.

The poacher was still at it. He'd made his last kill no more than a day or two ago, just over the ridge from the mine site, at dawn or dusk when Chuck and the students weren't at the mine.

Chuck blinked, blind with anger. He rose and turned his back to Clarence and Kirina and the students.

"Let's go," he called over his shoulder, his voice dark with fury.

He strode down the mountain ahead of the students, his vision clearing but his rage continuing to burn white-hot in his chest.

He could do little about Nicoleta's murder beyond waiting for the police to act.

But as for the sheep killer?

That he could do something about.

TWENTY-FOUR

Chuck pulled the van to a stop in front of Raven House.

Half a dozen Estes Park police sedans lined the parking lot in front of the dorms. A shiny white recreational vehicle emblazoned with the words "Estes Park Police Department Mobile Command Unit" was positioned in the middle of the gravel lot. A group of uniformed officers stood outside the command vehicle, arms folded, observing the return of the van.

The students stared, speechless, at the officers, prompting Chuck to say as he parked, "I'll head over and see where things stand."

"What about Clarence?" Sheila asked from the back row.

Clarence, in the passenger seat opposite Chuck, looked straight ahead and said nothing.

"They'll be talking to him, too," Chuck answered.

"But what about his knife?"

Chuck gripped the steering wheel, his knuckles turning white. "There's nothing at this point—*nothing*—linking the blood found between the dorms with what happened last night. For now, I'm sure, the police are focusing all their efforts on the murder." He shut off the engine. "Straight to your rooms, please. Wait there until you're called for your interviews. Then you can head over to the lodge cafeteria for dinner; I'm sure the dining hall will be closed."

He climbed out of the van without waiting for anyone to respond. The gathered officers parted as he approached the command vehicle. At Chuck's knock, Hemphill opened the door and motioned him inside.

The new-vehicle smell of off-gassing plastic filled the interior of the vehicle. Everything was bureaucratic gray and off-white. Formica cabinets and countertops lined the walls except where a small table and facing bench seats were bolted in front of the vehicle's sole window. A built-in television, tuned to a news channel and muted, glowed from the wall of cabinets opposite the table. Below the television, a two-way radio sat on a small counter.

Chuck recognized the only other person in the vehicle, the older cop, Harley, who'd come to Estes Park from St. Louis. Harley sat in a wheeled office chair at a counter running the width of the rear of the RV. He nodded at Chuck before going back to studying a pair of laptop computers arranged in front of him. A wire led from one of the computers to a small microphone on a plastic stand.

Chuck took in the high-tech interior of the vehicle. "Pretty nice setup for a town your size," he said to Hemphill.

The officer waved dismissively. "Homeland Security money." He slid into the bench seat on the far side of the small table and motioned Chuck to the seat opposite him.

Chuck slid behind the table. "Arrested anybody yet?"

Hemphill opened a narrow notebook on the otherwise empty table and pulled a pen from his front pocket. He laid the pen on the notebook.

"I take it that's a no," Chuck said.

"Correct." Hemphill pointed out the window at the students, who worked with Kirina and Clarence, unloading the gear boxes and tools from the roof of the van and carrying them into Raven House. "Your crew, how well do you know them?"

"They're good kids, if that's what you're asking," Chuck said. "Friendly, outgoing. Nothing about them suggests any involvement in what happened last night."

Hemphill put his hands on the table and leaned forward. "Nothing?"

The hair on the back of Chuck's neck stood up.

The officer cleared his throat, still sitting forward. "Parker tells me this is the first time he's ever had a college group like yours stay here for the summer. Said he didn't think much about it to begin with. It was extra income for the resort, making use of the old dorm. He says he's had the international college student worker program for several years now, so he figured American students would be fine." Hemphill paused. "But he says your kids have been pretty active—at night."

"Active how?"

"He used the term 'cross-pollination.' Said that, from what he'd heard—" and from what he'd *seen*, Chuck thought, remembering the binocular case on Parker's windowsill "—there was lots of movement back and forth between the two dorms, between your students and the international workers."

"Huh," Chuck said. He'd caught enough snippets of conversation between the students over the summer to know Parker's report had an element of truth to it. The students and the international workers ate together in the dining hall behind the dormitories, and they socialized together in the evenings outside the dorms as well, tossing horseshoes and sharing music playlists. It made sense that the commingling between the Raven House and Falcon House residents extended beyond Clarence's start-of-summer hook-ups with Nicoleta.

Hemphill continued. "Parker says he thinks the most active one of all was your brother-in-law."

"You've been after Clarence from the start, because of his knife. But he's got nothing to do with this."

Hemphill lifted a hand. "You have to understand. If we—"

"You're supposed to be working on finding the *real* killer," Chuck broke in. "Clarence isn't him."

Hemphill spread his hands. "I'm just giving it to you straight. Do you really think I'd be telling you this if I believed Clarence was the perpetrator? You know good and well if I thought he was the guy, I'd take him in without telling you a thing."

"Okay," Chuck said grudgingly. "Fine. Am I to understand

that, based on what Parker told you, you're going to focus on my entire group, not just Clarence?"

"Yes."

"Have at them, then."

Hemphill's brows came together in question.

"I want this thing settled as much as you do," Chuck told him. "I was there. I held her in my arms. I saw what happened to her." He worked his jaw. "I want to see whoever did that to her brought to justice."

"Fair enough," Hemphill said. "How about we start with you?"

TWENTY-FIVE

Chuck gripped the edge of the table as Hemphill said to Harley, "Come on over, would you?"

The older officer cradled one of the laptops and the microphone in the crook of his arm and rolled his chair down the narrow aisle. He slid the microphone to the center of the table and set the computer on the end of the tabletop in front of him. A wire ran from the mic to the laptop.

"You've already interviewed the workers from Falcon House?" Chuck asked.

Hemphill nodded.

"Learn anything useful?"

"You know I can't comment on that."

"But you told me what Parker had to say."

"Maybe I shouldn't have, but it involved your students."

"And me, by association."

"And you."

Fifteen minutes later, Chuck descended the metal steps from the command vehicle. The officers outside had dispersed. He stood for a moment, gathering himself.

He'd offered as much additional detail as he could to the brief description he'd provided at the scene of the killing, taking as his own Clarence's initial sighting of Nicoleta with the presumed killer behind the dorms, and describing to Hemphill, with Harley tapping away on the laptop, what had sounded like a quarrel between the two before they left the walkway and headed up the slope into the forest.

He headed across the parking lot to Raven House to summon Clarence for his interview, per Hemphill's request. Kirina was to follow Clarence, then each of the students.

"When do we tell them I texted you?" Clarence asked from where he sat on his bed when Chuck stepped into his room.

"And that it was me who first saw her, or, them?"

Chuck closed the door behind him before he spoke. "They're still working the scene. It'd be better if they come up with a suspect first. A *lot* better."

"All hell's gonna break loose when we tell them."

"If they figure out who did it soon enough, we won't have to."

Clarence twisted his hands in his lap. "I dunno."

"I told them everything you told me, so they know everything you know. All we're doing is protecting you from their preconceived notions."

"I guess so."

"You have to remember what Hemphill said to you at the mine site, the way he's been gunning for you."

Clarence pushed himself from his bed. "My story is that I didn't see anything. *Nada*. Right?"

"You can do this, Clarence."

"I hope."

"Just get through the interview and we'll move on from there."

Chuck laid out his plan to Clarence before following him downstairs to the lofted common room where Kirina was sorting cardboard boxes of finds from the mine. Heavy wooden tables, lined with folding chairs, took up half the room. A sagging couch and worn easy chairs surrounded a mismatched pair of battered coffee tables in the other half. Tools and plastic storage bins were stacked in a corner.

Chuck waited until Clarence was out the front door before turning to Kirina. "The officer who came to the mine, Hemphill, is conducting the interviews. He wants to talk to you after Clarence."

Kirina stood at one of the tables, her hands resting on an unopened box. "How'd yours go?"

"I told them you were the only one from Raven House who came up the hill to see what was going on."

"Everyone was milling around in the halls. I ordered them to stay put." She looked straight at Chuck. "I saw Clarence when I went outside, before I went up the hill into the forest."

Chuck sucked in his cheeks. He glanced over his shoulder, making sure they were alone. "You saw what?"

"He was coming back down out of the woods, from farther over."

Chuck closed his eyes. He couldn't remember ever being more tired. "Clarence was at the scene," he admitted to Kirina, opening his eyes, his voice low. "I told him to get out of there because of how the cops had been after him, with his knife and all."

"You're *lying* to the police?"

"I'm protecting Clarence. People say everybody's treated the same these days. But guys like Clarence, with his earrings, his accent, the color of his skin..." Chuck let the end of his sentence dangle.

"There's been a *murder*, Chuck. The killer is still out there somewhere."

"I told the police everything Clarence saw, everything he heard. We're not withholding anything from them."

"Except who actually saw it."

"The truth is, he didn't see that much."

"I take it you don't want me to tell them I saw him sneaking back into the dorm."

"I'm not asking you to lie. I'm just saying, if you don't tell them that one part, he'll appreciate it, and so will I."

She took a deep breath and held it. "I like Clarence. I like him a lot. Still, I'm not saying I'll tell them, and I'm not saying I won't."

Twenty-Six

Chuck left Kirina and walked down the first-floor hallway past the students' rooms and out the back door. Up the slope behind Raven House, just visible through the trees, a pair of police officers knelt within the circle of crime-scene tape, sifting the forest floor with their fingers. Another officer stood back, tablet computer in hand, jotting notes. Nicoleta's body had been removed from the scene. The officers' meticulous work wasn't so different from his own as an archaeologist, as if both the past of an ancient society and the modern-day death of a young woman could somehow be reduced to dry, recorded notations and a collection of evidence bags.

He swallowed hard. Nicoleta murdered, no one yet arrested for her brutal killing, and here he was, withholding information from the police. But he was doing it for Clarence, he reminded himself. He would come clean the instant the situation warranted it.

He followed the paved path past the shuttered dining hall and the back of Falcon House, using the building as a screen to remain out of sight of Parker's office. He would talk with the resort manager soon enough, and with Professor Sartore as well, but he wanted, needed, to see Janelle and the girls first.

Janelle had texted during his interview that she and the girls had returned to the cabin without him after all—a good sign. He angled into the forest to the driveway and followed it up through the trees to the cabin, where Janelle met him at the front door. Behind her, the girls sat facing one another on the living-room floor, game computers in their laps, engaged in an interactive contest.

Rosie glanced up long enough to tell Chuck, "I'm beating her! I'm beating her!" before returning her focus to her tablet, her fingers flying.

"Not for long," Carmelita responded, her own fingers tapping frantically at her computer.

Janelle stepped onto the deck, closed the door behind her, and leaned against it. "How'd it go?" she asked.

"About what I expected. I told them all I could."

"What about Clarence?"

"They didn't get that specific."

"They will, though."

"Kirina may be telling them about him right this minute."

A quiver entered Janelle's voice. "Kirina?"

"She saw Clarence coming back to Raven House after I sent him away."

"And if she tells?"

"They're going to find out at some point. It'd just be better if it was after they catch somebody, or after we're out of here on Friday."

"They're still focused on Clarence?"

"Hemphill tried to make it sound like they aren't, but I'm not sure he was telling the truth. Can't really blame them, you know."

"I can blame them all I want."

"You said earlier it made sense for them to be focused on him, what with his knife and all."

"That was about the blood, not the murder—which happened *after* they found his knife."

"It's all still supposition, though. Nothing's really changed."

"*Nothing's changed?* We're talking about life in prison. The death penalty." Her upper lip trembled. "You have no idea, walking around in your white-man bubble. *Mami* and *Papi* thought they were doing us a favor, giving Clarence and me our *Americano* names, like that would make it all fine."

"*Janelle.*"

"Durango's okay. Lots of Latinos around. But Estes Park's

white as the moon."

"They're good people here, seems to me." Except for the poacher, Chuck realized with a fiery jolt.

"I'm not saying they're not. But when something goes wrong, it's only logical for them to start looking around at outsiders, at people who look different than they do." Tears rose in Janelle's eyes. "*Mi hermano.*" She stepped into Chuck's arms.

As he held her, Clarence appeared, walking up the drive through the trees.

He smiled up at them. "Hey, guys," he called with a relaxed wave.

Janelle ran down the steps to him. They embraced at the side of the truck. Clarence held her until she shoved him away and shook a finger in his face. "What's that on your breath?"

He raised his hands in self-defense. "A little nip, that's all."

"*A little nip?*"

"It's okay, sis. I waited until after the interview."

Chuck looked down at Clarence from the porch, thinking of what Kirina might be saying to Hemphill right this instant. He spoke from the deck railing, his voice hard. "They may want to talk to you again."

Clarence stepped backward, stumbled, and almost fell.

"You had more than 'a little nip,'" Chuck accused him.

Clarence's eyes flitted between Chuck and Janelle.

Janelle held out her hand. "Give it to me. *Now.*"

Clarence pulled a steel flask from his back pocket and handed it over.

She shook her head in obvious disgust as she took it. "I can't believe you."

She unscrewed the lid and upended the flask at arm's length. A stream of golden liquid cascaded to the graveled parking area in front of the cabin, splashing Clarence's feet.

He extended his hands. "That's Cuervo Gold," he pleaded.

The last of the flask's contents dripped to the ground. "I don't care if it's Cuervo Titanium." She screwed the lid back on the flask and threw it back at him.

As Janelle and Clarence climbed the stairs to the deck, Chuck said to Clarence, "I take it, based on your 'little nip,' your interview went okay."

"It went fine, *jefe*. I told them I was sleeping like a *bebé* last night. I acted all innocent—which was easy since I am."

Janelle faced him on the deck and snapped, "You really think they bought it?"

"Why wouldn't they?"

"Your *knife*, Clarence. The blood on the ground the night before."

"Oh, yeah." Clarence tilted his head. "That."

Janelle turned to Chuck. "What's next?"

Chuck said to Clarence, "You want to tell her?"

"Tell her what?"

"What we decided," he prodded.

Clarence brightened as he remembered. "Falcon House," he said to Janelle. "Chuck figures one of those guys is the killer."

Chuck explained. "On account of what Clarence heard last night. And saw."

"The argument behind the dorms?" Janelle asked.

"*Sí*," said Clarence.

"A lover's quarrel," said Chuck. "That's what he heard."

Clarence wobbled a finger back and forth. "That's what I *think* I heard."

Chuck told Janelle, "He's going to see what he can find out."

"He's *what*?"

"*No hay problema, hermana mia*," Clarence said. "I know everybody over there. I'm just gonna stop in, ask around, see what's what."

"See what's *what*?" Janelle rounded on Chuck. "You're telling me your big plan is to send Clarence into Falcon House to root out the murderer?"

"He's just going to stop in, like he always does."

"Yeah," Clarence seconded. "Like I always do."

Janelle took in the two of them. "You're nuts. Both of you."

"We have to do something," Chuck countered. "If we don't, they'll just build a circumstantial case against Clarence while the real killer goes free."

Clarence explained, "Either the killer took off and he's long gone—which means there's nothing we can do about it—or he's laying low at Falcon House, pretending he's just one of the guys."

Janelle clarified, "One of the *mexicanos*. That's all there are over there, when it comes to guys, right?"

"*Claro*. I'll wander around, *habla* a little *español*, see if anybody's acting nervous or suspicious or whatever."

Chuck told Clarence, "Remember, we can't talk on the phone or text each other anymore. I'll swing by and check in with you later, face-to-face."

"*Bueno*."

Janelle turned to Chuck, clearly dumbfounded. "That's it? You're going to send him into the middle of everything—while he's *drunk*?"

Clarence leaned forward, attempting to take the brunt of her wrath. "I'm not drunk." He tapped the empty flask in his pocket. "And I'm not gonna be, am I?"

Chuck added, "That's not the whole plan." He considered the cascade of events over the last forty-eight hours—Nicoleta's murder, the blood on the ground, his own entrapment in the mine, the collapse of the mine floor, the rotting bighorn sheep carcasses on Mount Landen. So many moving parts. "He's not the only one who'll be doing something."

Janelle shot Chuck a withering look. "Don't tell me you're thinking of going off and doing something risky, too."

"Clarence won't be risking his life in Falcon House, and I won't be taking any risks either."

"Then what's this other part of your big plan?"

"I'm going to do some research."

"Mr. Archaeologist," Janelle huffed. "Always something more to study."

Chuck recited his favorite quote from the first page of the very first archaeology textbook he'd been assigned at Fort Lewis College more than twenty years ago: "'An archaeologist's task is to amass evidence piece by painstaking piece, until the compendium of proof shines a bright light on the precise truth.'"

He held his breath while Janelle absorbed the words. Her eyes went to the tall ponderosas that shaded the cabin on all sides. She looked back at him and jutted her chin in defiance. "All I know is, I'm not staying here alone with the girls. If you're going off to do some *research,* then we're coming with you."

Twenty-Seven

"There's more you should know," Chuck told Janelle as he drove the truck out of the resort complex, headed for town. She sat opposite him in the front seat. Carmelita and Rosie, still engaged in their computer battle, sat in back.

Chuck described the scene he'd encountered in the fen on the north side of Mount Landen—the headless rams, the stench, the swarms of flies. As he finished, his phone vibrated in his pocket. He let the incoming call go to voicemail.

"You think the dead sheep have something to do with the murder?" Janelle asked.

"No, I really don't."

"And you don't think the puddle of blood and Clarence's knife have anything to do with it, either, right?"

"I don't know what to think anymore."

"Which is why we're on our way to the library."

"'An archaeologist's task...'"

Janelle looked at her hands. "It's too much to take in, all of this."

Chuck had been about to tell her of his entrapment in the mine, too, but she was frightened enough as it was. He clamped his mouth shut.

He parked in front of the library and turned to the girls, his arm over the front seat. "Time to turn those contraptions off."

"Awww," they grumbled.

He aimed a thumb at the library. "They say there's real, live books in there."

The girls looked through the windshield.

"We're at the library!" Rosie rejoiced. She bounced up and down in failed attempts to loosen her seatbelt.

At Rosie's side, Carmelita beamed. Chuck held a palm out to her and she gave him a high-five.

"Me, too," Rosie demanded.

She delivered his extended palm a ferocious slap. He shook his hand in fake pain before stretching to release her buckle.

Inside, Rosie took the hands of Janelle and Carmelita and tugged them down the hall toward the children's wing, where the three had spent a number of afternoons over the course of the summer.

Chuck checked his phone as he headed for the rear of the library. The call had been yet another from Sartore. He shoved his phone back in his pocket. He'd get back to the professor. But first: research.

He asked the librarian at the back desk if Elaine was in.

"She's on break," the young man replied. "Outside."

Chuck circled the building until he found Elaine seated on a discarded fiberglass desk chair against the chiseled stone wall of the library. A large, green dumpster shielded her from the traffic on Elkhorn Avenue. Her cane leaned against the wall beside her. Smoke curled from a cigarette hanging from the corner of her mouth.

Upon spotting Chuck, Elaine yanked the cigarette from her lips. "Now you know all my secrets," she said as he approached.

"I don't imagine I know *all* of them yet," he replied. "Nor am I sure I want to."

Her lined face broke into a grin and she released a phlegmy croak of a laugh before growing serious. "You've had a little excitement up your way."

"She was a nice young woman, by all accounts."

"They always say that in situations like this."

"Sounds like you know something about her I don't."

She took a drag on her cigarette and blew smoke in a long stream out the side of her mouth. "I've been around long enough to know that when someone dies, there's usually a reason for it—and the person who's dead is usually part of the reason."

"God, but you're a hard-ass, you know that?"

"The years tend to do that to you."

"If you're not careful."

"Careful's the last thing I've ever been in my life. Or ever wanted to be."

With an open hand, Chuck gestured to an invisible audience. "How to grow up to be one smart-as-a-whip, tough-as-hell broad, Exhibit A."

Elaine's watery eyes glowed. "I'll grant you, I'm pretty wise at this stage of the game."

"Or just wizened?"

Elaine honked, smoke escaping from her nostrils. "You're more of a hard-ass than I am."

"Just softening you up before I report back."

She pointed at a second discarded library chair, this one listing on a bent leg. "Pull up a seat, Indiana Jones."

Chuck settled into the chair with a heavy sigh. "It's good to talk to you."

"It's always good to talk to me. What'd you learn?"

He took a moment to work his thoughts backward past Nicoleta's murder, the dead bighorns, and his forced stay in the mine to the oozing black material and the white object in the bottom of the shaft. "I'm not really sure."

"That's not much of an answer."

He rubbed his eyes with his fingertips, realizing yet again how exhausted he was. "The rock went away near the bottom. Everything started falling apart and I fell in and this black stuff covered me up. I thought I was a goner." He knew he was rambling, but he couldn't help himself.

The tip of Elaine's cigarette glowed red in the shade of the building as she took a drag. "I don't understand a word you're saying." She blew smoke past him.

He straightened in his seat. "Sorry." He blinked hard a

couple of times. "In the mine, near the bottom of the vertical shaft, the rock gave way to something else."

He described the black gunk and how it had collapsed around him at the slightest touch. He did not mention the white object he'd spied deep in the crevice.

"Black *gunk*?" Elaine asked.

"Black...*stuff*. Not as runny as mud, but really wet. Saturated. And granular, like coffee grounds."

"Lots of it?"

Chuck shivered at the memory of the black material covering him in the pit. "Yes."

"You brought some of this 'gunk' back with you?"

Chuck looked away. "No."

"Foolish man." Elaine took a long pull on her cigarette, drawing it down to the filter, and dropped the stub in a metal can resting on the pavement next to her chair. She placed her hands on the hem of her dress at her knees. "I'm going to have to see some of it," she said, smoke seeping from her mouth with her words.

"You don't know what it is?"

She blew out the last of the smoke. "I've got an idea. But I'll have to see the real thing before I'll know for sure."

Chuck waited as a semi-truck and trailer rumbled by on Elkhorn Avenue. The thought of roping back down the vertical shaft filled him with less dread than he'd have imagined; he would need to descend only far enough to gather a sample of the black material.

He knew he had far more important things to worry about than some unexplained black stuff in an old mine, but there was still the coincidental-or-not timing of the puddle of blood and the discovery of the vertical shaft a few hours later to consider.

Besides, returning to the mine wouldn't take long, no more than three hours or so. He surveyed the wooded slope rising beyond Elkhorn Avenue at the north edge of town. It was still well before sunset, enough time to drive to the mine, grab a sample of the black material, and most likely get back before Hemphill finished interviewing the last of the students.

Janelle. No way would she let him leave her and the girls alone this evening. But she might appreciate a few hours away from the resort as well.

A rustle of wind swept across the parking lot, carrying with it the first hint of the coming evening chill. He needed to get going, but he had one more subject to cover with Elaine first.

"There's something else I ran across today," he said.

Elaine took hold of her cane and placed her gnarled hands on its polished head.

He told her of the drag trails off the mountain and the carcasses in the small meadow and his suspicion that the rams' horns were headed for the black market.

"Supply and demand," Elaine said when Chuck finished. "Capitalism at its worst."

"I have to figure it's someone from around here."

"Of course. I can think of plenty who would jump on a gravy train like that."

"Such as?"

"Lots of locals are jealous of the free-spending tourists who come here. They don't understand the visitors are on their one big vacation of the year."

Chuck knew plenty of people in Durango who felt the same way.

Elaine continued. "They start looking for easy ways to grab what they think ought to be theirs. Studies show the rate of employee theft from businesses is significantly higher in tourist towns than non-tourist towns. Which is to say, if you want to get a good look at suspects for this massacre you found, just take a walk up Elkhorn Avenue and look in the front doors of the gift shops and restaurants."

"That doesn't exactly narrow it down," Chuck said. He told Elaine the conclusion he'd reached with Clarence that the poacher almost certainly was a regular visitor to the park.

"That makes sense." Elaine turned her cane in circles beneath her hands. "I'll keep thinking. If I get any bright ideas, I'll let you know. In the meantime, your job, should you choose to accept it, is to bring me some of that black stuff—and to not kill yourself in the process."

TWENTY-EIGHT

Ninety minutes later, Chuck stood with Janelle and the girls at the eastern edge of the mine site. In front of them, the last of the evening sunlight burnished the forested foothills falling away to the plains beyond.

Janelle had agreed to Chuck's suggestion that she and the girls accompany him to the mine, where, he told her, he wanted to make sure everything was squared away now that the students had left the site for the last time.

"A chance to stay away from the resort a while longer? Count us in," Janelle said. "Besides, I've wanted to visit the mine all summer." She turned to the girls. "We get to see where Chuck and Uncle Clarence have been doing all their work."

"Yippee!" Rosie cheered. She and Carmelita bumped fists.

Chuck added, "If we hurry, we'll be there for sunset."

Janelle faltered. "It'll take until after dark?"

"Not by much. We'll have headlamps for the hike out, and the moon will be up, too. It'll be fun. And I'll feel good knowing everything's okay at the site."

"I know you're trying to do all you can to be invited back next year, but I'll be honest with you, Chuck—after last night, I'm not sure I ever want to come back here again."

"You won't have to. Sartore says he's lining up more field school courses at other parks," Chuck said. No need to mention the professor's threat that Chuck's job was on the line, pending how the rest of the week played out. "I just want to spend another summer with you and the girls, it doesn't matter to me where."

"Come on, *Mamá*," Rosie said, hanging on Janelle's arm. "Can we go up there? Huh? Can we?"

"Well," she hedged. She checked the sun, still well above the mountains in the western sky. "*Bueno. Vamanos.*" She patted Rosie's backside, sending her in the direction of the truck.

From the edge of the mine site, Chuck pointed out to Janelle and the girls the open swath of grass at the center of the Y of the Rockies complex. At the south edge of the fields, two hulking, log buildings, the lodge and conference center, were just visible in the fading light.

He took four headlamps from his rucksack, pulled one over his head, and handed out the other three to Janelle and the girls.

"While you watch the last of the sunset," he said, "I'll head into the mine and grab the floodlights and make sure everything's put away."

He threw his pack over his shoulder and followed the tracks to the mouth of the mine. He unlocked the door, pulled it open with a stubborn squeak, stowed the lock and key in his pack, and hurried to the end of the tunnel.

He clicked on the floodlights, their batteries recharged by the solar panels still set up outside. Working quickly, he strapped his seat harness around his waist and secured a dismantled length of ore cart track to one of the floor-base timbers so that the end of the iron track extended over the mouth of the vertical shaft. He clipped his anchored rope through a carabiner slung from the extended end of the track and edged backward into the opening. When the rope took his weight, he swung free, slowly rotating in the middle of the shaft.

He loosened his belay device and slid down the rope commando-style, equidistant from the shaft's four rock walls. Halfway down, where the streaks of black material first appeared, he locked the belay device and rocked his body back and forth, coming closer to the walls of the shaft with each swing. When he drew near enough, he grabbed a fistful of the crumbly black matter from the wall he faced. He pulled a Ziploc bag from his pocket, shoved the handful of black material inside it, and dropped the filled baggie down the front of his flannel shirt.

He looked up from where he hung, swinging, in the shaft. The beam of his headlamp followed the rope to the end of the ore cart track thirty feet above.

Nearly half an hour had passed since he'd left Janelle and the girls outside. Darkness would be falling by now, the girls drawing close to Janelle, who would be wondering what was taking him so long.

Was it possible that whoever had locked Chuck in the mine had followed the four of them this evening? No, he assured himself. He'd seen no sign anyone had been at the mine since the field school packed up, and, anyway, whoever it was probably wasn't that dangerous—they hadn't stayed around long enough to prevent Clarence from rescuing him.

He bounced lightly on the rope. The ore cart track held firm. The white object was only thirty feet below him.

He put his thumb to the release lever of the belay device, pressed it forward, and slid down the rope. As he descended, the black streaks widened to where they joined together just above the bottom of the mine shaft.

He kicked to rotate himself until he faced the crevice. The light from his headlamp angled into the cleft, creating hard lines of gray and black. He leaned sideways, craning his neck, but couldn't catch sight of the white object at the back of the narrow opening.

He put his thumb to the belay-device lever, ready to descend to the bottom of the shaft. He pressed the lever just as a shriek reached his ears. It was coming from the mouth of the mine.

Twenty-Nine

Chuck stilled his breathing.

A second cry echoed the length of the tunnel and down into the pit.

He aimed an ear toward the top of the shaft. When he heard a third shriek, he slumped in his harness, weak with relief.

Rosie was hollering his name.

"Chu-*uck*," she screamed a fourth time, breaking his name into two syllables. Her cry was distinct this time; she'd entered the tunnel.

"There's a hole!" he yelled back, terrified at the prospect of the girls scurrying ahead of Janelle and unknowingly coming upon the vertical shaft. "Careful!"

He peered upward. "Be careful!" he cried again.

Light from moving headlamp beams bounced off the back wall of the mine tunnel sixty feet above him, joining the steady glow of the floodlights.

"You hear me?" he hollered. "There's a hole!"

Janelle's voice came from above. "Chuck?"

"The hole I told you about, where Samuel fell," he called to her. "You'll see it ahead of you. Keep the girls back."

A head with a headlamp attached poked over the edge of the shaft. "What are you doing down there?" Janelle asked.

"I'm almost done. I'll be right up."

Janelle's head hovered over the edge of the shaft for a moment before it disappeared. He returned his attention to the problem before him.

He slid down the rope until he stood thigh-deep in the viscous black muck, his legs and feet instantly growing cold. He aimed his headlamp into the fissure. The white object was wedged, as before, where the crevice narrowed to nothing. And there, scattered in the crevice below the object, were light-colored sticks of various lengths and thicknesses.

Still attached to the rope, he edged sideways into the crevice. His back brushed the crevice wall, which collapsed onto his shoulders. The wet, black material dripped from his body and landed in the muck with wet plops.

He leaned into the crevice, his shoulders pressed against the fissure's narrowing sides. As the walls fell against him, he closed his eyes and reached blindly for something smooth.

He swam his hand through the muck, up, down, sideways, until his fingers bounced off something solid. He dug his toes into the black gunk and shoved himself forward a few more inches. He stretched full out, the black material gathering around him, and took hold of the object, his fingers finding purchase in depressions in its rounded shape.

He held the object against his chest and pushed himself backward with his free hand until he was out of the crevice. Once more he was covered in muck, soaked to the skin, and freezing.

Before he could swipe the grit-covered lens of his headlamp clean to look at the prize grasped in his hand, the wall of the shaft in front of him gave way, raising the level of black muck to his waist.

He shoved the object down his shirt and shrugged his pack around to his front. He dug out his ascending devices, attached them to the rope, wrestled his boots into the loops hanging from the devices, and commenced the arduous climb up the rope, this time hanging from the ore cart track above, safely away from the four crumbling lower walls of the shaft. He ascended from the gathering muck twelve inches at a time, the brisk climbing movements staving off the worst of the cold, his breaths coming in sharp gasps.

"Chuck?" Rosie called from above. "Is that you?"

He paused halfway up the shaft. "Sure is, sweetie," he called with forced cheeriness. "I'm almost there!"

The light of a headlamp illuminated him from above as he resumed his ascent. "Up from the primordial muck," Janelle observed.

When he reached the top of the shaft, she took hold of the shoulder straps of his pack and helped him clamber onto the floor of the mine tunnel. He unclipped himself from the rope and lay on his back while he caught his breath. The round object, enveloped in his T-shirt, rose and fell each time he inhaled and exhaled.

The girls stood well back from the open shaft, their headlamps aimed at him.

"What's that sticking out of your tummy?" Carmelita asked.

Chuck sat up as his breathing slowed. He reached beneath his shirt and removed something white. Though his headlamp was still covered in grit, the headlamps of Janelle and the girls lit the object in his hand. It was a skull, all right. The stick-like debris, now buried in the bottom of the pit below, undoubtedly had been the rest of the skeleton.

Janelle backed away until she was even with the girls. She drew them to her.

Chuck rotated the skull in his hand. The cranium was small, not surprising given the smaller stature typical of miners a hundred years ago. The skull's eye sockets, dark and vacant, sat close on either side of the sinus cavity.

"What's that?" Janelle asked, pointing.

Smack in the middle of the skull's forehead was a pea-sized hole.

Chuck reached with his forefinger to touch the edge of the perfectly round opening. The edge of the indentation was slightly concave where it entered the skull.

"A bullet hole," he said.

THIRTY

"That is *so gross*," Carmelita declared, the beam of her headlamp fixed on the bullet hole.

"Uh-*huh*," Rosie concurred, crossing her arms over her chest. "Gross, gross, grossy-gross."

Carmelita stepped forward. "Can I touch it?"

Rosie dropped her arms to her sides. "Yeah, yeah, yeah. Can we? Can we?"

Janelle turned her headlamp on the girls. "I'm sure you're not allowed to do anything with it."

Chuck cradled the skull in his hand. He couldn't see Janelle's eyes behind the light of her headlamp, but he knew by her calm tone of voice what was in them: complete and utter composure. Janelle's toughness was well earned—the girls' father, with whom Janelle had taken up as a rebellious teenager, had been a drug dealer in Albuquerque's South Valley until the day of his death by gunfire.

Carmelita and Rosie pressed forward on either side of Janelle, who held them back with extended arms. The girls focused the beams of their headlamps on the skull. Chuck wiped his headlamp lens and directed its light at the object in his hand as well.

The skull differed markedly from the ancient Native American skulls he encountered in the course of his archaeological work on federal lands across the Southwest. Those skulls featured receding jaw lines and wide nasal passages. The skull resting in his palm had a prognathous, or extended, jaw line and a narrow nasal opening associated with Caucasians. A thin, bony protrusion between the eyes known as a nuchal ridge also pointed to the skull's European ancestry.

Chuck rotated the skull to study the bullet's jagged exit wound.

Deaths in Colorado's hard-rock mines were commonplace.

Mountain-town cemeteries dating from the late 1800s were lined with the graves of miners who'd died of everything from tunnel collapses to carbon-monoxide poisoning to silicosis caused by rock-dust inhalation. Murder, on the other hand, was rare in the state's tight-knit mining communities—yet the skull in his hand revealed death by a deliberate hand.

Chuck turned the skull back around and rubbed his thumb across the small, dark circle in the center of its forehead. How had the miner come to be shot and killed?

Rosie leaned on her mother's arm while balancing on a couple of loosened floorboard planks. The planks squeaked against one another beneath her weight. The sound, similar to the squeak of the mine-mouth door, startled Chuck.

The baggie of sodden black material fell from his shirt as he scrambled to his feet, thinking of the locked door that had been eased closed in silence at the mouth of the mine just twenty-four hours ago. He peered down the tunnel past Janelle and the girls. The rectangle of starry night sky was visible at the mouth of the mine. The door was still open.

He shoved the baggie and skull into his pack and led Janelle and the girls down the tunnel at a fast clip, the rectangle of sky growing larger with each step. He increased his speed, almost jogging, as they passed the tunnel's halfway point.

"What's the rush?" Janelle asked, herding the girls as best she could behind him.

Though the end of the tunnel was less than a hundred feet away, the reinstalled floorboards seemed to stretch far ahead of him.

He broke into a run.

Thirty-One

Fifty feet to go. Thirty. Ten.

Chuck burst from the mine and stood, panting, between the ore cart tracks.

Janelle ushered the girls out of the mine behind him. "What were you thinking?" she demanded.

"Yeah," Rosie said, placing her hands on her hips. "What were you thinking?"

Chuck swung his headlamp all directions. No one was there.

"I was thinking," he said, grabbing Rosie beneath her arms, "how incredibly cute you and Carm are."

He spun Rosie around and around, his boots digging into the gravel between the tracks, the stars rotating above their heads.

"Whooo!" Rosie cried, grinning in the light of his headlamp, her legs flying free as she twirled.

Chuck slowed, set her down, and used her as a staff, leaning on her shoulder and bending forward. "You're not a little girl anymore, you know that?" he said between gulps of air.

"No, I'm not." She clapped her hands. "I'm a big girl." Displaying no signs of dizziness, she looked at Janelle, her headlamp lighting her mother's face. "I've always been a big girl, haven't I, *Mamá*?"

"In every way," Janelle agreed. She directed her headlamp at Chuck's grit-encrusted pack. "I thought archaeologists weren't supposed to mess with human remains."

"Generally, that's true." He straightened. "But if it was me who'd been murdered—even it was more than a century ago—I wouldn't mind if somebody tried to figure out what had happened."

She aimed her headlamp at his face. "This is your idea of making sure everything's 'squared away' around here, is it?"

He answered with a question of his own. "What say we get out of here?"

Two hours later, Chuck stopped the truck halfway down the cabin's driveway. He climbed out and looked up at the slice of sky showing between the trees lining the drive. Light from the moon, high in the eastern sky, nearly washed out the stars.

When he'd returned to the resort with Janelle and the girls half an hour ago, he'd spotted only a couple of police cars along with the mobile command vehicle still parked in front of the dormitory buildings.

After showering off his latest round of black grit, Chuck convinced Janelle—and himself—that she'd be okay on her own with Carmelita and Rosie for a little while.

"It should only take a few minutes to check in with Clarence and see how things went at Falcon House," he said.

She glanced out the front window at the dark forest surrounding the cabin.

"You can come along," Chuck said. "But..."

Behind her, in the tiny bathroom at the back of the cabin, the girls giggled as they brushed their teeth, wrestling for position in front of the sink.

She sighed. "Straight there and straight back."

From where he stood outside the truck at the edge of the driveway, Chuck's eyes fell on his grimy pack resting on the floor between the truck's front and back seats, lit by a sliver of moonlight angling through the trees. He would wait until he was on his way out of town to turn the skull over to park officials. He would also let them know about the ram carcasses rotting in the forest on the north flank of Mount Landen.

His thoughts returned, compass-like, to Nicoleta's murder, and to the fact that he'd put off checking in with Professor Sartore for far too long. He fished his phone from his pocket and punched up Sartore's number.

The professor answered before the first ring ended. "Chuck, I swear to God—"

"It's been nonstop here, professor," Chuck said. He hurried on, outlining the murder and its aftermath, knowing full well Sartore had been following events online as they unfolded.

"Shut everything down first thing tomorrow morning," Sartore said when Chuck finished. "I want those students out of there."

"I'll do my best."

"No, you won't 'do your best,'" the professor growled. "You'll get them out of there tomorrow, no ifs, ands, or buts."

"I'm afraid there is one 'but,' sir. The police are telling me they'd like the kids to stick around until they give the all-clear."

"That's illegal."

"Some of the kids knew the young woman who was killed."

"You mean to tell me the police are considering them as *suspects*?"

"I wouldn't go that far."

"I will not have my students held hostage," Sartore thundered. "I'll go to the governor if I have to."

"I've met twice so far with the officer in charge of the investigation. He sees himself as a tough nut, likes to play hardball. He's careful to not say the students have to stay, but he's suggesting it very strongly. I think he'd almost like it if you took him on."

"God*dammit*."

"My feelings exactly, professor. Not sure we have a choice in this, though."

Sartore grunted in defeat. "I'm driving up tomorrow, then."

"You really don't need to."

"Wrong. I *do* need to," Sartore said. "I was counting on you, Chuck. But you've failed me. You hear that? *You've failed me.*"

Chuck clamped his mouth shut. Best to ride this out.

"Stay close to those kids until I get there," the professor continued, his tone growing more reasonable in the wake of Chuck's silence. "All of them. And keep me posted."

"We'll be okay by Friday," Chuck said. "I'm sure of it. The police just have lots of people to talk to."

Sartore huffed. "I want to know everything as soon as you know it. I know you like to handle things on your own. Hell, that's why I hired you. But not now, not with this. These long stretches between calls? No more of that. You hear me?"

"I hear you, sir."

Hemphill stepped out of the mobile command vehicle when Chuck parked in front of Raven House.

"Where have you been?" the officer demanded, striding across the parking lot before Chuck could escape into the dormitory.

"Working. I've still got a job to do here."

Hemphill aimed a finger behind him. "Come with me."

Once again, they settled into the seats opposite one another at the small table inside the command vehicle. The interior lights were turned low, giving Chuck the impression he was seated with Hemphill in a quiet bar. The new-vehicle smell inside the RV had been replaced by the greasy odor of burgers and stale French fries.

Harley gave Chuck a weary nod from his seat at the rear counter. Even in the dim light, Chuck could see that Harley's eyes were bloodshot, his face drawn. Chuck could only imagine what his own face looked like after two nights with virtually no sleep.

Hemphill pressed his hands to his temples while Harley rolled down the narrow aisle in his chair and set his laptop and microphone on the table.

Chuck said, "I already told you what I know."

Hemphill flicked his fingers at the microphone. "Just a formality."

"You talked to all the students?"

"I did. Parker was right. Your group has been pretty busy this summer."

Chuck kept his tone even. "Nothing wrong with that."

"You're a hands-off kind of guy, that's what everyone says. You let your team leaders run things for you."

"That's what they're for. And they've done a good job. Things have gone smoothly enough."

"Up at the mine, maybe. But down here? It's been a full-on soap opera." The officer lifted a finger. "First off, there's your guys."

"Team Nugget," Chuck confirmed.

"Yep. Drinking, toking, having a good time."

"Doesn't surprise me."

Hemphill lifted a second finger. "The thing that surprised me was your girls. What your boys were to alcohol and pot, your girls were to bed hopping."

"With Team Nugget?"

"And Falcon House."

"The Mexican workers?"

"The younger ones, some of them, from the sound of things."

Chuck rested his fingers on the edge of the table. "None of what you're telling me speaks to the fact that it was the young woman from Falcon House, Nicoleta, who was killed."

Hemphill lifted a third finger and continued as if Chuck hadn't spoken. "Then there's your brother-in-law. He knew the victim. Intimately. But I expect you already knew that, didn't you? You just didn't feel like sharing that piece of information with us."

Chuck studied the tabletop as Hemphill went on. "He was up front with us about it. Told us he slept with her a couple of times at the beginning of the summer."

Chuck looked up. "But you haven't arrested him yet."

"That'd be the logical thing to do right about now."

At the end of the table, Harley cleared his throat. Hemphill gave the gray-haired cop a sidelong glance before returning his gaze to Chuck.

"Your brother-in-law takes the prize, I'll give him that," Hemphill said. "Out and about every night, and remarkably successful, too, from the sound of things—the way he measures success, anyway."

Chuck tucked his hands in his lap. It sounded as if Hemphill believed Clarence was innocent, which meant Kirina hadn't said anything about seeing him slipping back into the dorm after the murder. "What more can I tell you?"

"I feel like I've got a pretty good sense of him at this point."

"And?"

"I don't have any physical evidence tying him to the murder."

Harley shifted in his seat. "Not yet," he muttered.

Hemphill said, "As you can see, Harley and I have a difference of opinion regarding your brother-in-law."

"Damn straight we do." Harley crossed his arms tight across his chest. His face reddened in the muted light of the command vehicle.

"I respect Harley's opinion," Hemphill said. "In this case, however, I disagree with it—at least for now. But the minute I have cause to think otherwise, I'll come knocking."

"What you're thinking is one-hundred-percent correct," Chuck said. "Your right-hand man here—" he dipped his head Harley's direction "—is wrong. Clarence is no murderer. And as for his knife and the blood, he had nothing to do with that, either."

"I happen to agree with you," Hemphill said. "For now, like I said. I think Clarence is telling the truth." He looked straight across the table at Chuck, his eyes growing cold and hard.

"What are you looking at?"

"Don't you mean, 'Who are you looking at?'" Hemphill let a

beat pass. "You reported it. You found her."

"Which rules me out."

"Or rules you in."

Chuck's stomach lurched. He pointed at the microphone. "I thought you said that was only for show."

Hemphill said nothing.

Chuck lowered his head and spoke straight into the microphone. "The picture you have of me should be pretty clear by now. I run as tight a ship in my personal life as I do in my professional life. I've been in my cabin, up in the woods, with my wife and daughters every night this summer."

The muscles around Hemphill's eyes relaxed. "Everything you're saying is exactly what I've learned about you."

"Playing the tough cop? Seeing if I'd crack?"

The officer shrugged.

Chuck worked to corral his anger. "My students, you've got nothing on them, right?"

"So far."

"And, despite what Harley here thinks, you've got Clarence tagged as innocent, too."

"So far as well."

"And me."

"Yes."

"Leaving the focus of your investigation on the residents of Falcon House."

"Or an outsider."

"Which means my students are free to go."

"Day after tomorrow, Friday, as we discussed, if nothing changes. Except, possibly, for your brother-in-law."

"You're going to name him as an official suspect or something, to keep him from leaving?"

"At this stage, to be perfectly honest with you, I'm not sure."

Chuck pointed toward Falcon House. "Your murderer is sitting right over there, in his room. Figure out which one of those guys did it, and we can all go home."

Thirty-Two

Chuck glanced over his shoulder at the employee dormitory as he headed across the parking lot toward Raven House upon leaving the command center.

As he'd told Hemphill, the murderer had to be one of Parker's workers.

Right?

Chuck slowed.

The male workers living in Falcon House were Mexicans who, by all accounts, maintained low profiles and sought only to send their earnings south to their families—not exactly the murderous type.

But who else could it be?

He stroked his chin as he walked.

What about the librarian, Elaine? Immediately upon hearing about the black material in the mine, she'd sent Chuck back to retrieve a sample of the stuff for her. Why had she been so intent on sending him back to the mine? And why, ten years ago, had she retired from Denver to the cold, wintry Colorado mountains rather than the warm, sunny Arizona desert preferred by just about every other Denver-area retiree?

What of the emergency room doctor, Gregory, ogling Janelle at the hospital, then showing up unbidden at the cabin, ostensibly to check on Rosie? Who makes house calls these days? Did Gregory's big, showy SUV require truck tires? And did those tires have lightning-bolt-shaped treads? Chuck couldn't recall.

The Elk Foundation sticker on the SUV's bumper indicated Gregory was a hunter. How often, Chuck wondered, did the young doctor drive into the park to go "mountain biking"? Enough to poach half a dozen trophy rams over the course of the summer?

Gregory's irregular hours in the emergency room would

provide him the opportunity to visit the park whenever he wished, and as a hunter, he knew his way around a rifle. Still, as a well-paid doctor, what need could he possibly have for the extra income he would derive from selling Rocky Mountain sheep horns on the black market? Or could he be poaching simply for the thrill of the illicit game?

And as for the puddle of blood spilled between the dorms, who could get their hands on human blood more easily than a night doctor with the run of the Estes Park hospital?

Then there was Parker. How well, after all these years, did Chuck really know the resort manager? And what of the binoculars sitting on Parker's windowsill? What might Parker have seen through them that he hadn't admitted to Chuck—and that might have led him to murder one of his young, female employees in the dark of night?

Chuck shook his head. *Parker?* he chided himself. *Gregory? Elaine?* What were the odds any of them was involved in Nicoleta's murder, the puddle of blood, the hidden mine shaft, or the poaching of the bighorns?

He entered Raven House and found Clarence, along with Samuel, in Jeremy's room. Jeremy slouched on his twin bed as if it were a couch, his back to the wood-paneled wall. Clarence leaned against the worn bureau opposite the bed, while Samuel sat on the room's desk chair.

Other than a poster of a curvaceous female skier flying off a snow cornice somewhere high in the mountains wearing only skis, boots, and a bikini, the walls of the upstairs dorm room were bare.

Chuck stood in the doorway. "You made it through your interviews, I see."

Jeremy muttered from the bed, "Like we had any choice."

Chuck turned to Samuel. "They fed you dinner at the lodge cafeteria?"

Samuel's head bobbed up and down like that of a puppy. "The manager, Parker, stopped by our table. He said he was checking in, making sure we were doing all right."

Jeremy's lips curled up in a sneer. "He'd better be making sure we're doing all right, with his employees getting murdered right outside our dorm."

Ignoring Jeremy, Samuel asked Chuck, "Are we getting out of here tomorrow?"

"I still get the sense no one's going anywhere until Friday."

Samuel and Jeremy moaned.

Clarence, sounding fully sober, spoke up in Chuck's defense. "Someone's been killed. They need time to investigate."

Jeremy shoved his tongue against the inside of his cheek, making it protrude rhythmically a couple of times, then snickered and mouthed the word "*someone*" to Samuel.

Samuel squirmed and glanced away. Chuck glared at Jeremy. Clarence, to his credit, said nothing.

Samuel looked at Chuck. "What's up for tomorrow, then?"

"I'm afraid I haven't gotten that far." He turned to Clarence. "Can we talk?"

Ignoring Jeremy, Chuck nodded a goodbye to Samuel and headed down the hall with Clarence.

When they were in Clarence's room with the door closed behind them, Clarence asked, "What'd you get out of Hemphill?"

Chuck spun the chair from the desk and sat down with his back to the window. "He doesn't think you did it. The other cop, Harley—the one with all the homicide experience—disagrees."

Clarence perched on the edge of his bed. "He made it clear he couldn't believe it when Hemphill let me go after my interview."

"Learn anything from your visit to Falcon House?"

"Not really. They're scared, like everyone else. They didn't want to do much talking. But they loosened up after a bit."

"The girls or the guys?"

"Both. We compared notes. They claim they're as in the dark as we are."

"Nothing more specific?"

Something flickered in Clarence's eyes. He leaned back on his elbows in an unconvincing display of nonchalance. "It wasn't all wine and roses over there, let's just put it that way."

Chuck waited.

Clarence cleared his throat. "The old cop isn't the only one who thinks I'm guilty," he explained. "I was hanging in the hallway, just talking, when Nicoleta's roommate, Anca, came out of her room. She came after me when she saw me, screaming, yelling. The others had to hold her back."

"She knows about you and Nicoleta, from earlier in the summer?"

"They're in doubles over there, two to a room. She had to stay out of the way when Nicoleta and I were doing our thing. So yeah, she knew. No way she couldn't."

Chuck pointed toward Jeremy's room. "Everybody else knows, too."

Clarence sat up. "I was with her at the start. But it wasn't just me. People pretty much lined up at her door as the summer went on, from what I heard."

"How much of that did you tell Hemphill?"

"Everything. I said I liked her, didn't know why anyone would want to hurt her."

"The line of people at her door could have resulted in hurt feelings somewhere along the way, don't you think?"

"I heard some of the guys at Falcon House weren't exactly pleased—not that they turned down any opportunities with her or anything. And I imagine Anca got tired of sleeping on the floor in other people's rooms."

"You really told Hemphill all of that?"

"Yes."

Chuck frowned. Hemphill hadn't shared any of that information with him. What else had the officer heard in the course of his interviews that he hadn't told Chuck?

Clarence continued, "I told him the truth about everything except...last night." He paused. "They're pretty fixated on you, too, you know."

"He asked about me?"

"Sure. Plenty."

"What'd you tell him?"

"I told him you were the most stand-up guy I knew, that there was no way you would ever have done it."

Chuck nodded his thanks.

Clarence went on. "I think you're right. It's one of those Falcon House guys. As far as which one, though, how's anyone ever going to know?"

Chuck hung his head and spoke to the floor. "We really don't know anything yet, do we?"

"We know it wasn't you or me—or any of our guys. They're partiers, sure. Drinkers, skirt chasers."

"Like you," Chuck said, looking up.

"Like just about every warm-blooded male I've ever known. But they're not killers."

"I want you to stay as close as you can to those Falcon House guys. Keep your eye on them. One of them did it. That has to be it. We just have to hope they'll slip up at some point."

Chuck left Clarence and moved on to Kirina. She opened her door at his knock, crossed the room to her bed, and settled her computer on her lap.

He closed the door behind him. "What's the latest from the outside world?" he asked, eyeing her laptop.

"Sartore is freaking out. He's posting stuff online, asking questions on the one hand and trying to smooth things over with the parents on the other. Basically, he's making a total mess of everything."

"You've been sending replies?"

She shook her head. "Nothing I could say would help the situation."

"I just talked to him. He was pretty fired up."

"He already posted that you told him we're stuck here till Friday."

"Are you okay with that?"

"I knew Nicoleta. Sure, I'm okay with it, if it means finding out who killed her."

"You knew Nicoleta?"

"Of course, I did. She was pretty social. She knew everyone in Raven House. But I have no idea who might've wanted to kill her."

Chuck sighed."Sartore told me he's going to drive up here tomorrow."

"You should be glad. It'll take some of the pressure off you."

Chuck hadn't thought of it that way. He nodded. "How'd your interview go?"

"The officer was kind of gruff. But it went all right, I guess. Didn't take too long." She tilted her head toward her room window, its curtains open. "I saw you go back into the command post with him a few minutes ago. What'd he want?"

"Thanks to you, he had nothing to say about Clarence sneaking back into the dorm."

She waved off Chuck's gratitude. "I understand what you're doing and why you're doing it. Clarence didn't kill Nicoleta. We all know that. Better to keep the cops' focus where it should be."

"They're going to zero in on Falcon House tomorrow, sounds like. On the workers."

"That's good to hear. What do you have in mind for us for tomorrow?"

"I'm not sure. Any thoughts?"

"I guess we could stay here, finish up cataloging the last of the finds, see if we can spot anything with the Falcon House workers ourselves."

"We can make like Sherlock Holmes," Chuck said. "Sniff around, solve the case on our own."

"Stranger things have happened."

THIRTY-THREE

"Let's just leave," Janelle said when Chuck returned to the cabin. "*Ahora mismo*. They haven't charged Clarence with anything. Or you. We can be out of here in fifteen minutes and back in Durango by dawn."

The girls were settled in their twin beds in the back bedroom. Janelle sat on the living-room couch next to Chuck.

"They'll put out an arrest warrant for Clarence," Chuck said. "For me, too."

"Clarence didn't do anything," she pleaded. "Neither did you."

"He slept with her, Jan."

"He *what*?"

"He slept with Nicoleta. Earlier in the summer. He was the first of many, sounds like."

"He slept with the murdered girl?" Janelle repeated in disbelief.

"You know full well what he's like."

She rose, crossed the room, and plopped into one of the kitchen chairs. She propped her elbows on the table, using both hands to push her hair away from her face. "What else do you know that I don't?" she asked.

Chuck left the couch and slid into a kitchen chair opposite her. "He's being as open as possible with the cops. That's why they haven't taken him in yet. But the longer things go with no other suspects..."

"They're wasting their time on him."

"Add his having slept with her to the discovery of his knife with the blood, and it's a wonder he's not in custody already." Chuck reached across the table, offering Janelle his hand. "We have to get some sleep. We'll figure things out in the morning."

"We really can't leave?"

"If Clarence runs, he's all they'll focus on."

She tucked her hair behind her ears and took Chuck's hand. He pulled her to a standing position and they climbed the stairs to the loft together, her arm tight around his waist, drawing him close.

Chuck spent much of the night staring out the skylight, cursing himself for his inability to sleep as Janelle tossed and turned beside him. Finally, just before dawn, his eyes closed and he fell into a deep, dreamless slumber.

Rays of morning sun angled through the skylight when Janelle shook him awake. He sat up, groggy and confused, and squinted at the bright yellow rectangle of sunlight on the wall.

In an instant, everything came flooding back. He snatched his phone from the bedside table. It was after ten o'clock. He had voicemail from Kirina asking where he was, from Professor Sartore demanding that Chuck check in with him yet again, and from Parker, who said he'd thought of something he wanted to tell Chuck.

"I've got to get going," he told Janelle, swinging his feet to the floor.

"Breakfast first."

"No time." He waved his phone at her.

He dressed, splashed water on his face, and ran his fingers through his hair, pressing it into place.

He opened his laptop on the kitchen table and skimmed the emails piling up from the students' parents. The field school blog, though filled with excited chatter by the students, contained no new information. The *Estes Park Trail-Gazette* website offered little solid news in its lead story beyond the murdered cashier's full name, Nicoleta Barstolik, her age, twenty-two, and her nationality, Bulgarian.

Janelle looked over Chuck's shoulder at his computer screen until he closed it. "You really have to go?"

He rose and turned to her. "You shouldn't stay here either.

I'll leave the truck for you. In fact, there's something I'm wondering if you could do for me."

He went outside and returned with the baggie of black material he'd collected from the mine shaft. Janelle held it in her hand while he explained, "There's a research librarian, Elaine, the one I talked to yesterday, who wants this. I'm wondering if you could—"

She cut him off. "Let me get this straight. We've got a murder, Clarence under suspicion as Jack the Ripper, cops all over the place—" she waved the bag in Chuck's face "—and you want me to deliver a bag of dirt to some librarian for you?" She stopped, her eyes lighting on the baggie in her hand. She turned the bag, studying it. "What is this stuff, anyway?"

"It's from the mine. The librarian wants to see it."

"Because...?"

"She thinks she might know what it is."

"And this has what to do with the murder, exactly?"

"I've been wondering about the timing of the blood on the ground and finding the hidden shaft in the mine the very next day."

Her mouth turned down. "This is just something to keep me and the girls busy, isn't it?"

"And away from the cabin," he agreed, content to follow Janelle's lead. "You've probably seen her down there. She's the one with the cane."

Janelle gave the bag a shake. "This doesn't matter. Don't you see? The only thing that matters is getting out of here."

"The only thing that matters is making sure Clarence doesn't get locked away for something he didn't do—which is exactly what will happen if we leave today." Chuck took hold of Janelle's free hand with both of his. "Tomorrow. Twenty-four more hours."

She pulled her hand away and tossed the bag on the kitchen table. It landed with a wet *plop* and slid a few inches, leaving a skid of black on the tabletop. She went to the sink, rinsed her hands, and turned to Chuck as she wiped the outside of the baggie clean with a paper towel. "Okay," she said, worry in her eyes. "I'll run your errand. I'll drop off your bag. Then the girls and I will 'lay low' in town. I won't make any trouble for you."

"Jan."

"I'll do whatever you say."

"*Janelle.*"

"But I want one thing in return," she said. She threw the wadded paper towel at him, her arm a flash of motion. He caught the towel against his chest as tears sprang to her eyes. "I want you to get down there to Raven House and look after my little brother."

Thursday

Thirty-Four

Chuck walked straight to the conference center. He fingered his phone in his pocket. Sartore wanted him to call, but he had nothing new to report. The professor could wait.

He climbed the stairs to the third floor and knocked on Parker's office door.

Parker stood at his office window with his back to Chuck, his binoculars to his eyes, the case open on the windowsill beside him. Chuck recognized the binoculars as Brunton Epochs, a technological marvel in the way they amplified available light to provide crisp, clear views, particularly at dawn and dusk.

Parker lowered the binoculars and turned from the window. "Thought maybe you'd gone into hiding."

"I'm tempted," Chuck said. He looked past Parker at the sunny day outside. "This summer was supposed to be easy. A vacation."

"Like you need one with your career—work when you want, as long as you want, on the jobs you want." Parker set the binoculars on the windowsill and dropped into his seat behind his polished desk.

Chuck let his gaze roam around the well-appointed office. "You haven't got a lot to complain about yourself." He rounded Parker's desk, picked up the binoculars, and focused through the window on the dormitories. As he watched, a kitchen worker in a white apron emerged from the rear of Falcon House and walked up the sidewalk toward the cafeteria building.

"You re-opened the dining hall?"

163

"People have to eat."

Chuck swept the binoculars past the string of commercial buildings lining Elkhorn Avenue and stopped at the Stanley Hotel, its clapboard walls blazing white in the morning sun. The hotel sat at the head of a sloping lawn on the far side of town, nearly two miles away. Tourists, ant-like in the binoculars' viewfinder, made their way up the broad stone stairway to the famously haunted lodge.

Chuck returned the binoculars to the sill and took a seat in front of Parker's desk. "Must be quite the view at night."

"A view's only worth so much." Parker shifted his weight in his chair. "I've been doing this for ten years, and I'm still not sure I'm cut out to be a desk jockey."

"How many employees are you in charge of?"

"More than a hundred, and they're every single one of them trouble—the ones in Falcon House most of all. The local workers go home at night, but with the dorm, it's like sitting on a volcano all summer." He aimed a thumb out the window. "I look over there when I'm working late, and they're scurrying around like mice, coming and going in their junker cars, lights flicking on and off in each other's rooms, slipping outside to get stoned." He whistled through his front teeth. "The things I've seen."

"Why don't you do something about it?"

"What is there to do? They're good kids for the most part. Adventurous, which is why they signed up to come over here in the first place. And they're hard workers, I'll grant them that. It's when the sun goes down, that's the problem—" he looked at Chuck over the top of his wire-rimmed glasses "—whether they're mine or yours."

Chuck let Parker's insinuation pass. "You said you'd thought of something."

"Right." Parker sat forward. "Not sure if it means anything, but...I came back up here the other night, after dinner, to do some work—the story of my summer, every summer. Anyway, I was up here pretty late." He paused. "It was two nights ago."

"The night of the blood."

"And the night of your brother-in-law's knife."

Chuck dug his fingernails into the supple leather arms of his chair as Parker continued.

"The view from up here is pretty...all-encompassing."

Chuck pointed at the high-tech Bruntons. "Especially with those."

"It's fun, actually, a lot of the time, looking around with them. People going in and out of the Stanley, cars coming down Trail Ridge Road."

"And here in the resort, too."

"It's good to keep an eye on things. And, like I said, the things I've seen...but all of it, you know—" he waggled his hand "—consenting." He looked away.

"Go on," Chuck urged.

The resort manager's eyes came to rest on the wooden bear sculpture in the corner, the creature's gouged-out eye sockets staring back at him. "It's not what I saw. The problem is what I didn't see."

Thirty-Five

"What *didn't* you see, then?" Chuck asked, playing along.

"I didn't see Nicoleta's roommate, Anca."

Chuck pressed his hands to his stomach, containing himself. It had been Anca who had come after Clarence in the Falcon House hallway.

Parker continued, "There's no smoking in the dorms, as you know. And of course, with the drought, there's pretty much no smoking allowed anywhere. One spark and—" he puffed his cheek "—*poof.*"

"But people still smoke."

"We can't prohibit it. You know the buckets, right?"

Chuck nodded. Red metal canisters, open at the top and filled with sand, were bolted waist-high to the light poles lining the sidewalk in front of the dormitory buildings. Smokers were to stay within ten feet of the buckets, and to put their butts out in the sand.

"Every night at ten o'clock," Parker said, "the TV goes off in the front room of Falcon House and she comes out for a smoke. Every single night."

"You do work late, don't you?"

"Never past midnight. My wife won't let me. But we're talking about Anca, not me."

"Nicoleta's roommate," Chuck confirmed.

"Ten p.m., on the dot. Except for two nights ago."

"I'm not really sure—"

"Maybe it doesn't have anything to do with anything," Parker said. "But she never showed. I mean, it's gotten to the point where, when I've been working this summer, I've started anticipating ten o'clock. I know she'll come out, have her smoke, go back inside. When she goes through her routine, it's like everything's okay in my world. I can keep working, go home, whatever, but the earth's still turning, I'm going to make it through another summer season, know what I mean?"

"Except for two nights ago."

"It was odd, that's all. I was sitting right here." Parker turned ninety degrees to a small computer table with a keyboard tray and oversized monitor, demonstrating how easy it was for him to glance out the window while he worked. "Ten o'clock came and went. Ten-fifteen. Ten-thirty. I finally went home, but it was unsettling."

"Somebody doesn't smoke a cigarette, and you call that 'unsettling'?"

"I know. Believe me, I get it. You're not sure what to make of it, and neither am I. But I can tell you this, Chuck: five hours after Anca's a no-show, the cops were scooping up a bunch of what apparently is human blood, just back of where she usually has her smoke."

"And twenty-four hours later, her roommate is dead, in almost the same place."

"Which is why I wanted you to know, seeing's how it's your brother-in-law's knife the cops are parading around." Parker stopped, but it was clear there was something more on his mind. "He's got a real obvious body frame, your brother-in-law."

Chuck pictured Clarence's short, stocky build, his pot belly, and his long, dark hair. "One that's easy to spot in binoculars, I suppose."

"Even at night," Parker said.

"You saw him the night of the blood?"

"No."

"The night before last?"

"Not then, either."

"Good."

"But I saw him other nights. Lots of other nights. Your brother-in-law, from what I've seen, has gotten around quite a bit this summer."

"Making his way over to Falcon House?"

Parker nodded. "Several of the girls' rooms. Lights on, lights off. Curtains open, curtains closed. Doesn't seem to matter to him."

"If it makes you feel any better, he told the police."

"As well he should have."

"You don't miss a thing around here, do you?"

"Oh, I'm sure I miss plenty. But I consider it part of my job to catch as much as I can."

Chuck angled back toward the cabin after exiting the conference center. Upon entering the trees, he turned and made his way through the forest to the back of the dormitories, avoiding Parker's long-lensed gaze. Above the dining hall, the crime-scene tape was gone, the place where Nicoleta's body had lain impossible to pick out on the slope. The mobile command vehicle and police cars were gone, too, as if the murder never had taken place.

He entered Raven House through the back door and found the students at work alongside Clarence and Kirina in the common room, with its knotty, aspen-plank walls running all the way to the second-story ceiling. Finds from the mine site, most dug from beneath the collapsed cabin, lined the front room's wooden tables. Each item was stored in an annotated Ziploc bag. The students talked among themselves while they toted their laptops from find to find, typing up written descriptions of each.

By the end of the course, the students were to have completed full logbooks of everything recovered from the mine site, including discovery date, grid location, and physical description. Based on the fact that all twelve students were working when Chuck entered the room, it was clear they still had plenty to do.

Chuck stuck around for the remainder of the morning, growing increasingly antsy as the minutes ticked by. He couldn't stop thinking of the errand he'd sent Janelle on with the girls. What would Elaine make of the black material? Would she recognize something about it that would shed light on the hidden shaft, the puddle of blood—even the murder?

THIRTY-SIX

"I recognized it the instant I saw it," Elaine said, leaning on her cane as she settled in her chair beside the dumpster. "It was what I suspected."

Unable to restrain himself, Chuck had left the students in Raven House at the beginning of lunch hour. He drove the field school van to the library, where Elaine abandoned the research desk and led him to her break site at the side of the building, a brown leather purse over her arm.

She leaned her cane against the wall, extracted the baggie of black material from her purse, and set it on the ground before lighting a cigarette. Chuck drew up the bent library chair he'd used yesterday afternoon and sat down.

Elaine exhaled a long stream of smoke, a dreamy look on her face. "Two a day," she said. "That's all I allow myself." She leaned her head back and closed her eyes. "The first drag is always so fucking great."

The legs of her maroon pantsuit rode up on her calves, showing thick ankles. She sat up straight, elbow on folded arm, cigarette hovering in front of her face, and eyed Chuck through a tendril of smoke. "Your wife's a real beauty. Quite the catch."

Chuck nodded in agreement.

Elaine toggled her head, her face alight. "And those two little girls. Darlings."

"I'm afraid I can't take credit for them."

"It's better for girls to take after their mothers. I took after my father, and look what happened to me."

Chuck spoke without thinking. "I bet you were quite the looker before..." He faltered.

"Before this?" She indicated her twisted frame with a wave of her cigarette. "Polio. I was one of the last to ever get it. I was the age of your girls, or thereabout. Go figure."

"Something tells me it didn't keep you out of mischief."

"That's one of the good things I got from my father."

"I'll have to keep my girls away from you, then."

"I imagine you'll help them find plenty of mischief on your own. Especially the younger one; she's going to be a handful."

"She already is."

"The minute I saw your wife and girls, I knew you were a lucky man." Elaine paused. "Are you sure you don't want to keep it that way?"

"What do you mean by that?"

She pointed at the baggie on the pavement beside her chair. "This stuff has some bad juju to it. I can feel it."

Chuck studied her. She didn't seem the type, not remotely, yet she was talking in riddles just like Sheila—and as if she knew of the skull and skeletal remains at the bottom of the mine.

"I've been lucky enough so far," Chuck said. "I'm willing to take my chances."

Elaine sighed, smoke escaping her lips. "Of course you are." She tapped ash from the end of her cigarette and settled back in her seat. "Okay, then," she said, as much to herself as to Chuck. "Ever heard of Thomas Walsh?"

"Walsh? Afraid not."

"You said you're from Durango. The Thomas Walsh Public Library is just over the mountains north of you in the little town of Ouray."

"Sorry, never heard of him."

"But you've heard of the Hope Diamond."

"Who hasn't?" He fixed his eyes on the black material in the Ziploc.

She smiled. "Patience," she said.

She took a pull on her cigarette before continuing. "Once upon a time, Thomas Walsh was one of the richest men in America, if not *the* richest. For many years, Walsh was one of

Colorado's most famous self-made men, but hardly anyone remembers him anymore."

"Except you."

"I like what he did for the people of Ouray. He was a humanitarian of the highest order. Treated his employees better than any mining boss ever before him, or since."

"Finally," Chuck said with another glance at the plastic bag. "Mining."

Elaine blew a stream of smoke straight up into the air. "Not at first. He started out as a hotelier in Denver's early days. He had his own place, owned it free and clear. All he had to do was run his hotel and have a nice life. But the gold bug bit him instead."

"The gold bug?"

"It got people in different ways. Take Horace Tabor. He ran a mercantile in Leadville during the gold-rush years. He made his fortune grub-staking others, which was a fine way to go. Didn't even have to get his hands dirty. But that sort of thing wasn't for Thomas Walsh. He wanted to do it all by himself. And when he got the fever, he got it bad. He was smarter than your average prospector, though. Most of them headed into the hills and started digging and panning wherever they wound up—and just about all of them ended up broke and hungry and empty-handed in a matter of weeks."

Chuck leaned forward and put his elbows on his knees, warming to Elaine's tale despite himself. "But that wouldn't do for our guy."

"No. Our man Walsh made a study out of the gold rush. He taught himself geology, mineralogy, anything that would help him in his quest. He left his wife and kids in Denver and headed into the mountains. A year passed. Another. Still another."

"*Three years?*"

"Try ten. He prospected for a full decade, the fever burning in him all the while. He wouldn't stop. Eventually, he worked his way to the San Juan Mountains, the most rugged and remote mountain range in Colorado, in the far southwest corner of the state, down where you live."

"Ten years," Chuck said. "By then the rush was over."

"Long over," Elaine concurred. "Which, ultimately, is what led to his success." She held her cigarette at her side between her fingers. "Everywhere he went, he was too late. The big discoveries had already been made. By the end of his decade of searching, mines were going bust all around Colorado. The lodes had been found, dug, carted out. Horace Tabor had made his fortune and was busy building opera houses and hobnobbing with governors and senators. But Walsh still prospected. He took breaks a couple of times, back in Denver, played at being a family man again, ran the hotel with his wife. But he kept studying, kept scheming, and, before long, he'd be back at it in the mountains, putting to work the latest of what he'd learned."

"Until he got to Ouray," Chuck said.

"Which, like everywhere else, was all played out by then."

"But he figured something out."

"Ouray was where his studies finally paid off—resulting in his enormous fortune. He built the library in Ouray, and the hospital, too. Eventually, he left the mountains with his riches. Denver wasn't good enough for him anymore, so he headed east to Washington, D.C. Back then, that was where the wealthiest Americans gathered. He built himself the most opulent home ever constructed in America—sixteen thousand square feet of pure decadence. And his two kids?" She tut-tutted.

"Not good, I take it," Chuck said.

"All that money, from a father they'd hardly seen while they were growing up, flowing into their pockets just as they hit adulthood? You tell me. The oldest, a boy, drank too much. He went on to get hooked on opium along with his wife, a high-

173

society girl, the daughter of the publisher of the *Washington Post*. They were both killed when he drove his car into a brick wall.

"And then there was Evalyn, the daughter. She held herself together a while longer. She hosted parties at her parents' home in Washington that were legendary for their excess, with seventy-five-foot-long banquet tables loaded with every conceivable delicacy. To be invited to an Evalyn Walsh party was to have truly made it in young Washingtonian society. And when it came to her own personal adornment, nothing was too ostentatious, or too expensive. When his only daughter was twenty-five, Thomas Walsh gave Evalyn the world's most famous gemstone, the Hope Diamond, as a wedding present. She treated it like a dime-store trinket, hanging it around the neck of her Great Dane, once even losing it in the cushions of a couch.

"It was she who put the final exclamation point on the curse of the Hope Diamond. Not long after her daddy bought it for her, the Walsh family fell from grace. The money ran through Thomas' fingers like sand until, finally, it was gone. At about the same time, Evalyn's husband left her for another woman, sending Evalyn on a downward spiral, addicted to alcohol and opium like her brother. She sold the Hope Diamond to support her drug habit, and finally died of pneumonia."

"What became of her father?"

"As you might guess, he'd been happiest during the years of his quest, when he was alone with his pickaxe, roaming the mountains. He didn't know how to handle himself once he became rich and everybody wanted a piece of him. When the money ran out, he sold the house in D.C.—it's the Indonesian Embassy these days—and moved back to Denver, where he spent time as a guest lecturer at the Colorado School of Mines, explaining to eager young engineers what he'd figured out over the course of all those years in the mountains."

"Which was?" Chuck asked.

Elaine picked up the bag of black material and tossed it to him. "What's that look like to you?"

"Coffee grounds."

"And coffee grounds are worthless, are they not?"

He nodded.

"That's what everyone else thought, too."

THIRTY-SEVEN

Chuck squeezed the Ziploc between his fingers as Elaine continued.

"By the time Walsh made it to Ouray, he'd seen thousands of played-out mines. He went way up into the San Juans, to a high mountain cirque called Yankee Boy Basin that was lined with abandoned shafts.

"The Yankee Boy mines had produced marginal amounts of silver, not gold, and they'd gone bust years before. But thanks to all his research, Walsh noticed something different about the mines in the basin. The tailings dumped down the mountainside during the digging of a mine usually are gray—the color of the hard-rock interior of the mountain. But the tailings from the played-out silver mines in Yankee Boy Basin weren't gray, they were black. And when Walsh picked up a handful of the stuff and worked it between his fingers, he found it had the consistency of—"

She allowed Chuck to fill in the blank: "Coffee grounds."

Elaine tapped the air with her cigarette in approval. "Geologists were just figuring out back then that gold exists in numerous forms," she explained. "There's the pure kind, shiny and yellow, in the form of grains and nuggets. But there are other forms as well, wherein gold is mixed with other minerals and is not readily apparent to the naked eye. One of those hidden forms is gold suspended in an ore known as calaverite, which looks as gray and unremarkable as any worthless mineral. When calaverite containing suspended gold is exposed to oxygen and moisture, however, a chemical reaction takes place. It turns from gray to black, and becomes loose and crumbly."

The plastic bag weighed down Chuck's hand.

"In fact," Elaine went on, "that's exactly the process by which gold becomes recognizable to the human eye. Over eons, air seeping through fissures into mountains oxidizes gold in its impure form, turning it into a black, slag-like material. The slow leaching action of water over millions of years turns that black slag into pure gold.

"The silver miners above Ouray unwittingly exposed just such a mixture of tellurium ore and gold to oxygen when they dumped the tailings down the mountainsides. The mixture went through the next steps of the process—oxygenation and leaching by rain and snow—in the years after the mines were abandoned. The first discovery of a large deposit of calaverite was in California in 1868. That was several years after the Pikes Peak gold rush petered out. Most prospectors were long gone, but the timing happened to be perfect for Walsh, who was still on the hunt, and still keeping up on the latest findings in the mining world. As soon as he crumbled that first handful of abandoned tailings between his fingers in Yankee Boy Basin, he recognized it for what it was."

"Gold," Chuck said.

Elaine pointed at the black material. "It looked just like that."

Chuck hefted the baggie. "But this never has been exposed to the outdoors."

She gave him time to figure it out.

"Oh," he said. "Right. There's no need for sunshine. Just air. Oxygen." He closed his eyes, remembering the current of air that flowed constantly into the mouth of the mine, as if drawn by a fan.

"I suspect," Elaine said, "that the vertical shaft you told me about has helped speed up the process. I'd be willing to bet there's a fissure in the mountainside somewhere below the horizontal tunnel. Outside air flows into the tunnel and down the shaft and exits out the lower fissure. Essentially, the mine is one big air convector."

"You think the shaft was gray-walled all the way to its bottom at first?"

"It couldn't have been dug if the stuff was as loose and crumbly as you say it is now."

"But something made them turn and dig vertically."

"They probably were following a small vein of pure gold ore that eventually played out."

"When, in fact," Chuck said, "the last of the pure gold died away into calaverite—that is, into gold in its less-refined state."

"According to what I learned while poking around online this morning, that stuff you've got in your hand is probably ten percent gold."

He held out the bag. "*This?*"

"Add cyanide and it leaches right out—which is exactly what Walsh did in Yankee Boy Basin. He bought up the old claims for the whole valley, hired the best miners in the area by paying them double what anyone else was paying, and set to work. In its day, Walsh's Camp Bird Mine was the most productive gold mine on earth, and it stayed that way for years."

"A mother lode," Chuck said.

"Made of coffee grounds."

Elaine smiled, but Chuck did not. He looked down at the black crumbles that had hidden a skull all these years, with a bullet hole straight through from front to back.

Thirty-Eight

Someone had been killed for the black, crumbly grounds in Chuck's hand. That much was obvious. The hole in the forehead was the smooth entry of a bullet fired from at least a few feet away; a shot from point-blank range by someone committing suicide would have resulted in a fractured entry point.

The homicide was a cold case—very cold—but it deserved investigation nonetheless.

The skull was stowed in his pack in the back of the truck. He looked across the parking lot at the Estes Park Police Department. Should he head over there right now and report his discovery?

As soon as he asked himself the question, he knew the answer: Of course not.

In the midst of the homicide investigation, there was no telling what Hemphill would make of Chuck's showing up with news of a gold strike and evidence in hand of yet another murder. The skull had waited, undiscovered, for a long time. It could wait a little longer.

Elaine waved her hand to catch his eye. "I'm still here."

"I...I... ," Chuck stuttered, blinking himself back to their conversation.

"You don't sound very excited."

Chuck shook the baggie. "You're the one who said this stuff's got bad juju attached to it."

"I was joking," she said, though something in her voice said she wasn't. Not entirely.

"What more do you know about the Cassandra Treasure that you haven't told me?" he asked.

She pinched the crease in one of the legs of her pantsuit and tugged it into place. "I called someone," she admitted. "When you first showed up."

"If there's something you know, I need to know it," Chuck said. "I *deserve* to know it." He held out the Ziploc. "That's why I brought you this."

"I dated him when I first moved to town," Elaine said. "You'd be surprised what this old girl can get up to."

"I'm not sure I want to know."

"It didn't last long; we wore each other out in no time. He's a mature guy, like me, from one of the oldest mining families in the area. His people worked claims all around here."

"And you called him because...?"

"Because of your story. I hadn't thought about the Cassandra Treasure since the girl came in asking about it way back when. But you got me thinking—what if it was true?"

"You thought this guy might know something?"

"He answered right away, like he'd been waiting for me to call." She smirked. "I have that effect on people."

"You didn't tell him anything, did you?"

"Your secret's safe with me. I just said I'd had someone come into the library asking about this thing called the Cassandra Treasure, and wondered if he knew anything. He said he hadn't thought about it for decades, not since the fifties, when he was just a boy."

"The 1950s?"

"That was the last time any real mining activity was going on around here. He said there was all this talk of a big strike by somebody or other back then, but no one seemed to know anything about it, and finally the talk just died away. He figures that's where the rumor of the treasure came from."

Chuck furrowed his brow. Nothing seemed to fit. "That's all?"

Elaine shrugged. "As far as the mine's concerned."

It took him a moment. "The slaughtered rams?"

"You asked me to do some thinking about that, too."

"I'd almost forgotten."

She tapped the side of her head with her finger. "Not me. You did a good job, as far as you got with your thinking."

"That whoever's doing it is a park regular?"

"Yes."

"And?"

She took her cigarette from her mouth and held it up between her thumb and forefinger, watching the smoke curl from its tip. "We all rotate through the library," she said, lowering the stub. "Two hours at a time, from the research desk to the children's desk to the front desk. Last night, after you left, I moved to the front desk for the end of my shift. There's a view of Elkhorn Avenue out the front doors. It occurred to me that anyone who regularly enters and leaves the park is going to have to drive up and down Elkhorn, too."

Chuck pressed his lips together. Elaine was right. "It's the only route through town."

"I watched the traffic and thought through the various vehicles that pass by the front of the library," Elaine went on. "I tried to figure out which ones would go on into the park for whatever reason." She dropped her cigarette into the can at her side and looked down at it longingly. "It took me a while," she said, raising her eyes, "but I figured it out."

Chuck held his breath.

"Jake's." Elaine quoted the words stenciled on the doors of a vehicle Chuck had seen in the park several times over the course of the summer: "*Only Wrecker Service in Estes Park.*"

"Of course," Chuck said. He nearly dropped the baggie. How could he not have come up with the answer on his own?

He'd passed cars stalled on the side of Trail Ridge Road numerous times throughout the summer because their oxygen-deprived engines, tuned for sea-level driving, couldn't handle the high rate of speed that inexperienced, flatland drivers demanded of them while ascending the highest paved through-road in North America. The result was a shortwave radio call for aid by a passing ranger followed by a visit from Jake's wrecker service.

Chuck stood and clapped Elaine on the shoulder. "That's got to be it."

Elaine beamed. "I'll leave it to you to pass that information along to the right people."

Chuck nodded. He would—soon enough.

"But first," Elaine said. She arched an eyebrow at the baggie in his hand. "A few backpack loads of that stuff, before you tell the rangers, would make you a very wealthy man indeed—and no one would ever have to know."

Chuck stepped back. "Don't tell me you're looking for a handout."

She raised her shoe with the three-inch lift attached its sole. "Do I look like I'm in need of a pile of money to run away somewhere and live the high life?" She settled her foot back on the pavement. "Nope. I already have everything I want."

"I have everything I want, too."

"Maybe you should give it a little time, just to be sure." A corner of the librarian's mouth twitched. "You have to promise me one thing: that you'll think long and hard about that little girl of yours. You and I both know she deserves the best." Elaine paused, then said, "Who's going to pay her medical bills?"

"Rosie? What are you talking about?"

Elaine took hold of her cane, her knuckles turning white. "I don't mean to be nosy," she said, "but I couldn't help overhearing. After your wife delivered the bag to me, your little girl asked her if they were going to the hospital next, to see her doctor."

THIRTY-NINE

Chuck drove straight to the medical center, fighting the unreasonable fears Elaine's comment had unleashed in him. Logic said all was well with Rosie—he'd received no text from Janelle. Nonetheless, he couldn't help punching the gas as he drove across town.

He spotted the pickup parked in the hospital's visitor parking lot. Gregory's SUV was nowhere to be seen. Chuck slotted the van into a space and marched across the pavement.

He breathed a sigh of relief when he saw the four of them upon rounding the corner of the hospital building. Janelle, the girls, and Gregory sat at a window table in the hospital's ground-floor cafeteria. The edge of the table rested against a floor-to-ceiling wall of glass overlooking a small, street-side courtyard. Janelle and Gregory sat opposite one another, the girls beside them. Carmelita, next to Janelle, nudged a balled-up paper napkin around her cafeteria tray with a plastic spoon. Rosie nestled beside Gregory, her shoulder pressed against the doctor's beefy bicep.

Rosie was the first to catch sight of Chuck. She leapt from her chair, a picture of health, and waved frantically at him through the plate-glass window.

Chuck stopped in the middle of the sidewalk. Gregory caught his eye and froze, a paper cup halfway to his mouth. Janelle twisted in her seat and glowered at Chuck. Rosie glanced at her mother and returned to her seat.

Chuck squared his shoulders and resumed his approach, entering the cafeteria through a side door.

It was past one o'clock. The room was quiet, most tables empty after the lunchtime rush.

He couldn't help but notice how natural Janelle looked with the young physician. Chuck touched a finger to one of his sideburns, where gray hairs sprouted. More than once, in the months since he'd become the girls' stepfather, strangers had told him how cute his granddaughters were.

Gregory, wearing blue hospital scrubs, rose from his seat with his hand outstretched. "Chuck, right?" They shook. "Here, let me pull up an extra seat for you."

While Gregory grabbed a chair from a neighboring table, Janelle fixed Chuck with an icy glare. When he shrugged in self-defense, her glare turned icier. Gregory returned with a straight-backed chair. Chuck nosed it up to the end of the table between Janelle and the doctor. The tabletop was littered with the remains of their meal. How long had Janelle and Gregory been relaxing and talking here together?

The doctor cleared his throat. "I was just telling Janelle, er, your wife, uh, how well Rosie's doing."

Chuck nodded stiffly. "Thank you."

"Do you think...would you like to grab some lunch? This place is pretty popular. Good prices, great food."

"No, thanks."

Gregory swallowed. "So, what brings you downtown?"

"Errands."

An awkward silence followed.

"Well," Janelle said finally, "I guess we should get going."

"Of course," Gregory said. He stood abruptly, bumping the edge of the table. "Whoa." He grabbed the table to steady it. "Sorry."

Neither Chuck nor Janelle replied. Janelle said to Carmelita and Rosie, "Gather your things, please."

The girls stacked their paper cups and plates and plastic utensils on their cafeteria trays. Gregory picked up his tray and said to Janelle, "Thanks for stopping by. I think it was a good idea." He reached to touch her shoulder but dropped his hand to his side instead.

Chuck clasped Janelle's shoulder. "We appreciate what you did for Rosie the other night," he said to Gregory.

Janelle looked down, busying herself with her tray.

The doctor offered a strained chuckle. "No trouble. No trouble at all. That's what I, er, we do here." He cast his eyes around the cafeteria.

Janelle stood, lifting her tray and shrugging Chuck's hand from her shoulder. "Chuck is absolutely right," she said to Gregory, her voice flat. "We owe you our thanks, taking such good care of Rosie the other night, then checking back with us not once, but twice, to make sure she's doing all right. That's what I call true patient care."

"It's nothing," Gregory said. He turned to Rosie. "How could I not make sure you were doing okay?" He raised his palm to her for a high-five.

Rosie slapped the doctor's hand. "Howdy do, cowboy," she said.

Gregory and Janelle exchanged tight smiles. Chuck forced himself to smile, too.

"Come on," Chuck said to the girls. "I'll help get your trays to the kitchen."

Janelle waited until she and Chuck were outside and around the corner of the building before she whirled on him.

"How *could* you?" she hissed as the girls walked ahead of them along the sidewalk.

"How could I what?" Chuck asked innocently.

"You know very well *what*. There's no excuse for what you pulled in there."

His jaw tightened. "All I did was come looking for you. The librarian overheard that you were taking Rosie to the doctor. I had no idea what—"

"Don't try that with me," Janelle cut in. "If you *ever* think it's okay to spy on me, I'll...I'll..." She sputtered to a stop.

"I was just trying to find you."

"You were *spying*, Chuck. All you had to do was call."

"Radio silence, remember?"

"That's between you and Clarence, not you and me, and you know it."

She was right, but he couldn't bring himself to admit it out loud, not quite yet. "The librarian said you were headed over here."

"Gregory called and offered to check her again. You have to get over this, Chuck."

"I have. I am," he said, stumbling over his words. "I wasn't sure what to expect, and then there you were, having lunch. I'm not really jealous—not that I shouldn't be. I mean, look at you." He took in her fitted blouse, her shorts cut high on her slender legs, her sandals showing off her bare feet.

"You're not going to get off that easy," Janelle said, the edge to her voice diminishing.

"You and I both know what that guy's after. An emergency-room doctor checking in on his patients? Who ever heard of that?"

Janelle shrugged. "I was...well, yeah."

"I guess you, I, should be flattered. Handsome, skier-dude doctor way up here in the mountains? The guy deserves his own TV show."

The sides of Janelle's mouth ticked upward. "Stop."

Chuck intoned, "Surviving avalanches by day, saving little girls by night. It's '*Doc Gregory*,' Tuesdays at eight, seven Central."

She grinned and shoved him off the curb. "I said, stop."

He stepped back up to the sidewalk and slung his arm around her shoulder. "I'm sorry," he said as they followed the girls into the parking lot. "I really am."

"I don't like how prickly things have been between us."

"Neither do I. But it's kind of to be expected. The murder, the blood, the cops and Clarence—it's a lot to deal with."

"I'm not talking about that. I'm talking about us." She stopped and turned to him. "You just need to remember one important thing. You won. Understand? *You won*. It's been more than a year now, and I'm more in love with you than ever." She slipped her arm around his waist. "Can't you just enjoy your victory?"

She drew him to her.

"Whoop, whoop, whoop!" Rosie crowed from where she stood at the open door of the truck, observing their kiss.

She held the skull up in front of her face and rotated it side-to-side as she cheered.

FORTY

Chuck shook his head, unable to hide his smile. So much for keeping the skull away from the girls. He should have figured on Rosie's curiosity leading her back to it.

He let Rosie and Carmelita finger the bullet's entry and exit wounds before tucking the skull back in his pack and taking it with him in the van to the resort, following Janelle and the girls in the truck.

Janelle turned the truck left, past the lodge and conference center, headed for the cabin. Chuck continued on around the grass fields.

Several employees were gathered in front of Falcon House. Four dark-complexioned men were dressed for work in white aprons and short-order-cook hats, while three young white women wore street clothes. They stood next to an old sedan parked in front of the employee dormitory. Wildflowers were tucked beneath the wiper blades against the car's windshield. A small bouquet rested on the hood.

Chuck saw, as he parked, that the employees surrounded Clarence.

The employees looked warily at Chuck as he approached from the van. Clarence appeared unfazed in their midst.

Chuck held out his hands in a peace-making gesture. "I'm sorry about what happened with Nicoleta," he said, stopping before them.

A stout, young woman, dishwater-blonde hair hanging straight down the sides of her face, spoke with a thick Eastern European accent. "You was there, yes?"

"That's right. I was."

"I am Anca." The young woman's voice caught in her throat. "Did she say some things, some words, to you before she...?"

"I'm sorry," Chuck said. "No, she didn't. She couldn't speak.

And...and that was all."

"No one else was there?" Anca asked.

"I heard her scream. I ran to her, but I was too late. Whoever did it was gone."

"You have no idea who does this thing?"

"No."

She aimed a finger at Clarence. "Earlier, I think it was him. I try to—How do you say it in this country?—rip his face off. But the others, they tell me no." Her glance took in her co-workers. "They say this guy, he a good guy, and I know, inside me, they are right." Her voice quivered. "Then I say it must to be you. You was there. You was with Nicoleta. But they say you could not do that to Nicoleta and stay with her, that the polices would know."

"Your friends are right," Chuck said.

"But Nicoleta, she is died." The young woman teared up.

"The two of you were roommates, right?"

"Yes."

"Were you good friends with each other?"

"I have done some things with her, but she was many of the time on her own."

"And the night before last, when she...she...?"

"I was no with her that night. For the first time of the whole much summer, I go to the town with some of the other peoples for to a restaurant and a bar, like I was told the polices. No more television watching, finally. I was very much happy. It was a much fun town on the night. I was asleep, for not long, in another room, and then there was a scream, and I look in our room, and she was not there..." Anca's voice trailed off.

Chuck thought of the many nights Anca had been forced to spend in other workers' rooms. It sounded like it had almost become routine. "Nicoleta had many other friends?"

"With your people."

"*My* people?"

"Your student peoples, the—How do you say it?—the partiers." Anca gave Chuck a calculating look.

He bristled. "None of my students had anything to do with it. Not Clarence, and not anyone else."

"This is what you are saying to us."

"The police don't think so, either."

She blinked away her tears. "I am not caring about these polices. If I am learning who has done this thing, I will take care of it on myself." She reached into a large cloth handbag hanging from her shoulder and lifted a handgun into sight, just above the top of the bag.

Chuck stepped back. "Whoa."

At the sight of the gun, the four men turned on their heels and made for Falcon House. The two other young women exchanged worried glances while Clarence edged to Chuck's side.

"Please," Chuck implored Anca. "Put that thing away. There's no need for that."

The young woman slipped the handgun back into her bag.

"Where'd you get that?" Chuck asked her, dumbstruck.

She shrugged. "Is easy. Is America. My father, he tell me I must to have gun in this country. And now, with Nicoleta, I know he is right." She touched the bouquet of flowers left on the sedan in Nicoleta's memory. "Where I come from, this killing never happen."

"I—" Chuck began. He looked at Clarence, then at the three young women. "I just came over here to tell you, all of you, how sorry I am. I know there was some...fraternization...between Raven House and Falcon House residents over the summer. But I've had no indication from the police, or from anyone else, that it had anything to do with Nicoleta's—" He stopped, started over. "I want you to know I'm with you, we're with you. We want to do everything we can to—"

Chuck stopped again, his eyes darting toward the sound of

vehicle tires crunching on the gravel road. He, Clarence, and the three young women watched as Parker drove his bright blue pickup to the front of the dormitory and parked.

The resort manager climbed out of his truck and addressed the group as he walked up to them. "I saw you talking over here."

Chuck looked across the fields at Parker's office window, visible in the top floor of the conference center. He glanced at Anca, her gun-bearing satchel over her shoulder. Surely it was against resort policy for employees to be armed.

The three young women shuffled their feet. "We are talk about Nicoleta," Anca told Parker. She pointed at Chuck and Clarence. "They speak with us. Is all okay."

The other two young women looked anywhere but at Parker.

"You've probably done enough talking for now," the resort manager said.

Anca bowed her head and stepped back. The three young women pivoted and headed for Falcon House.

Chuck rested his fingertips on the hood of the sedan. "It's Nicoleta's?" he asked Parker.

"It is. She bought it at the beginning of the summer, planned to sell it before she went home. A number of them do that each year so they can get around."

"They're turning it into a memorial?"

"It's a reminder for people. I'm sure her keys are in her room, but that's still off limits. Meantime, it's sitting out here for all the world to see and focus on."

Chuck looked at the car, eyes narrowed, tongue pressed against the roof of his mouth. "You should have it towed," he told Parker.

"Chuck's right," Clarence agreed. "Out of sight, out of mind."

"Hmm," Parker said. "That's not a bad idea. I suppose we could move it over to the maintenance yard."

"Where's that?" Clarence asked.

Chuck answered for Parker. "Behind the lodge, through the trees from our cabin." He looked at the resort manager. "No telling how long the cops are going to take to finish their investigation. Meantime, you can bet the car's going to get more and more attention."

"I know." Parker folded his arms and frowned at the sedan.

"No time like the present," Chuck prodded.

"Oh." He loosened his arms. "Right."

Parker reached for his phone to call Jake, proprietor of the only wrecker service in Estes Park.

FORTY-ONE

Chuck took Clarence by the elbow while Parker made his call.

"There's something I want to show you," he said. He explained his suspicion regarding Jake as he led the way to the van.

"You really think it's him?" Clarence asked.

"There's a lot of logic to it. Hopefully, we'll find out in a few minutes." Chuck reached inside the vehicle. "Meantime..." He handed the baggie of calaverite to Clarence.

"What's this?" Clarence asked.

Chuck aimed a finger west, at the mountains and the mine, high above town. "There's gold in them there hills."

He described his retrieval of the black material from the shaft and explained what Elaine had said.

"You've got to be kidding," Clarence said when Chuck finished. "We're rich!"

"Sorry. Rocky Mountain National Park is rich. Not that anything will happen. There's no mining allowed within park boundaries."

Clarence stared at Chuck in disbelief. "You're going to tell them?"

"Of course."

Clarence lifted the baggie. "You say it's ten percent gold. A few loads of this..." His voice died away in wonderment.

"Not gonna happen."

"So what *will* happen?"

"It'll be pretty big news at first, I imagine. They'll have to plug the tunnel with concrete or something to keep out treasure hunters like you."

"You're nuts, man."

"It's not ours to take."

Clarence tossed the baggie back to Chuck. "I'm telling you, you're an idiot."

Chuck returned the plastic bag to the van and motioned Clarence to his side. "There's something else you should see."

With Clarence at his shoulder, he unzipped his pack and took out the skull. "Somebody already died because of the gold in the mine," he said, handing the skull to Clarence. "I don't want you or anyone else to be next."

Clarence touched the bullet hole in the forehead. "*Jesucristo*," he breathed. He looked over his shoulder to be sure Parker was still occupied on the phone. "You found this in there, too?"

"In the bottom of the shaft, along with the rest of the skeleton."

"What do you think happened?"

"I have no idea." He took the skull back from Clarence. "See how small it is? It must have been one of the miners. It'll be up to the rangers to figure out, if they ever can." He returned the skull to his pack.

"I can't believe you, of all people, are gonna turn that thing in—the gold, too—and just walk away."

"I admit I'm tempted. But, at this point, I just want to get us out of here."

Clarence groaned. "I almost forgot about all that for a minute." He tore his eyes away from Chuck's pack. "Guess I ought to get packed up—and hope they let me leave with everybody else tomorrow morning."

Clarence disappeared inside Raven House. Parker ended his call, climbed into his truck, and drove back around the fields. Chuck stowed his pack out of the way against a far wall of the Raven House common room, then returned to the van and busied himself emptying trash from it and sweeping out its floor with a whisk broom while awaiting Jake's arrival.

Thirty minutes after Parker's call, the long, black flatbed wrecker bounced through the front entrance to the resort and headed around the fields to the dorms. Parker followed in his pickup.

Chuck closed the rear doors of the van as the wrecker pulled to a stop behind Nicoleta's sedan. He walked toward the tow truck as the driver descended the ladder-like steps from the cab, grasping the handles on either side of the door. The driver hopped to the gravel lot, pulled a baseball cap from the back pocket of his grease-stained coveralls, and tugged it over his close-cropped, salt-and-pepper hair. He looked to be in his late fifties, lean and fit, his face browned by the sun. His green eyes sat close on either side of a long nose. The collar of a white T-shirt showed in the V of his coveralls. He wore leather work boots, the treads of which Chuck wanted badly to see.

"You must be Jake," Chuck said to him.

"That'd be me." Jake's voice was reedy and high-pitched.

"I'm an old friend of Parker's," Chuck said. "Nice truck you got." He took in the wrecker with an admiring gaze. "Diesel?"

"Gas. Got the V-10 in her."

"Ford's best."

"Step on her, she'll bark," Jake agreed.

"I'll leave you to your work," Chuck said, addressing both Jake and Parker as the resort manager approached from his pickup. Chuck let his eyes rove over the flatbed a second time and asked Jake, "Mind if I have a look?"

"Be my guest."

Chuck set out around the wrecker. He checked the front tire first. Its lightning-bolt-shaped tread matched the marks in the dirt of the Fall River Road pullout. Of course, the tire's sidewall featured the logo for Goodyear, the most popular truck-tire manufacturer in the country.

While Jake and Parker knelt at the back of Nicoleta's car, surveying its undercarriage, Chuck made his way around to the driver's side of the tow truck. A large, rectangular toolbox, painted black to match the rest of the truck, was bolted to the vehicle's frame just behind the cab, beneath the flatbed. The box was a foot and a half wide, two feet tall, and nearly five feet long—easily long enough to contain a rifle.

Chuck looked across the top of the flatbed. Jake and Parker still crouched behind Nicoleta's car. Keeping his eyes on the two men, Chuck gave the handle inset beneath the lid of the toolbox a stiff pull. The handle was locked. It didn't move. He yanked upward on the lid, but it held fast, too.

His fingertips came away from the toolbox covered with dry, black flakes. He put his fingers to his nose and sniffed. Nothing. He studied the toolbox. More of the flaky material, rough and textured in contrast to the box's smooth, shiny black paint, clung to the front wall of the steel box just below the lid.

Jake rose from the back of Nicoleta's car and made his way along the driver's side of the wrecker. Chuck stepped backward with a good-natured wave. He angled across the parking lot to a metal trash can next to the sidewalk. Using the body of the van as a shield between the trash can and Jake and Parker, Chuck retrieved one of the students' discarded sack-lunch bags he'd gathered while cleaning out the van. He rummaged inside the brown paper bag until his fingers closed around an empty sandwich bag. He folded the small plastic bag into the palm of his hand and hurried back around the van as Jake maneuvered the wrecker, its reverse signal beeping, until its tail end nearly touched the rear of the sedan.

Leaving the engine running, Jake climbed down from the driver's seat and worked a set of controls behind the cab, tilting the flatbed to the ground with a loud grinding noise. When he'd seated the end of the flatbed on the gravel behind Nicoleta's sedan, he slid beneath the car to attach chains from the wrecker to its frame.

While Jake lay beneath the sedan and Parker looked on, Chuck rounded the far side of the truck and crouched beside the black metal toolbox. He held the lip of the open sandwich bag to the side of the box and scraped with his fingernails at the black material. Tiny flakes fell from the metal box into the clear plastic bag. When he held up the bag, however, he found he had far less than he needed.

He put the open bag back to the toolbox and scraped harder. Even so, little of the black material fell from the box into the baggie. He slid a credit card from his wallet and used it to scrape at the side of the toolbox. The plastic card bent as he worked it back and forth, but the material still clung to the metal. Growing desperate, he eyed the parking lot, spotting small bits of broken glass and a discarded beer-bottle cap, flattened into the gravel by passing vehicles.

He grabbed the bottle cap and used it to scrape at the toolbox, counting on the idling engine and Jake's work with the chains to cover the noise he made. This time, sizeable flakes of the black material cascaded into the sandwich bag.

Chuck crouched to peer beneath the flatbed in time to see Jake wriggling out from under the sedan. Parker extended a hand and pulled the wrecker owner to his feet. Chuck sealed the plastic bag, stowed it in his pocket, and made his way back around the front of the truck to the two men, calming his breathing as he approached.

Across the parking lot, Clarence reemerged from Raven House and stood glaring at Jake.

Chuck caught Parker's eye. "I take it Hemphill gave you his okay?"

The resort manager nodded. "As long as we don't tamper with the inside."

Jake announced, "Its brakes are set. We'll have to drag it up onto the bed."

Chuck asked him, "Been doing this a long time?"

"Too long. Can't say as I ever towed a murder victim's car, though." Jake turned to Parker. "I heard lots of people liked her."

"She liked lots of people," Parker said. "That might be a better way to put it."

"Hormones," Chuck commented.

Jake spat on the ground. "Tell me about it. I got a couple of girls in college. Private schools, expensive as all get out. They're good girls, mind you. But I swear, the things they tell their mother, it's enough to turn me three shades of green." He waggled his hands over his ears. "I've got to the point now where I don't even listen. I just write the checks and stay out of it all."

"You have to tow a lot of cars to put two kids through college," Chuck observed, keeping his tone light. "Especially private schools."

The wrecker owner dipped his head in agreement. "Seven days a week, all summer, every summer."

"I've got two daughters of my own. Youngsters. But I'm already dreading the tuition payments."

"You just gotta make sure they don't do too good in school," Jake said. "My wife, she pushed my girls hard. Straight A's for the both of them, which gave them these ideas of how they had to go way far away to these fancy schools back east." He popped his tongue off the roof of his mouth. "Me, I'm just along for the ride."

"Bad grades," Chuck said with a definitive nod. "Got it. Maybe I can even convince my girls to drop out before they finish high school."

Jake's face cracked into a tight-lipped smile. "There's your ticket." He made his way to the control station at the side of the truck, put his leather-gloved hands to the levers, and called to Parker, standing beside the sedan, "Holler if she starts sliding off line, would you?"

Jake depressed a metal handle, engaging the winch with an angry whine. Chuck put his fingers to his ears and backed away.

He crossed the parking lot and stopped on the far side of the van, where Clarence joined him.

"Learn anything?" Clarence asked.

"The tire treads on the wrecker match the ones in the pull-out—same as half the truck tires sold in America over the last five years. As for his boots, I haven't gotten a good look yet." Chuck pulled the sandwich bag from his pocket and displayed the dry, black flecks nestled at its bottom. "But I've got this."

He and Clarence went around to the back of Raven House, out of sight of the parking lot. Chuck dribbled a few drops of water from an outside spigot into the sandwich bag and worked the bottom of the bag between his thumb and forefinger until the flakes dissolved in the water. He raised the bag. The solution in it was bright pink, almost red.

FORTY-TWO

Chuck opened the bag and sniffed at the few drops of solution inside. He held the bag out to Clarence, who took a noseful.

"Anything?" Chuck asked.

Clarence shook his head.

"Me neither. I was hoping for the scent of something, maybe the sheep carcasses, from the meadow."

"Doesn't matter though, does it?" Clarence pointed at the bag. "It's blood, from the wrecker, *verdad*?"

Chuck nodded. "It was smeared and dried on the side of a toolbox behind the driver's compartment."

Clarence's eyes glowed with grim satisfaction. "You've got him, then."

"But what do I do with him?"

"Tell the rangers. Show them what you found."

"He'll just deny everything. He's a local. He'll get off, no question."

"He won't dare do any more killing, though."

"That's not good enough."

"You could confront him."

"Like in the movies?"

"Ask him some questions. You'll see it in his eyes."

"Then what?"

"Then you can—" Clarence stopped as the loud whine of the winch and clanking noise of the flatbed lowering into place ended. Seconds later, the wrecker door slammed.

Chuck and Clarence poked their heads around the corner of Raven House and watched as Jake fired up the engine and rumbled away with Nicoleta's sedan atop the flatbed.

"Too late," Clarence said.

Over the next forty-five minutes, Chuck made his way from room to room along the first-floor hallway in Raven House, checking in with the students as they packed. Despite—or perhaps, in some odd way, because of—Nicoleta's murder, the students rode a wave of energy, flitting from room to room and hurrying up and down the stairs and in and out of the bathrooms at the end of each hall.

Only a few of the students planned to travel back to Durango in the van the next morning. The rest, driving their own cars or having arranged rides from Estes Park, would spend the two weeks between the end of the field school and the start of the fall semester with family or friends.

Sheila came down the hall carrying a cardboard box.

"Are you going back in the van tomorrow?" Chuck asked her.

"Yes. Then on home from there for my healing ceremony."

"Your what?"

"My grandfather is a *hatáli*, a medicine man, from Two Gray Hills," she said, naming the Navajo reservation district on the Arizona-New Mexico border famous for its intricately woven rugs.

"Let me guess—if your grandfather is a medicine man, your grandmother must be a weaver."

Sheila's broad face broke into a smile. She tossed her long, silky, black hair over her shoulder. "Yep. Dezba Natani. A couple of galleries in Durango carry her rugs. Have you seen them?"

"Afraid not. I'll have to check them out." He looked her over. "You come by your belief in skinwalkers honestly, don't you?"

"Of course." She grew serious. "My grandfather does my cleansing every summer, before school starts. He's been doing it for me since I was little. But now, after..." She left a space where Nicoleta's name should have been. "I really need it."

"Your morning walks up the hill aren't enough?"

"They've helped me make it through the summer. There's a flat spot up there with a break in the trees where I can see all the way across the valley. But I haven't gone back up there since... since..."

Chuck steered the conversation away from Nicoleta's murder. "Healing ceremonies involve sweat lodges, right?"

"Only for the men. Mine just has a lot of chanting and incense burning and waving eagle feathers around. It's kind of goofy, but it works. Gets me ready for the school year."

Chuck smiled. "Sounds fun. Maybe he'd do one for me, too."

"He would, you know. He does lots of them for *bilagáana*—for white people, I mean."

Chuck stepped aside to let her pass. "I want you to know how much I've appreciated having you in the course this summer."

"It's been good," she said. "I mean," she hedged as she headed down the hall, "it's been better than I expected."

Chuck climbed the rear stairs to the second floor. Bits of conversation came from an open doorway as he walked down the hall.

"Yes," said a young woman's voice. "Gold. Seriously. That's what he said."

"The whole summer? You're telling me we've been—" The second voice, that of another member of Team Paydirt, cut off as Chuck passed the doorway. He kept moving, pretending he hadn't heard anything, and strode straight to Clarence's room.

The door was open. Clarence lay sprawled on his back on his unmade single bed, his eyes closed, a travel mug, its spill-proof lid snapped into place, balanced on his chest with both hands.

"Clarence," Chuck snapped. "What's it been, less than an hour?"

Clarence sat up, his eyes unfocused. Chuck closed the door behind him, crossed the room, and sniffed the mug. *Tequila.*

"What did I tell you last night at the cabin?" Chuck demanded.

Clarence squeezed the bridge of his nose with his fingers. "Just a little, *jefe*. To help me relax."

"The last thing you need to do right now is relax. Don't you get it? We'll be out of here tomorrow—as long as we keep our-selves together. Just one more night, Clarence."

"One more night of wondering if I'm gonna be locked away for the rest of my life."

Chuck glared at him. "You told everybody about the gold."

"Just Samuel. You didn't say I couldn't."

"He already told everyone else."

Clarence shrugged. "So what? You said it was going to be big news. Didn't seem like it was a secret or anything."

Chuck ripped the mug from Clarence's hand. "Give me that." He looked around the room. "Where's the bottle?"

Clarence's eyes grew steely. Then, in sullen defeat, he jutted his chin at his desk on the opposite side of the small room.

Chuck opened the desk drawers one at a time until, in the bottom drawer, he came upon a quart bottle of Cuervo Gold sloshing with tequila. "It's like I'm your babysitter," he grumbled.

He grabbed the bottle by its neck, shoved the drawer closed with his foot, and wheeled on Clarence. "I'm sure you've got more booze around here somewhere. *Don't touch it*, you hear me?"

Kirina poked her head out of her room when Chuck passed on his way down the hall, headed for the dumpster out back with Clarence's mug and bottle.

"Let's talk," she said, waving him into her room and closing the door behind him. Half-filled duffle bags covered the lino-leum floor. A stuffed backpack leaned against her bed.

"Is it true, about the mine?" she asked.

He ignored her question and held up Clarence's bottle. "Did you know about this?"

She looked away.

"Of course, you did." He eyed the side of her face. "But you told me how much you like him, didn't you? Far be it for you to get him in any trouble." He paused. "And, yes, it's true."

She turned back to him. "I heard it looks like dirt, but that it's really gold."

"Ten percent of it is. Or so I'm told. Not that it'll do anyone any good. It's park property. I'll let them know about it after everyone leaves tomorrow morning."

Kirina whistled. "Who'd've thought?"

After tossing the tequila in the trash, Chuck walked across the fields, headed for the conference center. His phone dinged with a text from Janelle.

Hard to get much done with the girls. You coming?

Back soon, Chuck texted back. *Stopping to see Parker first.*

"Saw you headed this way," the resort manager said after Chuck knocked on Parker's office door and entered.

Chuck looked out the picture window. In the distance, the afternoon sun flashed off the windows of Estes Park's downtown buildings. He took a seat in front of the desk. "All you ever do is creep on people."

"Moving my office up here was the best idea I ever had. I don't miss much."

"Except Nicoleta's murder."

"Which is why I'm spending even more time looking out my window now." He shook his head. "I can't wait for tomorrow to be over."

"Hemphill's what all of us are waiting on. I haven't heard a thing from him today, have you?"

"He didn't have much to say when I talked to him about moving Nicoleta's car. Maybe he's getting ready to pounce. That's what I'm hoping, anyway."

"He has to wait for the lab reports, the autopsy, all that. Could be a while."

"I'm not so sure about that. She was knifed, or maybe garroted or whatever they call it, that's obvious enough. And the killer took whatever he used with him. What else is there to study?"

"For one thing, what the victim was doing before she was killed. I'm sure Hemphill will want to know if she slept with anybody in the hours leading up to her death."

"Ohhhh."

"If the autopsy turns up anything, I think you...we...can count on lots of DNA requests."

"Both dorms?"

"I expect so."

Parker made no effort to hide his disgust. "Kids today. I swear."

"This from the guy who chased after every girl in Durango 24/7."

"That was different. I never caught any."

"Your failure makes you hate others' success?"

"I don't hate *you*."

"What's that supposed to mean?"

Parker leaned back and clasped his hands behind his head. "Look who you showed up with this summer. Give me a break, buddy."

"Janelle?"

"Yes, *Janelle*. She's the talk of the town." Parker's eyes grew bright. "Or of the hospital, anyway."

Chuck sat forward. "What's that supposed to mean?"

The resort manager jerked a thumb toward the window behind him. "The new ER doc."

"You saw him?"

"He drove right by. His SUV is hard to miss."

"He made a house call. He was checking up on Rosie."

"While you were away."

"He was there when I came back. There was nothing going on."

"Of course there wasn't," Parker said.

FORTY-THREE

Chuck kicked a piece of gravel out of his path as he made his way up the driveway to the cabin. The afternoon sun sliced through the trees. Insects buzzed in the ponderosas growing close on both sides of the two-track.

What would happen, he asked himself, when he revealed what he'd learned about the gold in the mine and turned over the skull to park officials? No doubt they would get in touch with the Estes Park Police Department, Officer Hemphill included.

Chuck shook his head. He was too tired to care what Hemphill might do at that point.

But what about Jake and the dead rams? Exhausted though Chuck was, anger flared in him.

He knew how things would go after he made his report: Jake was bound to hear what was up, and he would ditch any evidence that could be used against him. He would get off, at best, with a warning—and there was nothing, absolutely nothing, Chuck could do about it.

He cursed as he walked on up the drive to the cabin. Tracking the drag path to the fen, finding the tire tracks and boot prints, gathering the flakes of dried blood from the side of the toolbox within feet of Jake—all for nothing.

At the sound of his footsteps on the deck stairs, Rosie ran out the front door and dove into Chuck's arms. His heart warmed as he pulled her to him.

"*Preciosa mia,*" he whispered in her ear.

Rosie giggled. "*Preciosa mia tambien,*" she whispered back.

He led her by the hand into the cabin. Boxes lined the kitchen table. Folded pants and shorts and jackets covered the sofa and chairs. Janelle came out of the back bedroom carrying an armful of the girls' brightly colored blouses. She aimed an upward breath at a lock of hair that had fallen across one eye. When that proved unsuccessful, she laid the blouses over the back of the couch and pushed the loose length of hair behind her ear.

She wore knee-length yoga pants and a tight nylon top that accentuated her trim figure. She gave Chuck a weary look.

He saluted. "Private Bender, reporting for duty."

"About time." She displayed the cabin with a sweep of her hand. "Lots to do."

They set to work, the girls pitching in, as the afternoon gave way to evening. They finished packing not long after dinner, boxes and duffle bags stacked in the living room, ready to be loaded in the bed of the truck for the drive home the next day.

Chuck grabbed a beer from the refrigerator and wandered out to the front porch. He took a long swallow from the bottle, the cold brew tickling his throat.

Things would happen fast in the morning. He would see the students off first, along with Kirina and, he could only hope, Clarence, who would drive the van to Durango. Next, he would check in with Hemphill, to make sure there was nothing more the officer needed from him before he, too, left for home with Janelle and the girls. He would stop by park headquarters on the way out of town to drop off the skull and sample of calaverite, and fill park staffers in on what he'd learned about the mine and the slaughter of the bighorns on Mount Landen.

The forest surrounding the cabin was calm and quiet in the interlude between the last of the sun-warmed upslope breezes of daytime and the cool winds that fell from the high peaks and swept through the broad valley at night. A cricket sounded beneath the deck. The last light of dusk gave way to full dark.

Chuck thought of Nicoleta struggling to breathe before dying in his arms. What if the police never found the young woman's killer?

He thought of the bullet hole in the skull he'd found in the mine shaft. The odds of solving that long-ago murder were slim indeed.

And he thought, again, of Jake and the dead rams—and realized the wrecker owner's guilt was the one thing he could do something about.

He set his beer on the deck railing. Pulling his phone from his pocket, he looked up the 24-hour number for Jake's Wrecker Service online, punched it in, and brought the phone to his ear.

Forty-Four

Jake answered on the second ring. Chuck explained that Parker accidentally had directed the wrecker owner to leave Nicoleta's car in the wrong spot in the maintenance yard.

"It's in the way of a piece of heavy equipment he needs to get to first thing tomorrow," Chuck said. "He wants you to come back out and move it tonight."

"I don't think I left it in the way of anything," Jake said.

"I haven't been there, so I wouldn't know. But he said to tell you he'd pay you double, since it's after hours and all."

"Double? I like that. But why's he got you calling me?"

"He's busy with the murder investigation. Something's up. I'm not sure what."

A note of excitement entered Jake's voice. "Are the police out there again?"

"I'm guessing they're on their way. You might get to see them make their big bust if you get here quick enough."

"Give me fifteen minutes," Jake said. "I'll meet you at the yard."

Chuck stuck his head inside the cabin, muttered Parker's name, and, sounding disgruntled, explained to Janelle that he had to leave for a few minutes.

The girls lay on their backs on the couch, their heads hanging off the cushions, watching television upside-down, their bare feet pointed at the ceiling. Rosie looked at Chuck and rubbed her stomach in an exaggerated circle. "I'm hungry."

"We just ate an hour ago," Chuck said.

Janelle spoke over her shoulder as she headed for the kitchen. "Get back as quick as you can."

Chuck grabbed a mini-Maglite from the truck toolbox and hurried through the forest, aiming the small flashlight at the needle-covered ground ahead of him. Shadows flitted away from the light into the thick grove of trees standing between the cabin and maintenance yard.

Two hundred yards south of the lodge and conference center, the yard sat in an opening carved from the forest. A wide, dirt drive extended through the trees to a paved rectangle lit by overhead lights and surrounded on three sides by open-faced sheds lined with vehicles and maintenance gear. Chuck stood on the pavement beneath the lights and squinted into the shadowy sheds, spotting two well-used pickup trucks painted Y of the Rockies blue, a pair of Bobcat front-end loaders, a mini-excavator, a scissor-style platform riser, roll after roll of chain-link fencing, and piles of weathered lumber. Nicoleta's sedan sat where Jake had left it, at the far end of one of the sheds, well away from any stored equipment.

The rev of the wrecker's engine sounded from the foot of the driveway. The wrecker negotiated a ninety-degree turn in the trees behind the conference center, then straightened and accelerated, its headlights illuminating the gravel drive leading from the turn to the yard. Chuck faced the glare of the oncoming lights and used his flashlight to wave Jake onto the rectangle of pavement.

The wrecker rolled to a stop. Its air brakes belched and its engine died. Jake climbed to the ground, leaving the driver's door open and the key hanging on a ring in the ignition. He doffed his cap and scratched his head as he approached, his eyes on Nicoleta's sedan. "Just what I figured. I left it out of the way of everything."

"Yep," Chuck said. "I called and checked with Parker when I saw where it was parked. He said to tell you he was sorry, that he must have remembered wrong. Since you were already on your way, though, he asked if you could help get one of the Bobcats trailered for tomorrow."

Jake's mouth lifted in a flinty smile. "He knew I'd charge him for the call no matter what. Trying to get his money's worth out of me."

Chuck pointed past the end of the far shed row. "He said the trailer's around back."

Jake grunted. "Guess we'd best have a look."

He climbed up to the open driver's door of the wrecker, leaned inside to grab a metal flashlight from the passenger seat, and hopped back down to the pavement.

Chuck followed Jake a few steps toward the end of the shed before stopping. "You go ahead," he told him. "I'll make sure Parker's right about the key being in the ignition of the Bobcat. I don't trust him at this point, and we're wasting our time if he's wrong."

"Suit yourself," Jake said before disappearing behind the shed.

Chuck ran in silence, balanced on the balls of his feet, back across the pavement to the wrecker. Shoving his flashlight in the rear pocket of his jeans, he hoisted himself up the two ladder-like steps to the driver's side of the cab and plucked the ring of keys from the ignition.

He leapt to the ground and stepped to the front of the long, black toolbox bolted just back of the driver's door. The hole for the key in the toolbox handle was far smaller than a standard ignition keyhole. He fanned the ring's dozen-plus keys on his palm. Half of those on the ring were long ignition keys. The others were shorter.

He flipped through to the first of the shorter keys and tried it in the toolbox-handle keyhole. The key's thick tongue didn't even begin to slide into the slot.

"Ain't seein' no trailer at all," Jake hollered from the far side of the shed row.

Chuck hustled around the front of the truck so his voice would carry to the wrecker owner. "What's back there?"

"Nothin' but a bunch of weeds. They're waist high."

"Maybe he meant on around to the very back," Chuck called.

"Don't look like a vehicle's ever even been driven back here. Good God almighty." When Chuck didn't respond, Jake grumbled, "Okay, then. I'll go on and make the full loop."

Chuck ducked back around the truck and worked his way to the next small-sized key. This one sank to its shoulder in the keyhole but did not budge when he tried to turn it in the lock.

He flipped to a third small key. This one, too, slipped in to its shoulder. This time, when he twisted, the key turned. He pulled the handle and the toolbox lid rose.

The interior of the box, shielded from the overhead lights by the truck's flatbed, was black with shadow. Chuck aimed his flashlight inside it.

Atop a plastic rifle case resting at the bottom of the toolbox, wedged against one another in a neat row, were eight Rocky Mountain sheep horns, six full curl, two three-quarters.

Packed around the horns to hold them firmly in place were beige nylon stuff sacks, each about a gallon in size, secured at their necks by cinch cords. The outsides of the sacks, designed for use by campers to hold stuffed sleeping bags, were smeared with black.

Gripping his Maglite in his teeth to light the interior of the toolbox, Chuck loosened one of the bags and reached inside. His fingers dug into material that was moist and had the consistency of coffee grounds. He drew a handful of the material from the bag into the beam of his light.

He gasped, the flashlight falling from his mouth into the box. There was no doubt—it was calaverite.

He did some quick mental math. The nylon bags, lined against the horns, took up the full length of both sides of the five-foot-long toolbox, perhaps twenty bags in all. If each bag contained roughly a gallon of calaverite, and if Elaine's ten-percent estimate was correct, then the bags held some two hundred ounces of gold—more than a quarter of a million dollars' worth.

Chuck shoved the handful of gold-infused ore back into the bag, cinched it shut, and retrieved his flashlight.

Before he could close the toolbox lid, he was blinded by a flashlight beam aimed at his face.

"What the hell you think you're doing?" Jake growled.

FORTY-FIVE

Chuck dropped the metal lid with a *clang*. The ring of keys rattled against the side of the box.

"I was looking for tools," he said. "No keys in the Bobcat. Figured maybe we could hotwire it."

"Bull*shit*," Jake said. He flipped his long flashlight and gripped it by its head, the flashlight's beam turning his curled fingers blood red. Somewhere along the way, he'd paused to light a cigarette, now clamped in the corner of his mouth.

"I been wondering about you," Jake said, the cigarette bouncing up and down as he spoke. "All your questions." He jerked his head in the direction of the sheds. "And no trailers back there neither. Parker don't know nothin' about this, does he?"

Jake patted his empty palm with the heavy flashlight and took a threatening step forward.

Chuck backed away from the toolbox. "I don't know what you're talking about. I'm sure if we call Park—"

"Shut your trap," Jake snarled. He took another step forward, drawing even with the box. Keeping his eyes fixed on Chuck, he fumbled with his free hand until he found the ring of keys. He spun the key in the toolbox handle to the locked position and dropped the key ring in his coveralls pocket.

Chuck's heart was in his throat, his mind racing. He'd hoped—even expected—to find the evidence of Jake's poaching. But the calaverite?

Chuck took another step away from the toolbox, recalling the gouges he'd spotted halfway down the vertical shaft, where the black striations began. He'd assumed the cavities were the result of the calaverite having fallen away from the walls of the shaft. Now he knew otherwise. The black material, dug from the shaft walls, had wound up in Jake's toolbox.

Somehow, Jake had learned about the gold, and had discovered the hidden vertical shaft at the back of the mine. Entering the tunnel at night over the last few weeks would not have been a problem for Jake; the mine door had been unlocked all summer. Hiding what he was up to would have been easy, too; he had only to loosen one of the floorboards at the end of the tunnel and slip down the ladder into the shaft, then re-secure the plank when he finished before dawn.

Assuming Jake knew the immense value of the gold he'd taken from the mine—and how could he not?—Chuck's situation was precarious indeed.

Chuck slipped his right hand, black from handling the calaverite, behind his back. He jutted his chin at Jake. "You're the scumbag who's been slaughtering the park's sheep," he said, focusing on what Jake was sure to see as the lesser of his transgressions, "for your daughters' tuition money."

Jake's eyes flicked to the toolbox. "I ain't sayin' nothin' to you." He tapped the metal lid with the butt end of his flashlight. "You didn't see a goddamn thing in this here box, you got it? If you know what's good for you, you'll keep your mouth shut. You got no proof. You got *nothin'*."

"You really think you can get away with it?"

"There's plenty enough sheep to go around. A little culling's exactly what them animals up there need. Hell, the park people been talking about thinning them out for years."

"Justifying your own greed. No surprise there."

Jake's eyes flashed beneath the brim of his cap. He lifted his flashlight, ready to strike, but came up short when Chuck asked, "What's in the bags, Jake?"

The wrecker owner eyed Chuck. "Sand," he answered after a beat. "To anchor guns for sightin' in at the range. I'm vice president of the gun club."

Chuck said, disgusted, "The vice president of the Estes Park Gun Club is a lazy, good-for-nothing *poacher*."

"I'm telling you for the last time," Jake said, flat-lipped. "Keep your nose where it belongs." He took the cigarette from his mouth and aimed it down the gravel road toward the lodge and conference center. "Get on out of here. *Now*."

Chuck cocked his head in defiance. "I'm not going anywhere."

"Suit yourself." Jake shoved his cigarette back between his lips and turned away. He tossed his flashlight into the cab of the truck, climbed behind the steering wheel, and slammed the door.

Chuck returned to the toolbox and pulled hard on the handle, but the lid was securely fastened.

The tow truck's engine roared to life. As the truck lurched forward, Chuck jumped onto the lowest of the steps leading to the driver's door, clinging to the metal handles on either side. He climbed the second step to the door as Jake swung the wrecker in a tight circle in the paved center of the maintenance yard. Chuck let go of one of the handles long enough to try the door, but it was locked.

Jake ignored Chuck's face in the truck's side window. He lined up the wrecker with the road and floored the engine, his left hand fixed on the steering wheel, his right hand working the truck through its gears, gaining speed.

The truck bounced from the raised pavement to the dirt drive, the stiff recoil nearly causing Chuck to lose his grip on the side handles. Jake bent forward, hunched over the steering wheel, as the truck flew down the drive, trees flashing by on both sides.

Chuck ducked to avoid being swept from his perch by an outstretched branch, then swung his body forward and threw his torso across the windshield. He stared through the curved window and gave the glass a solid *thwack* with his palm.

Jake jerked backward and lost his grip on the steering wheel. The wheel spun a quick half turn before he caught it. The truck yawed left, skidding on the gravel, as Jake fought for control. Chuck twisted atop the hood as the truck skidded into the ninety-degree turn in the road behind the conference center.

The wrecker spun around. Its front passenger wheel plunged into the bar ditch lining the side of the road. The truck pivoted over the buried wheel and lifted into the air with a tremendous wrenching of metal.

Chuck flew off the hood to the ground, his fall cushioned by a thick stand of brush growing at the edge of the road. He tucked and rolled, his head striking the trunk of a small ponderosa as he tumbled past it. He came to a stop in a patch of scrub oak at the edge of the forest. Behind him, the truck groaned and settled on its passenger side, half on the road, half off.

Chuck tentatively moved his arms and legs. No broken bones. He put a hand to the side of his head to find blood oozing from a cut where the tree trunk had gouged his scalp.

The driver's door of the wrecker, facing the night sky, opened. The truck's headlights produced enough ambient light for Chuck to watch as Jake clambered out of the cab and slid down the windshield to the ground, his cigarette still clamped in the corner of his mouth. Chuck crouched in the brush as Jake peered past him into the dark forest. The truck engine, no longer running, ticked as it cooled. The smell of spilled gasoline filled the night air.

Behind the waist-high screen of scrub oak, Chuck pulled his phone from his pocket, holding it low to the ground.

Jake took a drag on his cigarette, released the smoke. "I know you're in there," he said.

Chuck pressed buttons on his phone, shoved it back in his pocket, and rose, showing himself. "You deserve what happened just now. You killed those sheep."

"Damn right I did. God didn't put them there just to prance around and look pretty. He put them there to make use of."

"But you left their carcasses to rot in the forest. You didn't even use the meat."

For the first time, a note of uncertainty entered Jake's voice. "I'm done with all that now. I won't be doing it no more."

Chuck made a show of extracting his phone from his pocket. "Too late. I'm calling the police."

"Be my guest. Won't nothin' come of it." Jake took his cigarette from his mouth and pointed it at the toolbox bolted behind the cab of the truck. "You can't do nothin' without no evidence." He faced the wrecker, his cigarette raised.

"No," Chuck yelled. "*Don't.*"

Forty-Six

Jake flicked his cigarette at the spot where the crumpled hood of the upended wrecker met the ground. "Glad my insurance is all paid up," he said.

A tongue of orange flame raced beneath the truck, followed by an oxygen-sucking *whoomp* from the engine compartment. Flames climbed around the sides of the wrecker and leapt, crackling, into the night air.

Jake shot Chuck a cruel smile, his face framed by the flickering light of the flames curling from the truck's engine compartment. He set off at a brisk walk down the drive toward the conference center, disappearing into the darkness, as the fire enveloped the cab of the truck.

Chuck dashed around the truck and climbed the wrecker's undercarriage hand over hand, flames flickering around him. He reached into the open driver's door to grab the key ring from where it hung in the ignition.

Black smoke enveloped him as he sidestepped along the truck's drive shaft to the toolbox. He climbed higher, leaning against the underside of the flatbed. He pulled his flashlight from where it was still wedged in his back pocket and aimed its beam at the ring of keys, flipping to the one he'd used earlier.

The smoke grew thicker as he unlocked the toolbox, threw open the lid, and latched onto two ram horns as they tumbled from the sideways box along with the sacks of calaverite. He pinned the horns to his chest and pulled the heavy rifle case out of the box.

He jumped to the ground and ran from the burning truck, kicking one of the fallen sacks of calaverite ahead of him. Free of the smoke, he stopped and filled his lungs with fresh air, the sack of calaverite at his feet, the horns and case clutched in his arms.

The truck exploded behind him, the force of the blast sending him sprawling to the road. The horns and rifle case tumbled to the ground. He covered his head as flaming bits of metal fell around him.

A sudden quiet followed the explosion. Chuck rose to his knees. The light of the crackling flames, bright around the burning truck, revealed a metal culvert extending beneath the road a few yards away. Chuck ran to the drainage pipe and shoved the horns, rifle case, and sack of calaverite deep into its black mouth.

He turned to see the scrub oak at the edge of the drive beside the truck burst into flames. He watched in horror as the fire climbed from the brush into the branches of a tall, roadside ponderosa. The water-starved tree lit up like a Roman candle, the flames sweeping upward from branch to branch. The heat of the fire radiated off Chuck's face. In seconds, the flames leapt up the slope to the next ponderosa in the forest.

Chuck calculated the advancing flames' natural line of travel. From the first ponderosa to the second, and on up the forested slope, the fire would burn straight for Janelle and the girls in the cabin, less than three hundred yards away.

He sprinted into the forest, paralleling the flames. Already the blaze had a twenty-yard head start on him as it burned from tree to tree up the slope.

A sudden gust surged past him, drawn by the voracious appetite of the flames. Ponderosas exploded into fireballs one after another, sending blasts of heat rolling back past him before the breeze again rushed into the fire. Light from the exploding trees probed the forest ahead, illuminating his way.

Digging for traction in the soft forest duff, Chuck gained on the conflagration. Dodging tree trunks and leaping fallen logs, he drew even with the head of the fire, then, as he neared the cabin, drew a few yards ahead of the blaze.

He burst from the trees onto the driveway in front of the cabin just as Janelle and the girls, lit by the oncoming flames, rushed across the deck and down the front stairs. Chuck dove into the driver's seat of the pickup while Janelle hoisted the girls into the back seat and tumbled in behind them.

Chuck grabbed the keys from the console, fired up the engine, and executed a T-turn off the parking area, the rear bumper ramming the trunk of a tree with a solid *chunk*. Flaming cinders floated past the windshield as he threw the truck into drive and floored it, spinning the pickup back onto the driveway. Smoke obscured the beams of the headlights as he sped along the two-track away from the cabin and accelerated down the driveway through the forest.

Twenty-five yards ahead, an arm of the racing fire leapt the rutted drive, leaving a solid sheet of flames in its wake.

FORTY-SEVEN

Chuck gripped the steering wheel and gunned the engine, aiming for the wall of flames. The girls screamed from the back seat as the truck rushed into the blazing barrier.

For a long second, all was black and flickering orange. Then the pickup broke through the fire. Burning embers fell away from the hood as they sped down the drive, the acrid scent of wood smoke thick in the truck's cab.

The headlights lit the driveway, now free of fire, as it descended through the trees. Chuck glanced in the rearview mirror. The girls clung, whimpering, to each other.

"It's okay," he told them. "It's all right. We're safe now."

"What happened?" Janelle asked from her seat beside the girls, her voice shaking.

"Truck wreck. The fire took off from there. I've never seen anything move so fast."

"Parker?"

"No. A tow-truck driver."

"Did anybody get hurt?" Carmelita asked.

"The driver wasn't injured," Chuck told her. Unfortunately.

Janelle looked back at the flames obscuring the driveway. "The cabin," she moaned.

"It's gone," Chuck said. "Or it will be." Shame sliced through him—he had set in motion the chain of events that had led Jake to start the fire.

"My dollies!" Rosie sobbed. "My clothes!"

"Hush, *bambina*," Janelle consoled her. "We're safe. Understand? That's all that matters."

In his side mirror, Chuck caught sight of the flames climbing into the night sky above the forest canopy. He twisted his hands on the steering wheel, unable to convince himself that what he saw was real.

They exited the forest behind the lodge and conference center. Guests' faces plastered the lodge's rear windows. Chuck swung the truck around to the front of the lodge, where a stream of fire trucks and volunteer firefighter vehicles turned into the resort entrance and poured down the entry road to the open valley floor.

He spun the wheel, skidding away from the oncoming vehicles and speeding along the road around the grass fields toward the dormitories. He glanced over his shoulder, taking in the clogged entry road behind them. "We can't get out of here right now," he told Janelle.

He slid to a stop in front of Raven House, hopped from the truck, and looked back the way they'd come. A broad stretch of forest behind the lodge and conference center was ablaze, flames leaping more than a hundred feet into the air. Across the fields, the screech of sirens from emergency vehicles intermingled with the roar of the flames as firefighters aligned their trucks in a defensive perimeter around the two massive log structures. Guests streamed from the lodge, past the emergency personnel, and onto the grass, most dragging suitcases or lugging duffles, many with youngsters by the hand.

Chuck swallowed, his mouth parched, reminding himself over and over that it was Jake who had flicked his cigarette beneath the wrecker, igniting the blaze.

The flames already extended well beyond the cabin. If the fire maintained its present speed, it would burn its way up and out of the broad valley that was home to the resort in less than an hour. From there, it would cross the boundary line into the national park. Not until running out of fuel upon reaching tree line high in the Mummy Range would the flames die out. A huge swath of forest—ponderosa lower down, white fir and blue spruce at higher elevations—would be incinerated.

Janelle and the girls climbed out of the truck, huddling near

Chuck as they took in the awful spectacle. He drew them close. Rosie wrapped her arms around his waist. He cupped the back of her head in his hand. "The fire can't get to us here," he told her.

Janelle looked west, past the dormitories and dining hall, at the dark forest rising beyond. "You're sure?"

Chuck pointed to the southwest, equidistant between the cabin, by now surely burned, and the dormitories. "The valley slopes uphill away from us. The fire should keep running that way."

"Good." Janelle pressed her palm to Rosie's head over the back of Chuck's hand. "Let's go find your uncle," she told the girls.

"Yeah," Carmelita whispered, her eyes fixed on the fire. "Uncle Clarence."

Chuck turned with Janelle and the girls to find the students filing out the front door of Raven House carrying their personal belongings. Kirina and Clarence followed the last of the students down the front steps and away from the building.

The girls ran to their uncle, who knelt and pulled them to him. He stared over their heads at the towering flames to the south.

Next door to Raven House, the international workers made their way out of Falcon House and gathered at the edge of the fields.

More guests emerged from the cabins and condos arrayed along the north side of the fields, opposite the lodge and conference center. Additional emergency vehicles flowed through the resort entrance—wildland fire trucks, police cars, and more private vehicles of volunteer firefighters, magnetic lights flashing on their roofs. The vehicles joined the defensive perimeter around the historic log lodge and conference center, closest to the flames.

Chuck counted the students as they made their way onto the green expanse of fields in front of Raven House. Eleven.

He hurried over to Clarence and Kirina as they joined the students. "We're one short. Who's missing?"

Clarence and Kirina scanned the students.

"Sheila," Kirina said.

Chuck clenched his jaw. "Check her room, would you?"

Kirina ran back inside as a firefighter, hustling across the fields in floppy rubber boots, approached from the direction of the lodge. His large stomach pressed against his fluorescent-yellow slicker and waterproof pants. Sideburns extended below his broad-brimmed helmet.

"I'm Lieutenant Robinson," he said between heavy breaths, coming to a stop midway between the students and the employees from Falcon House and addressing both groups. "I need all of you to remain where you are, out here on the grass where it's safe, until we can find a way to get you into town. A shelter is being arranged at the high school."

Jeremy spoke up. "What makes you think it's safe where we're at?"

The lieutenant aimed a thick finger at the fire. "As long as it maintains its course, you'll be fine out here in the open."

"And if it doesn't?"

"We'll deal with it then. The fire is still very active behind the lodge. We're concentrating our resources there right now."

"Yeah, but—" Jeremy began.

The firefighter held up a hand. "I have to keep moving." He set off toward the resort guests grouped at the north end of the fields.

Chuck turned to the students. "You heard him," he said, aware that the employees from Falcon House, huddled twenty yards away, were listening as well. "We're okay out here in the fields."

"For now," Jeremy said, prompting several students to cast apprehensive glances at the flames rising to the south. Smoke billowed into the sky above the fire, obscuring the stars.

"That's right."

"I don't see why we should wait," Jeremy insisted. "I say we take the van and head for town."

"You heard the lieutenant," Chuck said. "We won't be going anywhere for a while. Besides, all roads through and around Estes Park will need to remain clear for emergency vehicles." The students stood so close together their shoulders touched, their eyes on Chuck. "I suggest you make some calls, let your folks know you're safe."

Samuel held up his phone. "I've been trying. I can't even get a text to go through. The system's crashed or something."

The students groused to one another until Chuck waved his hands for quiet. "I'm sure it's programmed to let emergency traffic through first." He pointed at the leaping flames. "Big as this is, I wouldn't be surprised if we won't be able to text or make calls for quite a while, maybe all night." He took a breath. "The thing for you to understand is that you're safe, all of you. We're in for a long night, but we'll be okay. Even if the fire circles around, it won't get to us out here."

"It might circle around?" Samuel asked, fear in his voice.

Chuck toed one of the students' duffle bags resting on the grass in front of him. "That's why you brought your stuff from your rooms, right? Just in case."

Kirina exited Raven House, leaving the front door open behind her, the lights of the common room shining onto the front steps. "Sheila's not in there," she hollered.

At Chuck's side, Clarence drew a sharp breath.

FORTY-EIGHT

Clarence put his mouth close to Chuck's ear. "I was with her," he said, his voice low.

Chuck blanched. Before he could respond, he spotted Parker's bright blue pickup speeding around the fields, headed their way.

Jeremy scoffed, "Look there. It's Peeping Tom, come to make our day."

Clarence's words echoed in Chuck's head as he turned to Jeremy. "Peeping who?"

"The jerk with the binoculars glued to his face." Jeremy directed an accusatory finger across the fields at Parker's office window, a black rectangle beneath the eaves of the conference center. "*Pervert*," he concluded forcefully.

Chuck drew his lower lip between his teeth and bit down hard. Nicoleta, dead. Sheila, missing. And Parker's admission of his long history of failure with the opposite sex.

Chuck gripped Clarence's arm. "Don't go anywhere. We've got to find Sheila."

He left the students to meet the oncoming truck. He halted abruptly when he saw a second figure in the passenger seat.

Parker slid the truck to a stop in the middle of the road and climbed out, slamming the driver's door behind him. A wiry-framed man exited the passenger side of the truck—Jake.

They met Chuck at the edge of the grass, halfway between the employees and students, Parker's eyes blazing.

"Jake found me," Parker snapped. He jerked his head at the fire. "What the hell did you do?"

"*Me?*" Chuck said. "It was Jake. *He* started it."

Jake crossed his arms, his face set.

"Don't try that with me," Parker said to Chuck. "He told me how you tricked him into coming out here, and how you threatened him with some crazy idea about his being a poacher. He said you made him wreck; that the fire started from leaking gas."

"Jake threw his cigarette at the wreck to start the fire and cover his tracks."

"What tracks?"

"He *is* a poacher. He's been killing sheep, rams, for their horns, up on Mount Landen."

Parker wind-milled his arms at the raging fire, the firefighters building their defensive line around the lodge and conference center, the dozens of guests staring at the flames from the fields. He stuck his finger in Chuck's face, inches from his nose. "You've destroyed *everything*," the resort manager cried. "Don't you understand that? Everything I've worked for."

"I'm telling you, Parker," Chuck said. "Jake started it. Deliberately. There were horns in a lock box, and the rifle he used."

Jake smirked.

Parker took half a step away from Chuck. "Horns? A rifle?" He snorted. "Do you even know what you're talking about?"

"Parker, please," Chuck begged.

Jake's smirk twisted into an oily grin.

Chuck started over. "There's...there's..." He almost said the word aloud: gold. But what good would that do at this point? Parker already considered him crazy.

The resort manager drilled into him: "It hasn't been lost on anyone in Estes Park that the murdered girl died in your arms, Chuck. *In your arms.* Plus, there's your brother-in-law's knife." Parker waved at the flames. "And now this. I thought I knew you. I *trusted* you."

"I didn't start—"

"Shut up. Just *shut up*. At this point, I don't care who started what." Parker held his palm out to Chuck. "Stay away from me. You've done enough." He surveyed the guests gathered around the edge of the fields. "I've got to make sure everyone's accounted for."

Chuck bit his tongue. *Sheila.* He couldn't say anything to Parker about her, not now.

As Parker's gaze roamed from the students to his Falcon House employees, Anca detached herself from the group of workers and approached, her satchel over her shoulder, heading straight for Jake.

"You," she said, fire in her eyes, stopping in front of him. "Why is it you that is here?"

Jake pointed at Chuck. "Him. I'm here because of him."

Parker looked from Jake to Anca. "What?" he asked. "Who?"

The young woman reached into her handbag. Chuck caught her eye, silently willing her to restrain herself. He was a step ahead of Jake at this point—at least, he believed he was—and he wanted to keep it that way.

Anca hesitated. She jutted her elbow at Jake, her hand still in her bag, and told Parker, "He know her. He know Nicoleta."

Jake deflected Anca's allegation with a flip of his fingers. "Of course, I knew her. That piece-of-crap car of hers. Twice she had to call me."

"You towed her?" Chuck asked.

Jake turned to him. "Didn't have to. Idle adjustment the first time. She was conked out way up on Trail Ridge. The second time was a flat. I shot some No Leak into her tire and pumped it back up. Didn't have to tow her in either time. I'm telling you, I saved her a ton of money."

"You told Hemphill?"

"It didn't have anything to do with the murder," Jake said.

Anca said to Chuck, "I was on the Trail Ridge Road with Nicoleta when the car, it would not run. The car-worker man is right, he made it go again."

"The second time?" Chuck asked her.

"I was not there." Anca's eyes narrowed with distrust as she looked at Jake, her hand still in her shoulder bag.

Jake turned to Parker. "Let's get this over with."

Anca rooted around inside her cavernous bag.

Chuck stepped between her and Jake. Janelle listened from a few steps away, the girls pressed to her sides. He faced Parker and spoke. "Get what over with?"

"Citizen's arrest," Parker said.

"*What?*"

"You lied to Jake to get him to come out here, right?"

"Yes, but—"

"And you attacked him."

"I tried to keep him from—"

"The result of which is your burning down the resort."

"I didn't—"

"You're under arrest, Chuck," Parker said.

"It's *him*," Chuck insisted. "It's Jake. Don't you see? I didn't do anything!"

Parker looked from Chuck to Jake. "It's just...I think..."

Jake rolled his eyes. "Jesus, Parker." He shoved his hand into the front pocket of his coveralls. The pocket was easily large enough to hold a pistol.

Chuck balled his hands into fists. He'd had enough. He lowered his shoulder and charged. Jake's eyes widened, the whites around his irises bright beneath the streetlights. Chuck struck Jake in his midsection and drove him hard into the ground before he could withdraw his hand from his pocket.

Chuck grabbed Jake's wrist and pulled the wrecker owner's hand into the open to find that Jake gripped not a gun but a closed switchblade. Chuck clung to Jake's arm, but Jake flicked his wrist in a well-honed movement, making a five-inch blade appear at the end of the knife handle.

Jake twisted his hand upward. His wrist turned in Chuck's grip. The blade, razor-sharp, nicked Chuck's forearm, drawing blood. Chuck drove his fist into Jake's nose, slamming Jake's head backward into the turf. Blood spurted from beneath Chuck's fist and Jake lay still, on his back in the grass, the knife falling free from his hand.

Ignoring the blood oozing from the cut on his arm, Chuck slid Jake's knife out of the way with the side of his shoe as he fished his phone from his pocket. He punched *play* on the phone's recording app and held the phone close to Parker's ear.

Chuck's voice issued from the phone's tinny speaker: "You deserve what happened just now, with your truck. You killed those sheep."

"Damn right I did," Jake responded.

Parker listened to the recorded conversation, then Chuck's cry of alarm when Jake flicked his cigarette at his truck, starting the fire, and Jake's calm voice: "Glad my insurance is all paid up."

"Satisfied?" Chuck asked Parker, shoving his phone back in his pocket.

"My God," the resort manager said.

"I'm all for your citizen's arrest. You just had the wrong guy." Chuck kicked Jake's foot. "Tie him up. And do a good job of it. It'll be a while before the cops will be able to deal with him. I'm sure you've got something in your pickup."

Jake moaned and rocked back and forth in the grass, beginning to come around. Blood leaked from his pancaked nose.

"You got it," Parker said. He headed for his truck.

Chuck drew Anca aside. "What else do you know about this man—" he pointed at Jake "—and Nicoleta?"

"At the Trail Ridge Road, he look at Nicoleta and me a lot," she said. "His eyes, they have hunger." She shivered with obvious distaste. "That is how we say it in Bulgaria."

"And Nicoleta?"

Anca hesitated. "She make joke about it. She call him cowboy. Big, tough, American western man."

Chuck considered the number of people he'd heard Nico-

leta had slept with over the summer, and the gold-infused calaverite now smoldering behind the conference center, before his
thoughts returned to what Clarence had just said to him about
Sheila. The clock was ticking.

Parker made his way back across the grass from his truck, a
coil of rope in hand.

Chuck turned to the students and Janelle and Carmelita and
Rosie. He indicated Jake on the ground behind him with a tilt of
his head. "I'm sorry you had to see that. But, trust me, our sheep
poacher had it coming." He extended his fingers, loosening his
bruised knuckles. "You all know Sheila's missing."

"The Navajo girl?" Janelle asked.

Chuck nodded. "Clarence and I are going to look for her."

"Find her," Janelle said, gathering Carmelita and Rosie to
her. "Hurry."

He addressed the students. "You're safe here, all of you, outside, like the lieutenant said."

Chuck waved Clarence to him and they set off for Raven
House. "What do you mean, you were 'with her'?" he asked out
the side of his mouth.

"It was after you left. I was...she was..."

"*Clarence*," Chuck prompted him.

Clarence's words came in a rush. "She came to my room. She
said she'd been waiting all summer, that this was the last night
and she couldn't wait any longer. She closed the door behind her."

Chuck stepped through the front door into the empty common room at the front of Raven House.

Clarence stopped in the open doorway behind him. "I told
her to leave, but...but...she started to unbutton her shirt."

Chuck turned to him, incredulous. "What'd you do?"

"I sat there, on my bed. I'd been drinking. You know that."

"We had an agreement. Nothing with the students. *Nothing*."

"Which is exactly what I did. I took her by the shoulders and

I moved her to one side and I got the hell out of there."

Chuck breathed. In, out, in, out. "And now, she's gone."

"I don't know where she went."

Chuck tugged Clarence past him into Raven House and spoke to his back as they made their way across the common room. "You left her in your room? That's the last you saw of her?"

"I came back a few minutes later. She was gone. I went inside, locked the door, lay down. I was all in."

Chuck gritted his teeth. *The alcohol.*

Clarence continued, "I didn't wake up until I heard the sirens. I came outside with everyone else."

"She ran away," Chuck said, sure of it. "Into the woods. She told me where she went in the mornings. She said she hadn't been up there since the police investigation."

"If that's where she ran off to, the fire should've driven her back down by now."

"That's what you'd think."

They sprinted down the first-floor hallway and burst out the back door. A loud crack, distinct as a rifle shot, issued from the raging fire to the south. They set out up the slope past the dining hall, Chuck aiming his flashlight ahead into the trees, Clarence shining his phone light. They moved fast, straight uphill, passing the spot where Nicoleta had died in Chuck's arms. He swept his flashlight at bare tree trunks, dry grass patches, occasional low bushes. Nothing. Sheila could be anywhere.

"What was she wearing?" he asked Clarence.

Sheila's private spot above the dorms couldn't be far; she'd visited it during the few minutes the students had to themselves each morning between breakfast and when they reported to the van for the drive to the mine.

"A green shirt. It had a bunch of little buttons down the front that she—" He stopped, began again. "Tan pants with cargo pockets."

The clothes she'd been wearing when Chuck had visited with her in the Raven House hallway.

The forest floor climbed steadily. Chuck and Clarence wended their way up the slope between the trees. The growl of the fire grew louder as they climbed closer to the expanding periphery of the blaze. Wind whipped past them up the slope, drawn by the flames.

The forest floor leveled after a short, steep pitch. Chuck paused at the top of the slope, swinging his flashlight back and forth. Clarence stopped beside him.

They were a hundred yards from Raven House. The tiny plateau upon which they stood stretched thirty feet to where the slope resumed its climb out of the valley to the west.

Chuck cocked his head, sensing the breeze as it shifted around them. Rather than continuing to flow up the slope toward the fire, the wind moved one way, then the other, like liquid sloshing in a bowl, until, as if having made up its mind, it burst back across the narrow plateau from the west, tumbling past Chuck and Clarence and on down the slope toward the dining hall and dormitories.

A cloud of smoke followed the initial blast of hot air across the plateau. Coughing, Chuck bent forward, terrified. Where there was smoke, flames wouldn't be far behind.

He grasped Clarence's arm and turned at the edge of the plateau to sprint back down the slope to safety. There, beyond a break in the trees, just visible through the coursing smoke, was Sheila's view across the valley, the lights of the resort at the foot of the slope and those of Estes Park beyond.

The roar of the fire grew louder as the flames, having reversed direction with the wind, ate their way toward them, driven back into the valley by the cool night air flowing off the high peaks of the Mummy Range.

Squinting through the smoke, Chuck looked both directions

across the plateau, his smoke-filled lungs seizing.

Sheila wasn't here. They had to go.

Chuck started back down the slope. He came up short when a weak cry emerged through the roar of the flames.

FORTY-NINE

Chuck turned to Clarence. "You heard that?"

Clarence raised a hand.

"Help," the faint cry came again, from the north. Chuck ran full out across the plateau with Clarence at his side.

Chuck's flashlight beam cut a hard line that marked the north edge of the plateau. He slid to a stop and aimed his flashlight down the hill. The smoke lifted a few feet off the ground. Sheila lay on her back against the base of a small pine tree twenty feet below, her eyes shining in the beam of light.

She raised a limp hand. Her torso was twisted around the tree trunk, her shirt and slacks covered in dust.

Her eyes fell closed and her hand dropped to her side as Chuck and Clarence scrambled to her.

Chuck gripped her shoulder, his light bright on her face. "Sheila!"

Clarence, kneeling beside Chuck, pointed at her neck. "Same as Nicoleta."

A bright red cut ran from Sheila's left ear and disappeared beneath her chin.

Chuck nearly gagged. *Not again*. He tightened his grip on Sheila's shoulder. "Sheila," he urged, her name catching in his throat.

Sheila's arms lay unmoving at her sides. Her mouth hung open, her chin slack.

Chuck put his fingers to her neck. The cut beneath her jaw was shallow. Her pulse was strong below her jawbone, just above the cut, which continued beneath her chin and almost to her right ear.

The slash on Sheila's neck was far less severe than that of Nicoleta's fatal wound. Blood seeped, but did not gush, from beneath Sheila's chin, staining the front of her green blouse.

Chuck continued to probe with his fingers. He found a large, wet lump on the back of Sheila's head. When he took his fingers away from the lump, they were red with blood. "Somebody hit her, too."

Clarence shoved his phone in his pocket and reached beneath Sheila, sliding her away from the tree. "We've got to get her out of here."

The fire roared down the slope toward them, pressed by the down-rushing wind. Thick spirals of smoke, dark as molasses, curled above their heads.

Together, Chuck and Clarence lifted Sheila. They propped her limp body upright, her arms across their shoulders, and hurried down the slope toward the valley floor with her slung between them, her head lolling and her feet dragging.

The oncoming flames, no more than fifty yards up the slope behind them, lit the way ahead. Chuck looked back as they rushed down the hill. The fire was advancing faster than he and Clarence could move with Sheila draped awkwardly between them. The flames were only thirty yards away now, leaping down the slope from tree to tree like a blazing locomotive.

Chuck tripped over a branch, causing him to let go of Sheila and tumble down the hill, painfully knocking his head where he'd previously bruised it upon being thrown from Jake's wrecker. He came to rest sprawled on his back and watched from the forest floor as Clarence swung Sheila's body up and over his shoulder in a single, powerful move.

"Come on," he grunted to Chuck without breaking stride.

Chuck scrambled to his feet and followed as Clarence galloped down the slope, matching the speed of the pursuing flames.

The on-rushing fire lit the rear wall of the dining hall ahead of them. The flames were hot on Chuck's back. The smoke, flowing along the ground where the angle of the slope lessened near the bottom of the valley, seared his lungs. He trailed Clarence and Sheila along the side of the dining hall and out of the trees just as the fire reached the back wall of the building.

Chuck charged past the cafeteria and into the open, Clarence just ahead of him. He took a rasping breath. Human forms, hazy in the roiling smoke, lined the paved path leading from the dormitories to the dining hall. Waiting arms lowered Sheila's limp body from Clarence's shoulders and carried her past the dorms and across the parking lot to the grass fields.

Clarence sank to his knees on the path. Chuck looked back the way they'd come, his chest heaving. Flames snaked across the cafeteria's asphalt-shingle roof, spinning into the night sky like specters from the spirit world. He pulled Clarence up by the arm and they fled together to the fields.

Kirina and Parker crouched on either side of Sheila, who lay on the grass in the glow of an overhead streetlight. The students stood in a circle, looking on, while the workers from Falcon House hovered a few yards away in a tight clutch.

Chuck and Clarence elbowed their way inside the circle of students. Kirina looked up, stricken, her eyes darting from Clarence to Chuck and back to Clarence. "We thought...we thought..."

Chuck moved the students back, his arms outstretched. "She's going to be all right," he said. "She hasn't lost much blood."

Parker held his phone to his ear. "Nothing. I can't get through."

Samuel spoke from the circle of students. "None of us can."

"Keep trying," Chuck told him. "If we need to, we can get the firefighters to help." He knelt next to Kirina. "Her pulse was strong when we found her."

Kirina put her fingers to Sheila's neck. "Still is. The cut isn't deep." She stroked Sheila's forehead, her hand streaked with blood, her shoulders trembling.

Clarence leaned over them from above. "She called out.

That's the only reason we found her."

Janelle approached with the first-aid kit from the truck, the girls close behind her. She knelt next to Parker, snapped the case open, and set about applying gauze bandages to the wound on Sheila's neck, displaying the same calm assurance as when she tended to the girls' scraped knees and elbows.

Carmelita draped herself across Janelle's back and buried her face in her mother's long hair. Chuck reached a hand to Rosie, who collapsed against him. He rose and lifted her in his arms.

Rosie pushed herself away from him and pointed down at Sheila. "Will Dr. Gregory make her all better?"

"Of course, he will," Chuck promised.

"*Mamá* says you don't like him."

Chuck looked Rosie in the eye. "Don't like him? Ha. He saved your life, remember?"

Parker looked up from his phone. "She needs an ambulance, but—"

Samuel waved his hand and spoke, his voice urgent. "I just got through. Quiet!"

"We have a medical emergency," Samuel yelled into his phone. "We need an ambulance." He provided their location and a description of Sheila's injuries before lowering his phone and addressing the waiting group. "She said she'd send a police officer."

Chuck frowned. "An officer?"

"She said the ambulance isn't available."

"We only have the one," Parker said.

A siren sounded from downtown. Seconds later, a police car raced up the road to the resort entrance. At the bottom of the valley, fire trucks surrounded the lodge and conference center, blocking the main road, while firefighters directed defensive streams of water on the two buildings. The police car bounced over the curb separating the entrance drive from the fields and careened across the grass, headed for the dorms.

Chuck lowered Rosie to the ground. She went to Janelle while he stepped out of the circle of students. He waved his flashlight at the police car, which slid to a stop in front of him. Two figures emerged. The driver, lit by the overhead lights lining the fields, was Hemphill. Tall, broad-shouldered Dr. Gregory climbed from the passenger side of the car.

A large first-aid kit hung from the young doctor's hand. He hurried over to Sheila. Behind him, a rear door of the police car opened and a third person stepped out and rounded the car.

Chuck's boss, Fort Lewis College Professor of Anthropology Arturo Sartore.

Sartore's signature shock of long, silver hair, combed back from his wrinkled face, fell past his ears to his collar. He wore a short-sleeved dress shirt tucked into high-waisted khakis.

Chuck had forgotten Sartore was on his way to Estes Park. "Professor?"

"Chuck," Sartore said grimly. "I barely made it into town before all hell broke loose. I went to the police station and managed to catch a ride here."

Chuck turned and joined the circle of students. Gregory knelt at Sheila's side and pulled on a pair of latex gloves from his medical kit. Janelle sat back, allowing him to take over. Chuck aimed his flashlight at Sheila's head and torso, adding to the glow of the streetlight. Blood seeped from the gauze bandages swaddling her neck.

Janelle turned to Gregory. "Her pulse is steady. Her eyes have been fluttering; she's coming around."

The doctor touched Janelle's arm. "You've done a great job with her."

Color rose in Chuck's cheeks, this time the result of pride. He addressed Hemphill. "We found her up the hill in the trees."

The officer looked up at him. "*You* found her?"

"She was missing. Clarence and I went to—"

"*Clarence*?" Hemphill exchanged a glance with Sartore.

The professor told Chuck, "That's why the officer agreed to bring me here."

Clarence stepped back.

Chuck stared at Sartore. "What are you talking about?"

"Jim, Officer Hemphill, wants me to be here when he..." The professor fell silent, looking everywhere but at Clarence.

Chuck turned to Hemphill. "Be here for *what*?"

The officer rose from Sheila's side. "For Clarence's arrest," he said. He turned to face Clarence. "I'm here to arrest you for the assault and murder of Nicoleta Barstolik."

Clarence's face was ashen. "I'm innocent."

"The test came back positive for Nicoleta's blood on your knife. In addition to her fatal neck wound, she had a leg wound, sustained sometime before she died."

Clarence took another backward step. Hemphill waved his hand at the fire to the south and west, the firefighters surrounding the log buildings, the guests on the grassy expanse. "There's nowhere for you to go."

Chuck stepped to Clarence's side. "You've got it all wrong. You had Clarence's knife in your possession twenty-four hours before Nicoleta was killed, remember?"

The officer hesitated. "Doesn't matter."

"It damn sure does."

"There's plenty of knives out there."

"What is it you're alleging? That Clarence didn't manage to kill her the first time, so he left his bloody knife on the ground, called you on the emergency phone so you'd be sure to find it, somehow got hold of another knife, and used it to kill her the next night? And in the meantime, Nicoleta stuck around after he assaulted her—and kept his attack a secret—just to be sure he'd be able to finish the job? Is that seriously what you think?

What are you, crazy?"

The officer hesitated. "It's...we...I'm..."

"You haven't even got a case," Chuck told Hemphill. He laid a hand on Clarence's arm and made no attempt to hide his disgust. "Don't worry. You don't have to go anywhere. They've got nothing on you."

Clarence yanked his arm away from Chuck. Hemphill reached reflexively for the handgun at his waist. The officer's eyebrows shot upward as his hand grasped at an empty holster where his gun should have been.

Chuck looked past Hemphill to find Kirina backing away from the group, Hemphill's pistol held before her in both hands, her finger on the trigger.

FIFTY

Officer Hemphill spun to face Kirina, who sighted down the barrel of the gun at his chest, her face twisted in torment. "No," she said. She wiped tears from her eyes with her hand and re-settled it on the gun. "Not Clarence." She choked back a sob. "Not him."

Janelle put her arms around the girls, pulling them to her.

Sartore raised a placating hand. "Kirina," he said from where he stood among the students.

She swung the pistol, centering it on the professor. "*No*," she said, her voice suddenly fierce. "Don't you *dare* speak to me."

"We're here for you," Sartore soothed, his voice barely carrying above the roar of the flames consuming the dining hall and eating through the forest behind the dormitories. "*I'm* here for you."

"No, you're not. Not you," she said, backing away, the gun still aimed at the professor. "You, least of all."

Sartore's back straightened. "Okay," he said, his voice firm and unyielding. "That's enough." He held out a hand and stepped toward Kirina. "Give me that," he ordered.

The pistol wavered in Kirina's hands.

"You heard me," Sartore barked. "I'll have no more of this." He took another step toward Kirina. He was only a few feet from her now, his hand outstretched.

"No!" she cried, lifting the barrel until the gun was pointed at Sartore's face.

"Kirina," Clarence said. He had not moved from where he stood at Chuck's side.

Kirina swung the gun past Chuck, aiming at Clarence.

Rosie ducked under her mother's arm. "Not my uncle!" she screamed. She bolted across the patch of grass separating her from Kirina and threw herself at Kirina's legs.

Kirina jerked, spinning away as Rosie slammed into her. A loud report sounded and a burst of flame leapt from the mouth of the gun as the barrel swept in an arc in front of her.

Rosie tumbled to the grass at Kirina's feet. Kirina, still standing, stared open-mouthed at the discharged pistol in her hands.

Hemphill grunted and fell forward, clutching his shoulder.

A strangled sound came from deep in Kirina's throat. She turned and sprinted toward Raven House, dropping the gun. The pistol bounced once in the grass, spun up and over the concrete curb separating the fields from the road. The gun settled out of sight in the gutter as Kirina crossed the road and disappeared through the dormitory's open front door.

Janelle scrambled on her hands and knees to Rosie. Assured her daughter wasn't hurt, she crawled across the grass to Hemphill. The students fell back, their mouths agape. Gregory knelt with Janelle at Hemphill's side. Together, they rolled the officer to his back.

Sartore turned to Chuck. "I'm sorry." He looked at Hemphill and Sheila, broken and bleeding on the ground. "This is my fault. All of it," he said, his face downcast. "It's up to me to make things right." He set off after Kirina, his pace deliberate.

Chuck crouched at Hemphill's feet. "Say something. Can you talk?"

Hemphill squeezed his eyes closed. "Sure," he said through colorless lips. "I only got shot, that's all."

Gregory followed the slope of Hemphill's shoulder with his fingers. The officer winced.

"Entrance and exit wounds," Gregory said. "Not a lot of blood."

Janelle handed bandages to Gregory. Rosie huddled behind Janelle, a panicked look on her face. Carmelita put a reassuring arm around her little sister.

Parker said from Sheila's side, "Her eyes are open. She's trying to talk."

Chuck went to her. "Hey, there," he said. He wasted no time. "Do you know who did this to you? Do you remember?"

Sheila's mouth moved, but she made no sound.

Parker asked her, "Was it Clarence?"

Chuck glared at the resort manager.

Sheila's eyes went to Parker. She neither nodded nor shook her head.

Chuck crouched at her side. "You're going to be okay." He took her hand. "Just a name. That's all we need."

Her eyes fluttered and began to close.

"Let us know when you can," he told her.

Beyond the dormitories, the cafeteria roof fell in on itself with a loud *whoosh*. Smoke billowed from the building. Flames, rising from the forest, backlit the dorms on either side of the dining hall.

Chuck said to Parker, "You got her?"

The resort manager nodded.

Chuck stood and addressed the students, gathered a dozen feet away. "Keep at it with your phones. We need more police." He pointed at Jake, hogtied on the ground. "And keep your eye on him."

He turned to where Gregory and Janelle worked together, applying pressure to both sides of Hemphill's shoulder. He caught Janelle's eye and aimed his chin at the front door of Raven House. "Kirina didn't mean to do what she did. I'll see if I can get her to come back out."

"It wasn't entirely an accident," Janelle said.

"I worked with her all summer. She's not a murderer."

Janelle gripped Gregory's first-aid kit. "Could've fooled me."

Chuck looked away, thinking of "Peeping Tom" Parker, gun-toting Anca, and, finally, with grudging acceptance, Kirina.

He turned to Clarence. "You're in charge of the students." He set out for Raven House, remembering what Sartore had said:

This is my fault. All of it.

Chuck glanced down as he stepped over the curb to cross the road to the dormitory.

Hemphill's gun was gone.

FIFTY-ONE

Heat from the collapsed, blazing dining hall rolled between the dormitory buildings and struck Chuck full in the face as he crossed the road, walking away from the empty gutter and reasoning Sartore must have retrieved Hemphill's gun.

Black smoke speckled with red sparks lifted behind Raven House as Chuck hustled up the walk to the dorm. He stopped in the open front doorway. Fixtures hanging from the ceiling on long wires lit the common room. He took in the gear and tools piled in the corner, the boxes of finds on the wooden tables, his pack against the far wall. An open stairway climbed to a balcony cantilevered from the rear of the room. A closed door at the back of the balcony led into the second-floor hallway.

He stepped through the front door. The instant he entered the room, a loud *pop* sounded from the rear of the building and the lights blinked out.

He spun to face outside. The streetlights lining the fields went black. Seconds later, phones held by the students created small domes of light over the places where Sheila and Hemphill lay.

Chuck turned back to the common room and pulled out his flashlight. Lit only by the single, small beam and the light of flames from the burning dining hall flickering through side windows, the room was forbidding in its shadowy darkness.

The muffled sound of voices came from the second floor. Chuck slipped between the tables and crept up the stairs.

He turned off his flashlight and paused on the balcony, his back to the room below, facing the door to the second-floor hallway. He inched the door open. An invisible river of heat coursed through the doorway from the back of the building. A muffled conversation came from Kirina's room, halfway down the hall, its door open.

Eerie light from the blazing cafeteria building made its way through several open doors into the corridor. Chuck put his flashlight in his pocket and tiptoed down the hall, stopping just shy of Kirina's door.

Smoke curled along the ceiling from the rear of the building. He stifled a cough, his hand to his mouth, and turned his ear to the open doorway.

"...don't understand," Kirina said. "You *can't* understand. You'll never know what I feel for him, what he means to me."

"He's nothing but a creature of his own desires." A commanding voice. Sartore.

Kirina's response was sharp. "You don't know who or what he is."

Sartore's voice softened. "I know I wasn't there for you. I'm sorry for that. But these last months, I've worked hard to make it up to you."

"Don't give me that," Kirina said. "Your taking control of my life was never about me. It was always about you, your parents, your *mommy.*"

"It was never what you think," Sartore retorted. "And as for you, it's not too late, even now. We can get back to where we were at the beginning of the summer. I know we can."

"No, we can't," Kirina responded. "For good reason."

"I wouldn't call that...that...*brute* a reason."

"He's kind. He's funny. He's real."

"He's an animal, and you know it, addicted to his own base instincts. You're nothing to him but another conquest. You should have done to him the same thing you should have done—but didn't—when you locked Chuck in the mine."

"What? I was supposed to kill Chuck?"

"He'd served his purpose. He was a danger to us."

"It looked like he was doing what you'd hoped," Kirina said. "I followed him in my car and hiked in to the mine behind him.

I was afraid he'd come back out and see me. I did what I had to do; I locked him in so I could get away."

"You stopped thinking of your future, our future."

"I called you, didn't I?"

"Not until a few hours ago. Not until everything was out of control."

"He's the one who figured out what the floor collapse meant. I didn't even know until everyone started talking about it this afternoon. Don't you see? It was what you hoped, what you needed. He found what you wanted because I was smart enough *not* to kill him."

"But for Clarence, your lover, you were more than willing to kill, weren't you?" Sartore said.

The heat in the hallway was almost unbearable now, the smoke growing thicker. Sweat dripped from Chuck's brow, stinging his eyes and rolling down his neck into his shirt. He remembered the way Kirina, along with the other members of Team Paydirt, had looked at Clarence earlier in the summer—her eyes had been hungry. And just yesterday she'd told Chuck, "I like Clarence. I like him a lot."

Kirina spoke, barely whispering. Chuck leaned close to the doorway. "He isn't my lover," she said. "He wasn't my lover. Ever."

"Nicoleta. Wasn't that her name?"

Kirina said angrily, "She should have stayed away from him. But she claimed he was hers." Her voice turned bitter. "All she wanted was a green card. She was willing to do anything, with anyone, to get it."

"You put everything—*everything*—we've been working toward at risk."

"She was insane. Slashing her own leg, soaking his knife with her blood. She was going to threaten to tell the police he'd done it if he refused to marry her. It would have worked, too. I know it would have. She actually bragged to me about it, said there was nothing I could do."

A heavy silence carried from the room into the hallway. Chuck hung his head. *Kirina.* "The other girl," the professor said. "Her, too."

"*Sheila*," Kirina spat. "I spotted her leaving his room, her shirt half-buttoned. She saw me and ran. I chased her up into the woods and hit her with a tree branch. I had a length of cord from the dig in my pocket. I wrapped it around her neck. I could have finished her off. I should have. But...but..." She choked back a sob. "I'm not a killer. I'm *not* a killer. But what choice did I have?"

"*What choice?*" the professor erupted. "I've given you the opportunity to fulfill your grandmother's legacy, but you've turned into your grandfather instead."

"No," Kirina shot back. "I've turned into *you*, doing what's necessary to get what's mine."

"And now look what you've brought us to."

"Wrong. Look what *you've* brought us to. This fairy-tale idea of yours."

"I was right. What Chuck found proves it."

"It doesn't matter anymore. It's too late."

"No, it's not. No one knows anything yet. Everyone saw your shooting the officer for what it was: an accident. All you have to do is go back out there and say you're sorry. As for the girl, even if she thinks it was you, the cops will convince her it was Clarence. We're so close, Kirina."

"I can't do that. I won't."

"Clarence doesn't love you. He never has loved you. This is perfect, don't you see? He'll get what he deserves, what you know he deserves."

"I won't see him rot in prison."

"You'll be far away. We both will. And rich, fabulously

wealthy." A brief silence passed. "We're almost there," Sartore said. "It's actually better this way. They'll take Clarence, and we'll be free to take what is rightfully—"

"That's all you can think about, isn't it?"

"It's what my mother, your grandmother, wanted—for herself, for me, for you."

"But Clarence—"

Sartore broke in, his voice harsh. "*He doesn't love you*. He *never* loved you."

"No! *No!*" came Kirina's anguished cry, thick with heartbreak, startling Chuck. She flew into the hallway, her hands clamped over her ears, and came up short at the sight of him. "You," she breathed, lowering her hands.

Chuck stepped back. "I wasn't...I didn't..."

Before he could say anything more, a fireball launched up the rear stairwell and a blast of superheated air rolled down the corridor, punching him backward to the floor.

FIFTY-TWO

Kirina stumbled, thrown forward by the blast of wind. She found her footing, her back to the wave of heat, her hair blowing around her face.

The fireball dissipated at the head of the rear stairs. In its wake, a wall of flames climbed from the stairwell, setting the end of the corridor ablaze. The flames ate past the closed doors to the bathrooms at the far end of the hall and reached a pair of open dorm-room doors. The fire split in two, sucked into the facing rooms.

Chuck crab-walked backward down the hall away from the fire. Above him, long wisps of smoke gathered around Kirina's head like a witch's garland.

Kirina looked down at Chuck with sorrowful eyes. She turned and strode away from him, headed straight for the flames.

Chuck pushed himself to his feet. "Kirina! No!"

He charged after her, but the heat pumping down the hallway forced him to stop. He backed away as Kirina increased her pace, sprinting into the wall of fire.

She disappeared, swallowed by the inferno. The flames shifted and she reappeared, still running, her hair trailing, ablaze, behind her. Then the fire closed around her once more, this time for good.

Chuck fell back, mouth agape, as the fire resumed its march down the corridor. He stumbled backward through the thickening smoke, past Kirina's room, transfixed by the oncoming wall of flames.

Sartore stepped from Kirina's room into the corridor. He turned his back to the flames and aimed Hemphill's gun at Chuck's chest.

"Kirina," Chuck said, struggling to breathe the hot, smoky air. He pointed at the flaming hallway behind the professor.

"She...she..."

Sartore spoke without emotion. "She was weak. She didn't understand."

Chuck backed out of the hallway, retreating from the gun in Sartore's hand. He came up against the balcony railing. The professor followed Chuck onto the balcony.

"She was your daughter?" Chuck asked.

Sartore leaned his back against the door to the upstairs corridor, closing it against the smoke and hot air. He spoke with a slow, even cadence, as if time was of no importance. "In name only."

With the door shut, the relative coolness of the common room replaced the intense heat of the upstairs hallway.

Chuck wiped perspiration from his eyes. How long would the door hold back the flames? And what was the fire doing below, in the first-floor hallway? He glanced down from the balcony. Smoke poured through the open doorway leading from the lower corridor into the common room, but, at least for the moment, no flames ate into the room.

He considered reasoning with the professor about the imminent danger presented by the fire, but it was obvious Sartore didn't care.

Chuck remembered the excessive anger the professor had directed at him over the phone when things had begun to unravel earlier in the week. Now he knew the real cause of Sartore's rage.

"You used her," Chuck accused the professor. "You used Kirina, your own child."

"I gave her an opportunity. She chose not to accept it. But, fortunately, my backup plan—you—enabled me to learn what I needed."

That's why Sartore had called, after all these years, to offer him the field school position. "I found what you were after, didn't I?"

Sartore's eyes glinted. "Another of your many discoveries. That's what I appreciated about you as a student—so inquisitive, such a thinker—and why I selected you for this job. You and Kirina both. Between the two of you, I knew I'd strike gold—which is precisely what you did for me." Sartore looked Chuck in the eye. "And now you have before you the same opportunity I presented to Kirina. You can be as wealthy as you've ever dreamed, Chuck. Wealth you may share with your lovely young wife, your two little girls, and Clarence, too, should you so desire."

"The mine," Chuck said.

"My mother's discovery. Thanks to her hard work so many years ago, you have a decision to make—and you don't have long to make it."

Chuck stared at the gun in Sartore's hand, less than three feet away. The professor was sure to pull the trigger if Chuck tried to wrestle it away from him. Chuck risked a glance over his shoulder at the front doorway. Should he try to escape the dormitory? No. Sartore would gun him down before he reached the bottom of the stairs.

Chuck feigned a cough and pointed at the smoke gathering in the rafters. He slid along the railing and backed down the first step. Sartore followed, the gun thrust before him.

"What decision are you talking about?" Chuck asked as he took a second backward step.

"Whether to be a rich man, or a dead man."

Chuck continued backing down the stairs. "We both know the answer to that."

The professor followed. "You'll have to convince me you'll be good to your word."

"The gold."

Sartore nodded once, short and sharp. "From the beginning."

"And your mother?"

"My *brilliant* mother. She figured it out. She was one of the park's first female rangers, raised in Estes Park. Her family—my family—homesteaded here. Her grandfather worked claims all through the Mummies before the park was created. When my mother went to work for the park service in the 1950s, she explored the old claims in the park, her grandfather's and others, out of curiosity. One day, deep in Cordero Mine, she made an incredible discovery."

"Thomas Walsh," Chuck said.

In the dim room, the professor smiled, his eyes glowing. "My mother found exactly what Walsh found in Ouray."

"Calaverite."

"A massive pocket of it. But I needn't tell you that; you've seen it." Sartore's face darkened in sudden anger. "And then you had to go and tell everyone else." He regained his composure. "But there's still time. A few loads, before the authorities find out, will be more than enough for us."

"For *us*?" Chuck asked, nearing the bottom of the stairs. He glanced around the room, taking in the smoke pouring from the first-floor hallway and gathering overhead, the boxes on the tables, the gear bins and tools in the corner—and his pack, resting against the wall at the foot of the stairs.

He gulped. The skull stowed inside his pack and the 1950s lipstick container found beneath the floor of the mine tunnel. The two objects were related.

Chuck stepped backward to the last stair. His pulse, already racing, quickened even more.

The skull wasn't that of a small-statured, Civil War-era miner from a century and a half in the past. Rather, the skull was that of a woman who had been murdered just a few decades ago.

FIFTY-THREE

Chuck looked up at Sartore from the bottom step. "What was your mother's name?"

The professor's eyes took on a faraway look. "Sandy. That's what everyone called her. Her full name, though she never used it, was Cassandra."

Chuck blinked. *The Cassandra Treasure.*

"And your father?"

The professor's voice filled with contempt. "My *so-called* father. He was the only one who ever called her by her given name, when he wanted to humiliate her—which was all the time."

Chuck backed from the final step to the wooden floor of the common room. Sartore stood three steps above, his eyes clouded by the past. Beyond him, at the top of the stairs, the door to the second-floor corridor exploded outward. Flames burst from the upper hallway, enveloping the balcony and lighting the room.

Still backing away from the professor, Chuck angled between the tables toward the front door. Sartore descended the last of the stairs. Perspiration seeped through tendrils of hair plastered to his forehead. The flames consumed the balcony and licked across the ceiling above.

"My mother wanted to tell the park officials about her discovery," the professor said, the gun still trained on Chuck's chest. "She was convinced they would give her a share of the takings—and back then, they very well might have. But my father believed the park bosses would keep it all for themselves. My mother and father fought over the decision, ferociously. I was just a boy, hiding in the corner. My father made threats, waved a gun around, even threw my mother across the room. But she wouldn't leave him. She loved him no matter what he did to her. Then, one day, just like that, my mother was gone."

"He killed her?"

Sartore continued as if Chuck hadn't spoken. "I would give anything to know she didn't do what my father said. He told people she'd abandoned me and run off. He stayed in town for a while, started buying things for himself. Clothes, a new car. But people began to talk—until, one day, he didn't come home either.

"He'd mined enough of the calaverite to set himself up for the rest of his life. It was easy to disappear in those days. My aunt and uncle took me in, and I was left to listen to all the whispers behind my back."

"But you waited all these years," Chuck said.

"I left town as soon as I was old enough. I wanted to get away, live my own life—which is exactly what I've done, and exactly what I would have continued to do if I hadn't met Kirina's mother."

The horrible vision of Kirina being swallowed by the flames struck Chuck between the eyes. He forced the image to the back of his mind. "She really is—was—your daughter?" he asked again, playing for time.

He'd backed far enough between the tables by now to catch a glimpse of the fire advancing steadily down the first-floor corridor toward the common room. Overhead, flames from the second-floor hallway rolled far across the ceiling. Smoke gathered beneath the flames, twisting in wraith-like coils. Heat built in the room like an oven.

"Her mother left me when she became pregnant, though she never told me," Sartore said. "I didn't know I had a daughter until one day last year when Kirina called. She said she'd always known about me, that I was the reason she'd chosen to study anthropology. I agreed to meet her. When I saw her, I knew. She was my mother all over again. It brought back everything I'd lost. I understood then that I never should have turned my back on my mother's discovery, her dream."

"This whole summer was staged," Chuck said in amazement.

"I knew more of the gold had to exist, but when I visited the mine last fall, I found the tunnel was solid granite. I needed to deepen the search, figure it out. I was too old, but not Kirina—especially with your help. I proposed the field school idea to the park, talked up the public-relations potential, got them to bite."

"It was all a façade," Chuck said, recalling the professor's insistence that the students excavate the tunnel. "Except Kirina didn't turn out to be who you thought she was."

"In fact," Sartore replied, his disdain obvious, "she turned out to be more like my mother than I ever could have imagined."

"Lovesick, you mean."

"She was captivated by Clarence. Consumed. Enthralled. I told her there would be plenty of time for him later, but she couldn't help herself. I forced myself to believe everything would work out—until two days ago, when the police called with all their questions."

The flames reached the end of the first-floor hallway, climbed up the back wall, and joined the blazing balcony above. The temperature soared. Smoke hung thick in the room. Chuck took another backward step, edging toward the front door.

The professor trailed Chuck, his back to the flames. "And now you have the same opportunity as Kirina. You can make things right, for both of us."

Embers tumbled from the burning ceiling, blistering the varnished floor behind the professor. Chuck took small breaths to avoid searing his lungs. How far behind him was the front door? He dared not turn his head to find out. Instead, he looked Sartore in the eye. "Your mother," he said. "I found her."

The gun trembled in the professor's hand. "My *mother*?"

Chuck pointed at his pack, resting against the wall at the side of the room. "In there."

Sartore turned to the pack, his eyes growing round.

"It's everything you've spent your life wanting to know," Chuck said. "*Everything.*"

"What?" the professor sputtered. "How?"

Chuck tilted his head at the fire coating the back wall of the room. "There's no time." He pointed at his pack. "In there is—to you—my greatest discovery ever."

Sartore looked past Chuck at the open front doorway. Chuck held his ground, the heat in the room so intense his shirt burned his skin where it touched his chest.

A tear ran down Sartore's leathery cheek. He lowered the gun to his side, turned away from Chuck, and walked to the pack, his shoulders bowed.

Chuck backed to the front doorway. The cool night air poured past him into Raven House, feeding the flames.

Sartore set Hemphill's gun on the floor, lifted the pack, and rummaged inside it until he pulled out the skull. He held it before him, staring at the bullet hole.

Chuck gripped the doorframe, his eyes locked on Sartore. The breeze flowing into the building stopped. A millisecond later, a violent jet of superheated air blasted Chuck out the door.

FIFTY-FOUR

Chuck flew backward off the front steps as the Raven House roof collapsed into the common room and white-hot flames swallowed the professor.

Driven by the explosive blast of wind, Chuck tumbled across the front yard, his arms and legs flailing. He came to rest on his hands and knees, climbed to his feet, and ran away from the flaming building.

Janelle met him in the middle of the road in front of the collapsed dormitory. She held him in her arms, her cheek to his chest.

Chuck put his hand to Janelle's hair. Blood, dripping from the knife wound on his forearm, stained her shirt.

He leaned on her shoulder, his ears ringing from the concussive collapse of Raven House, as she helped him across the road, her arm tucked tight around him. Carmelita and Rosie met him at the edge of the grass. They wrapped their arms around his waist and buried their heads in his torso. Janelle's mouth moved, but he heard only high-pitched ringing. He looked around him, glad his eyesight, at least, was functioning.

Under Gregory's supervision, Clarence, Parker, and the students stood on either side of Sheila and Hemphill, preparing to carry the two patients deeper into the fields away from the fire. Falcon House, still standing, was engulfed in flames, as were the collapsed dining hall and Raven House.

Tornado-like winds, spawned by the flaming buildings, spun across the road and into the fields, pelting anything and anyone in their path with burning debris. A pair of fire trucks, dispatched from the lodge and conference center, raced around the fields toward the blazing buildings.

Clarence, Parker, Gregory, and the students lifted Sheila and Hemphill and hustled them away from the raging fire.

Janelle released Chuck. He caught his balance, his hands

resting on the girls' heads for support.

Janelle put a hand to his chest. "All right?" she asked, her words battering his eardrums as the ringing in his ears subsided. "Are you all right?"

He nodded but didn't speak, afraid to trust his voice.

She gathered his shirt in her hand and pulled him close. She stared into his eyes. "I love you," she said. Tears streamed down her cheeks. "Damn it all."

She pried the girls from his side. Taking them by the hand, she led them away from the fire. "Come on," she said over her shoulder to Chuck.

In front of Falcon House, the international workers retreated deeper into the fields as well—all except Anca. Nicoleta's roommate stood watch over Jake, who sat before her in the grass, his hands and feet drawn together with the nylon cord from Parker's truck, his wrists trussed beneath his ankles.

Chuck approached Jake and Anca on unsteady feet, his addled brain struggling to comprehend how Jake had known about the calaverite in the mine before anyone else.

Chuck spoke to Jake's hunched frame, his words echoing in his head, trying to come up with something, anything, that would get him talking. "You see what you did?" He aimed an accusatory finger at the burning structure that had been Raven House, ablaze behind him. "You just murdered two people."

Light flickered on Jake's face. Blood from his flattened nose covered his upper lip. "The girl got what she had coming to her. She shot a cop."

"That wasn't who she was," Chuck said, repeating his knee-jerk defense of Kirina despite what she had done to Nicoleta, and had attempted to do to Sheila.

The fire trucks rolled to a stop in front of the blazing buildings. Firefighters jumped from the trucks and set about unfurling hoses. A water tanker sped around the fields, joining the two trucks.

"You're telling me I was seeing things?" Jake insisted.

"Greed," Chuck said. "I see a lot of it in what I do."

But the word didn't describe Kirina, who'd been coerced into doing what she'd done by Professor Sartore, her father. Chuck shook his head to clear it as the ringing in his ears continued to diminish. The description of Kirina as greedy didn't fit her—but it fit Jake to perfection.

Chuck looked down at the wrecker owner. "Sometimes I find things people want real bad."

Jake stared at the fire trucks parked end-to-end in the road. He dug his heels into the grass, turning himself away from Chuck to face the firefighters as they worked.

A swirl of wind, launched by the fire, swept across the grass, flattening the stems to the ground before lifting them straight up. The heat from the spinning wind dried the sweat on Chuck's brow, but the perspiration returned as soon as the mini-tornado passed.

"It seems you found something this summer before I found it," he said to Jake.

Jake continued to eye the firefighters.

"Those *sandbags*," Chuck said. "For sighting in rifles at the gun range."

Jake flinched.

Chuck continued, "The dead girl, Nicoleta. You knew her."

Jake spoke without looking at Chuck. "I already told you that."

"But you didn't tell Hemphill."

The wrecker owner's shoulders drew together beneath his coveralls.

"Why not?"

"She was disgusting," Jake said, trembling.

Chuck bit his lower lip. Only Kirina had known, all summer long, that gold might be hidden in Cordero Mine. *Only Kirina.* He remembered, with a start, Jeremy disparaging her earlier in the summer: "One of those square-faced dykes who swing both ways."

He turned to Anca. "The people Nicoleta slept with—they weren't all men, were they?"

Anca shook her head, the movement slow and deliberate.

Chuck stepped in front of Jake. He caught Jake's gaze only for an instant before Jake lowered his head and averted his eyes, but that was enough for Chuck to see in them everything he needed to know.

Jake could have heard about the gold from only one person: Kirina. She had told Nicoleta about the possible riches in the mine; Nicoleta, in turn, had told Jake.

Chuck had overheard Kirina describe to Sartore, just moments ago, Nicoleta's all-consuming desire for a green card. The young woman from Bulgaria had been so determined to remain in America that she'd been willing to sleep with anyone and everyone who might provide a way for her to stay in the country. She'd even cut herself, soaked Clarence's knife with her blood, and called the cops anonymously, planning to blackmail him into marrying her. It was easy to see why Nicoleta would have slept with Kirina when the opportunity presented itself, and it was equally easy to see that someone as conniving as Nicoleta would have had no trouble prying lovelorn Kirina's big secret out of her. In fact, Kirina might well have told Nicoleta about the gold for her own purposes, promising Nicoleta a payoff in return for keeping her hands off Clarence.

But why would Kirina, bisexual or not, have slept with Nicoleta in the first place? Kirina was infatuated with Clarence, not Nicoleta. Rather than sleep with Nicoleta, Kirina should have resented Nicoleta for sleeping with her beloved.

Perhaps, Chuck reasoned, Nicoleta had been the next best thing for Kirina—a chance to get one physical step closer to Clarence, and to show him she, too, could play his game.

Chuck spoke to the back of Jake's downturned head. "How did Nicoleta pay you for the work you did on her car?"

Jake stumbled over his words, speaking to the ground. "She... she...I..."

Chuck's stomach climbed into his throat. "You killed her, didn't you?" he demanded.

He'd been right all along: Kirina was not a killer. So strong and competent on the outside, she was a lost soul on the inside, hopelessly infatuated with Clarence. At some point in the course of the summer, she'd sought physical solace in Nicoleta—solace that had cost Kirina her life.

Chuck had heard Kirina admit to Sartore that she had tried and failed to find it within herself to kill Sheila—but she'd never actually confessed to killing Nicoleta.

"*You murdered Nicoleta,*" Chuck repeated, standing over Jake. "She paid you in sexual favors for fixing her car, and she told you about the gold, trying to use the information to win herself a green card."

Jake's body stopped trembling as Chuck continued, glaring down at him. "You figured it out. You found the calaverite—the gold. No more tuition worries, especially when added to what you stood to make off your poaching. All you had to do was kill another ram or two and slip a few loads of ore out of the mine. But Nicoleta got her claws into you, didn't she? She wouldn't let go."

Chuck shuddered. It all made sense now. With the summer drawing to a close and her return to Bulgaria eminent, Nicoleta had worked two angles at once—cutting herself to blackmail Clarence, and threatening to reveal her sexual relationship with Jake as leverage over him.

The words of the librarian, Elaine, rang in Chuck's ears: "I've been around long enough to know that when someone dies, there's usually a reason for it—and the person who's dead is usually part of the reason."

Chuck stared at the back of Jake's head. "You agreed to meet her. She said you had to find her a husband, a visa, some way to stay here, or she'd tell everyone what you'd done with her. The two of you argued. You lured her into the forest and gave her a good shake, just to make her see reason. But she screamed instead. You were desperate. You had to keep her quiet." Chuck recalled the fluidity with which Jake had flipped open his switchblade a few minutes ago. "Your knife appeared in your hand as if by magic. You didn't mean to kill her; it just happened."

Jake looked up at Chuck, his eyes black and bottomless. He opened his mouth and howled like a caged beast, twisting his bound wrists. The cord securing him fell away and he scrambled to his feet.

Chuck stepped back, stunned. Jake had retrieved his knife from the grass and used it to cut through the cord binding his hands and feet without anyone noticing.

Jake swung his arm, aiming for Chuck's stomach, his knife flashing in his hand. Chuck leapt away. The instant the blade passed him, he danced forward on his toes and unleashed a straight-ahead left to Jake's face. His fist exploded against Jake's cheekbone, snapping Jake's head backward. Chuck followed with a right to Jake's body. Jake slashed backhand with his knife. Again Chuck leapt away—but not quickly enough.

Jake's knife ripped through Chuck's shirt and sliced his sternum. Blood poured down Chuck's chest and stomach, warm and wet. He grabbed Jake's knife arm as it reached the apogee of its swing and drove the knife into the ground, following with the full weight of his body.

Jake's knife hand crumpled in the turf with a snap as Chuck

piled himself atop the wrecker owner's arm. Jake screamed in agony, then bit down hard on Chuck's shoulder. Chuck threw himself atop Jake, freeing himself from the ripping teeth.

Jake's arm, bent backward ninety degrees at the wrist, was useless. Chuck raised a fist, ready to pummel Jake into submission, but Jake twisted away, dragging himself through the grass on his knees and elbows. He slipped free of Chuck's grasp and rose to his feet. Before he could take a step, Chuck grabbed him from behind and spun him around. Chuck reached for the back of Jake's head with both hands and, summoning all his remaining strength, yanked downward while swinging his knee up.

Chuck's knee met Jake's nose with a sickening crunch. An explosion sounded and bits of Jake's skull and brain tissue sprayed away into the night. At the same instant, a dart of pain followed the path of a projectile into Chuck's gut.

Chuck looked up to see Anca standing a few feet away, a look of horror on her face, her pistol held out before her, smoke rising from its barrel.

Jake fell from Chuck's grasp to the ground, a portion of his skull missing. Chuck collapsed to a sitting position beside Jake's inert frame. He put his hand to his flayed chest, took it away, and peered wonderingly at his palm, red with blood. He probed his belly with his fingers, finding a small hole seeping still more blood. A shard of the bullet from Anca's gun must have ricocheted into his torso.

He lay back on the grass and stared at the smoke floating across the night sky above him. The smoke was thick and black, but his mind was clear, the pain in his stomach negligible. Seconds later, Janelle and Gregory leaned over him, their faces drawn. Carmelita and Rosie appeared, too, kneeling, teary-eyed, at his head.

"Chuck," Carmelita cried.

"Daddy!" Rosie sobbed.

He stifled a groan. "I'm going to be all right," he managed. "I promise."

The girls quieted, their small hands stroking his hair.

Chuck closed his eyes and relaxed, confident in Gregory's capable hands, and surrounded by his family.

EPILOGUE

A dozen ewes topped the northwest ridge, followed by their calves. A pair of juvenile rams came last, sniffing the air and rotating their heads, on full alert.

The Rocky Mountain sheep worked their way across the north face of Mount Landen, nipping at bunches of brown grass on the high peak's treeless slope. The animals paused just below the rocky northeast ridge. The far side of the ridge fell away to a three-sided plateau topped by bent, rusted, ore cart tracks and a pile of logs where a cabin once had stood.

One of the calves trotted up and over the ridge crest. The remaining sheep hesitated, shoulders twitching, heads held high. When the calf did not race back over the ridge in panicked retreat, the rest of the herd followed, clambering up and over the crest one by one.

The ewes, calves, and pair of young rams fanned out on the east-facing slope, feasting on the low, dry grass that had grown untouched here throughout the long, hot summer. The animals grazed along the slope to the small plateau, where the rusted rail tracks led from a heavy, iron door set in the mountainside to the logs lying in a jumbled heap at the edge of the plateau. The mountain fell away from the plateau to foothills and on to plains stretching eastward to a flat, distant horizon.

The calves led the rest of the herd across the rock-strewn ground, kicking up their hind legs as they leapt the rails. The sheep spread out to browse again on the far side of the plateau, paralleling a dusty footpath leading around the peak to the paved highway that climbed the mountain's south flank.

The larger of the two young rams lifted its head to sniff at the last of the wood smoke rising from the burnt trees below, a reminder of the thick pall of smoke that had enveloped the high peaks of the Mummy Range for the last several days.

The ram lowered its head and made a playful charge at its fellow young male, forcing the smaller ram to flee across the rocky ground. The larger ram planted its hooves and shook its half-curled horns in victory as the first drops of rain fell from the bank of dark clouds that hung close over Mount Landen. The rams bent their heads to the tufts of bunchgrass on the mountainside as the drops fell harder, wetting the parched alpine slope and initiating the centuries-long process of healing the charred forest below.

ACKNOWLEDGMENTS

With this, the second installment in the National Park Mystery Series, I am ever more aware of the critical role my early readers play in improving the quality of my work. My utmost appreciation goes to my first reader, my wife Sue, and those whose blazing intelligence and strong editing skills join with Sue's to enhance my writing: Anne Markward, Mary Engel, Kevin Graham, John Peel, and, for spotting and correcting my police-procedural errors, Lt. Pat Downs of the La Plata County Sheriff's Department.

My thanks go to the smart, dedicated folks at Torrey House Press—Kirsten Johanna Allen, Mark Bailey, and red-pen-wielding Anne Terashima. I count myself lucky to be a member of the Torrey House team of authors, whose friendship and camaraderie I have come to cherish.

My thanks also go to America's independent booksellers, whose dedicated work to keep books and reading alive makes possible what I do, including Maria's Bookshop owners Andrea Avantaggio and Peter Schertz and their inimitable staff in Durango, Colorado, my home turf.

Finally, my heartfelt appreciation goes out to all those devoting their lives to preserving and protecting the wild places that define the western U.S., particularly wildland firefighters and the national park rangers and staffers who so capably balance the preservation of the West's most iconic lands with the introduction of those places to an ever-growing number of park visitors.

About Scott Graham

Scott Graham is the author of *Canyon Sacrifice*, the first installment in the National Park Mystery Series. Graham's previous book, *Extreme Kids*, won the National Outdoor Book Award.

Graham was raised in the Rocky Mountain town of Durango, Colorado, where echoes of Colorado's gold-mining past featured in *Mountain Rampage* resonate to this day. He has explored the high mountains of his home state his entire life, including numerous hiking, climbing, and backpacking trips deep into the Rocky Mountain National Park wilderness.

Graham has made a living as a newspaper reporter, magazine editor, radio disk jockey, and coal-shoveling fireman on the steam-powered Durango-Silverton Narrow Gauge Railroad. He is an avid outdoorsman and amateur archaeologist who enjoys mountaineering, skiing, hunting, rock climbing, and whitewater rafting with his sons and wife, an emergency physician.

About the Cover

Famed nineteenth-century landscape artist Albert Bierstadt painted "Rocky Mountain Landscape," a portion of which is featured on the cover of *Mountain Rampage*, in 1870. The painting is based on studies he made during a trip to the Estes Park region in 1863.

Bierstadt's paintings of geysers, waterfalls, and other magnificent topography in the Yellowstone area based on a trip there in 1871 played a significant role in Congress's decision a year later to preserve the region as America's first national park. Mount Bierstadt, a 14,065-foot peak south of Rocky Mountain National Park, is named in Bierstadt's honor.

"Rocky Mountain Landscape" hangs in the White House. It is used here by permission of the White House Historical Association.

About Torrey House Press

The economy is a wholly owned subsidiary of the environment, not the other way around.
—Senator Gaylord Nelson, founder of Earth Day

Love of the land inspires Torrey House Press and the books we publish. From literature and the environment and Western Lit to topical nonfiction about land-related issues and ideas, we strive to increase appreciation for the importance of natural landscape through the power of pen and story. Through our 2% to the West program, Torrey House Press donates two percent of sales to not-for-profit environmental organizations and funds a scholarship for up-and-coming writers at colleges throughout the West.

www.torreyhouse.com

ALSO BY SCOTT GRAHAM

CANYON SACRIFICE

Book One in the National Park Mystery Series

This page-turner brings the rugged western landscape, the mysterious past of the ancient Anasazi Indians, and the Southwest's ongoing cultural fissures vividly to life. A deadly struggle against murderous kidnappers in Grand Canyon National Park forces archaeologist Chuck Bender to face up to his past as he realizes every parents' worst nightmare: a missing child.

"This riveting series debut showcases Graham's love of nature and archeology, simultaneously interjecting some serious excitement. Recommend to readers who enjoy Tony Hillerman, Nevada Barr, and C.J. Box's Joe Pickett series."
— *LIBRARY JOURNAL*

"A gripping tale of kidnapping and murder…in a style similar to mysteries by Tony Hillerman."
—*ALBUQUERQUE JOURNAL*

"A riveting mystery…Graham takes readers intimately into the setting, his knowledge of the places he writes about apparent at every turn." —*DURANGO TELEGRAPH*

"A terrific debut novel…" —**C.J. BOX**, *New York Times* best-selling author of *Endangered*

YELLOWSTONE STANDOFF

A National Park Mystery
by Scott Graham

Forthcoming June 2016 from Torrey House Press

TORREY HOUSE PRESS, LLC

SALT LAKE CITY • TORREY

"All my life, I have placed great store in civility and good manners, practices I find scarce among the often hard-edged, badly socialized scientists with whom I associate."

—Edward O. Wilson
Pulitzer Prize-Winning Evolutionary Biologist

ONE

"Grizzly bears are not what you'd call predictable creatures. When they're surprised in the wild, they're as apt to rip somebody to shreds as they are to run the other way."

Yellowstone Grizzly Project junior researcher Justin Pickford, recently of Yale and Princeton—as he'd already boasted not once, but twice to Chuck Bender in the five minutes since Chuck had met him—didn't know the first thing about what he was saying. But as a brand-new member of the park's grizzly-research program, he clearly was pleased with the authority he'd granted himself to say it.

"In the case of the Cluster Team," Justin went on, "it just so happened the bear wanted to rip somebody to shreds."

Chuck, junior even to Justin as a Yellowstone National Park researcher, looked the young man up and down. Justin wore the requisite park-researcher outfit—sturdy hiking boots, Carhartt work jeans, untucked flannel shirt, bandanna headband. While his attire matched that of his fellow young researchers in the Tower Ranger Station meeting room, his scrawny, reed-thin physique did not. During his initial forays into the park's rugged backcountry in the weeks ahead, Justin would have to bulk up to attain the broad shoulders, trunk-like legs, and concomitant stamina of the three dozen other, experienced researchers in the room, or he'd be gone, back to the computer-tapping, paper-pushing world of academia on the East Coast.

Justin leaned toward Chuck and asked conspiratorially, "Have you seen the footage?"

Chuck glanced around the log-walled room. Folding chairs lined its scuffed, pine-plank floor. A platter of cookies and a three-gallon dispenser of lemonade sat on a table in back. The researchers, all in their mid- to late twenties, two males for each female, visited with one another in small groups, plastic cups in hand, waiting to take their seats upon the arrival of Yellowstone National Park Chief Ranger Lex Hancock.

Chuck turned back to Justin. "From two years ago?"

"Yep. The fall before last."

The video had been yanked from the internet the instant it appeared.

"Can't say as I have," Chuck said.

Justin's blue eyes glowed. "Want to?"

Chuck hesitated long enough to convince himself viewing the infamous footage qualified as worthwhile research. He nodded.

Justin cocked a finger and headed for a windowed door leading to the building's side porch.

As reflected in the door's glass panes, Chuck looked a lot like the other researchers—hiking boots, work jeans, flannel shirt—though his shirttail was tucked in and he needed no bandanna to keep his short, thinning hair in place. The door's reflection displayed his lean, weather-beaten frame, which spoke of his having survived much on the journey to his mid-forties, as did the deep crow's feet cutting from the corners of his blue-gray eyes to his silver-tinged sideburns.

Outside, the chilly air bit through Chuck's cotton shirt. It was eight in the evening, the second week of June, the days long and lingering in the northern Rockies. The sun, a white disk behind a thin veil of clouds, still hung above the tall stand of spruce trees rising beyond the parking lot to the west. He drew in his shoulders and shivered. How could it possibly be this cold?

Back home, at the edge of the desert in the far southwest corner of Colorado, daytime highs were in the nineties by now, and the nights, while crisp, weren't anywhere near as frigid as here in Yellowstone, where the last vestiges of winter held sway even as the longest day of the year approached.

"Let's make this quick," Chuck told Justin, rubbing his palms together. "Hancock will be here any minute."

Justin fished his phone from his pocket. "The video-frame sequence is every three seconds, but the sound runs in real time. That's what's so brutal."

The young researcher swiped the phone's face with his finger. "Martha forwarded this to me," he said. Martha Augustine was the backcountry coordinator for the Grizzly Project. "She said I should see it so I could decide for sure if I was in." He tapped at his phone as he talked. "It happened in the upper Lander Valley, at the foot of Saddle Mountain."

"A long way from where we're headed," Chuck said.

"Twenty miles or so," Justin agreed. "With the lake in between."

He held up his phone and stood shoulder-to-shoulder with Chuck. A paused video feed filled the phone's tiny screen. The trunk of a tree framed one side of the shot, a few feet in front of the camera. The remainder of the frame was filled with a view of a sloping meadow, brown with autumn. Dark green fir trees blanketed a hillside on the far side of the grassy meadow.

Justin punched play. A rasping noise issued from the phone's small speaker. Chuck cocked his head.

"That's the griz," Justin said. "Snoring."

A low-pitched grunt of alarm came next. The bear had awakened—and something had awakened it.

"The Cluster Team showed up, just doing their job," Justin explained. "Blacktail Pack had taken down an elk at the base of Saddle a week before; a GPS cluster of the wolves' transmitters told the wolfies as much." Justin used the informal term for the park's Wolf Project researchers. "The two members of the Cluster Team hiked in and rigged the camera to film the pack's behavior around the carcass. They were coming back to retrieve the camera and find out what they'd managed to record. Little did they know, the griz had chased off the wolves and was sleeping right on top of the kill."

A dark shadow covered the video feed, causing Chuck to flinch. When the video stream advanced to its next frame three seconds later, the shadow drew away to become the back of a grizzly bear's broad, brown head.

The bear remained still through the video's next three-second frame, its unmoving head captured from behind by the camera, the fur on its neck standing straight up, its stubby ears erect. A distinctive, V-shaped notch cut deep into its right earflap.

Over the sound of the bear's gravelly breaths came unintelligible human voices, those of a young man and woman. The tone of their conversation, relaxed and jovial, was that of co-workers comfortable in one another's presence.

A high-pitched peal of laughter from the young woman issued through the phone's speaker. The bear's head dropped from view when the next three-second frame clicked past. The animal growled deep in its throat, the pitch so low it rattled the phone.

The woman's laughter cut off in mid-peal. "Bear," she cried out. "There! See it?"

The bear reappeared on the video feed. The camera captured the grizzly's entire body, stretched full out as it sprinted toward the sound of the voices.

Chuck's heart tattooed his chest as three interminable seconds passed, the sounds from the phone that of the bear's harsh breaths as it charged, and that of the young man hollering, "Whoa, bear!"

The next screen shot captured half the bear's body as it angled out of the picture, still running flat out across the meadow toward the off-screen man and woman.

The grizzly woofed, a dog-like exhalation of warning.

"Stop!" the young man cried out. "I said stop!"

Chuck gulped. The man's exclamation should have given the bear pause. Instead, the bear woofed again, the sound farther from the camera, while the video feed returned to what it had been before, a serene shot of the meadow and forested hillside beyond.

Chuck squeezed his eyes shut, dreading what he knew came next. He wanted to plug his ears as well.

He forced his eyes open, taking in the immutable grass and trees on the phone's screen as a terrified screech from the young woman came over the speaker, after which her voice and the young man's joined together in a full-throated, "No!"

"Stop!" the man yelled a millisecond later. Then, under his breath, "Get behind me, Rebecca. Back up."

A savage roar shook the phone's speaker.